PENGUIN BOOKS

LIBERTY

W9-BNF-681

Garrison Keillor lives in St. Paul, Minnesota, home of his radio show *A Prairie Home Companion* heard Saturday nights on public radio stations coast to coast and overseas on Armed Forces Radio and on national networks in Australia, New Zealand, and the U.K. He is the author of several novels including the Lake Wobegon novels, and, most recently, of the bestseller *Pontoon*, as well as collections of stories (*The Book of Guys*), a political broadside, *Homegrown Democrat*, and three children's books, most recently *Daddy's Girl*. He is the editor of *Good Poems* and *Good Poems for Hard Times*. He wrote and appeared in the movie *A Prairie Home Companion*, directed by Robert Altman. His weekly column "The Old Scout," is syndicated to newspapers across the country and appears on Salon.com.

★ ★

Praise for *Liberty*

"Garrison Keillor is a force of nature."   —*The Dallas Morning News*

"Keillor's genius lies in the fact that after you finish reading this, you don't despair. He makes a strong case for the innate decency of the ocarina player, pig-manure vendors and even an odious governor and would-be member of Congress as they sweatily pursue their political ambitions. This is parody, of course, but—not for the first time—the bizarre reality of our actual politics outshines any parody that can be imagined."
—*The Washington Post*

"[Keillor's] novels are edgier, racier, and more satirical than his radio monologues. [*Liberty* is] a kind of literary vaudeville, fueled by words such as 'galoot' and 'Shnozzola' and Keillor's wondrously long, wandering sentences."   —*USA Today*

"Garrison Keillor's newest look at Lake Wobegon is a bit racier than usual . . . and chaotic in a beautiful way."   —Associated Press

"Fans of Lake Wobegon will find familiar characters sprinkled throughout *Liberty* and plenty of scenes set in the Chatterbox Café; and they will delight in the middle-Americana Keillor continues to purvey, although Wobegon seems to be getting a little less uptight and much steamier."
—*Independent Weekly*

Into the harbor of towers and seagulls sails the caravan
Fled from furious Europe and the disappointment of fathers
To find—Thee, our lady of Liberty, lighting the doorway.
Grant us mercy, dear Mother. We shed the old clothing
    of failure,
We rise up vibrant, dream-laden, bound for the west—
    Avant! Lovers of Liberty! The sunny uplands await
    and the fresh meadows.

—Emmett Lazarus

GARRISON KEILLOR

A LAKE WOBEGON NOVEL

PENGUIN BOOKS

To the memory
of Chester Atkins
who told stories
so beautifully

* *

PENGUIN BOOKS
Published by the Penguin Group
Penguin Group (USA) Inc., 375 Hudson Street, New York, New York 10014, U.S.A. • Penguin Group (Canada), 90 Eglinton Avenue East, Suite 700, Toronto, Ontario, Canada M4P 2Y3 (a division of Pearson Penguin Canada Inc.) • Penguin Books Ltd, 80 Strand, London WC2R 0RL, England • Penguin Ireland, 25 St Stephen's Green, Dublin 2, Ireland (a division of Penguin Books Ltd) • Penguin Group (Australia), 250 Camberwell Road, Camberwell, Victoria 3124, Australia (a division of Pearson Australia Group Pty Ltd) • Penguin Books India Pvt Ltd, 11 Community Centre, Panchsheel Park, New Delhi – 110 017, India • Penguin Group (NZ), 67 Apollo Drive, Rosedale, North Shore 0632, New Zealand (a division of Pearson New Zealand Ltd) • Penguin Books (South Africa) (Pty) Ltd, 24 Sturdee Avenue, Rosebank, Johannesburg 2196, South Africa

Penguin Books Ltd, Registered Offices: 80 Strand, London WC2R 0RL, England

First published in the United States of America by Viking Penguin,
a member of Penguin Group (USA) Inc. 2008
Published in Penguin Books 2009

1   3   5   7   9   10   8   6   4   2

Copyright © Garrison Keillor, 2008
All rights reserved

PUBLISHER'S NOTE
This is a work of fiction. Names, characters, places, and incidents are either the product of the author's imagination or are used fictitiously, and any resemblance to actual persons, living or dead, business establishments, events, or locales is entirely coincidental.

THE LIBRARY OF CONGRESS HAS CATALOGED THE HARDCOVER EDITION AS FOLLOWS:
Keillor, Garrison.
Liberty : a Lake Wobegon novel / Garrison Keillor.
p.   cm.
ISBN 978-0-670-01991-5 (hc.)
ISBN 978-0-14-311611-0 (pbk.)
1. Lake Wobegon (Minn. : Imaginary place)—Fiction.   2. Minnesota—Fiction.   I. Title.
PS3561.E3755L53 2008
813'.54—dc22   2008022145

Printed in the United States of America
Set in Aldus with Antic   Designed by Daniel Lagin

Except in the United States of America, this book is sold subject to the condition that it shall not, by way of trade or otherwise, be lent, resold, hired out, or otherwise circulated without the publisher's prior consent in any form of binding or cover other than that in which it is published and without a similar condition including this condition being imposed on the subsequent purchaser.

The scanning, uploading and distribution of this book via the Internet or via any other means without the permission of the publisher is illegal and punishable by law. Please purchase only authorized electronic editions, and do not participate in or encourage electronic piracy of copyrighted materials. Your support of the author's rights is appreciated.

1. THE GLORIOUS FOURTH

Last year's Lake Wobegon Fourth of July (Delivery Day) was glory itself, sunny and not too hot, flags flying, drummers drumming, scores of high-stepping horses, smart marching units in perfect cadence, and Ben Franklin, Sacajawea, Ulysses S. Grant, Babe Ruth, Amelia Earhart, and Elvis marching arm in arm along with Miss Liberty majestic in seven-pointed crown and wielding her torch like a big fat baton, plus the Leaping Lutherans parachute team, the Betsy Ross Blanket Toss, a battery of cannons belching flame boomboomboom from the crest of Adams Hill and Paul Revere galloping into town to cry out the news that these States are now Independent, God Bless Us All, and Much Much More, all in all a beautiful occasion in honor of America, and the only sour note was that so few in Lake Wobegon appreciated how truly glorious it all was, since Wobegonians as a rule consider it bad luck to be joyful, no matter what Scripture might say on the subject, and so in the swirl of color and music and costumes and grandeur you could hear people complain about the high cost of gasoline and shortage of rainfall and what in God's Name were they going to do with the leftover food. It was all eaten, that's what was done. More than seventeen thousand people attended and downed 800 pounds of frankfurters, 1800 of ground beef, a half-ton of deep-fried cheese curds, 500 gallons of potato salad, a tanker-truckload of Wendy's beer, but the next day the talk in the Chatterbox Cafe was not about exultation and the wonders of the great day, no, it was about the bright lipstick someone smeared on the stone face of the statue of the Unknown Norwegian and the word *RATS!* painted on walls and sidewalks and the innerspring mattress dumped on the lawn of Mr. and Mrs. Bakke, the work of persons unknown. People grumped about vandals and what made them do the bad things they do (lack of parental discipline, short attention spans) and maybe it's time to rethink the Fourth of July and pull in our sails a little and not give bad apples an arena for their shenanigans.

The Chairman, Clint Bunsen, was unfazed by this, having grown up with these people, and he weathered the petty complaints and dispatched his men to pick up the mattress and clean up the graffiti, and by the time March rolled around and the snow melted he was all set to go again and giving The Speech which the Old Regulars knew almost by heart and which went something like this: "July Fourth is the birthday of our country and deserves to be done right because, by God, it is a great country and it changed the world and if we can't even find a way to say that, then who are we? A bunch of skunks, that's who. When you neglect the details, you lose the big picture. For want of a nail the shoe was lost, for want of a shoe the horse was lost, and so forth. Like my father said, personal slovenliness is the doorway to cowardice and cruelty. Nobody cares about holidays anymore. Which is why—and I'm only giving my opinion here—the country is so beset by government lies and corruption and everybody out for himself and to hell with the future—because those people grew up thinking the Fourth was just a day to lie around on the beach and toast your weenie."

Chairman Bunsen loved the Fourth, he relished it, the booming, the chatter, the smell of cooking fires, the gaudiness, the good humor, the fiery delectations bursting in the sky, and he was happy to expand on this if you questioned the lavishness of it—Why two drum-and-bugle corps? Couldn't we cut back on the fireworks? Does it really take sixteen Percherons to pull one circus wagon? And why four wagons? Wouldn't two be sufficient? Why $1,200 for the Leaping Lutherans Parachute Team—wouldn't they appear gratis? Had he asked? Did we need to bring the Grand Forks Pitchfork Drill Team in? Couldn't we have found something just as good in Minnesota?—and he got very quiet and then started in on the subject of Getting The Details Right. "There was the guy who neglected to check his oil and the car overheated on the way to his girlfriend's and he was an hour late and she refused to date him again and if he had seen to business she probably would have married him instead of me. And I wouldn't be here. I'd be living it up in California. All because of lubrication." He cackled at his own story, nobody else did.

Clint Bunsen along with his brother Clarence ran Bunsen Motors on Main Street, the Ford garage in town, he was the ginger-haired, snub-nosed man in dungarees, and when he got wound up about the Fourth the O.R.s looked deeply into their coffee cups and listened.

The O.R.s were Carl, Lyle, Ernie, Berge, LeRoy, and Billy P., somber men with big rumps and great bellies that cried out for a pin-striped vest and a silver watchchain to accent the amplitude, and they sat in the corner booth at the Chatterbox and shot the breeze and bitched about their aching backs and their wandering children, but when spring came the Chairman climbed up on his high horse about the Fourth.

In other towns the Fourth was a parade of tractors and pickups led by a geezer VFW honor guard with four old ladies in a convertible, some dogs riding in a pickup, and a kid carrying a boom box playing "The Stars And Stripes Forever," but the Chairman insisted on upholding high standards despite all the guff he got. "It is not easy trying to sell grandeur and pizzazz to a bunch of sour old pragmatists," he said.

Last year's Fourth of July was G-L-O-R-I-O-U-S and the Old Regulars were his right-hand men who saw to the details. It was maybe no Latin Carnival with ecstatic dancing in the streets and men waving their shirts over their heads, but it was terrific in its own way. Absolutely amazing. Nothing else like it. Lake Wobegon's Fourth had not one but two national champion drum-and-bugle corps snap-bang-rattle-boombooming down Main Street, one of them in leather kilts, the Fabulous Frisbee Dogs of Fergus Falls, a unicycle basketball team whipping a ball around as they wheeled through fancy formations, a line of girls in illuminated glow-worm outfits, a dazzling float made of silver candy wrappers with a clown who juggled tabby cats, a fire-eater who blew flames fourteen feet long, local men and women dressed up as George and Martha, Abe Lincoln, Tom Jefferson, Teddy Roosevelt, Susan B. Anthony, Grant Wood's *American Gothic* couple, Uncle Sam on stilts, and four antique circus bandwagons with fantastic carved figures and bands seated atop them blazing away on "Muskrat Ramble" and "When The Saints Go Marching In"—pulled by Percherons, sixteen-horse hitches that took your breath away—plus the precision pitchfork drill team and the Betsy Ross Blanket Toss—ten Minutemen in powdered wigs and knee breeches holding a canvas net and throwing a woman wrapped in Old Glory thirty feet into the air, the Jubilation Marching Handbell Choir of Holdingford, forty white-gloved ladies, a bell in each hand, playing a rousing "Ode To Joy" as they strode along—and much more—contests, the Living Flag, yowsa yowsa yowsa, a magnificent fireworks display climaxing in a thunderous seven-rocket burst that spelled out W-O-B-E-G-O-N in the sky—and moments later, as an extra bonus, a fabulous thunderstorm. The Cable News Network sent a camera crew from Chicago—at Clint's invitation—people said, "Oh why would they bother covering a parade in Lake Wobegon?" and Clint said, "It can't hurt to ask"—and that Fourth of July night CNN broadcast it and the next day it was shown internationally and, all in all, it got 57 million viewers.

Fifty-seven million. Okay, so it was only forty-five seconds long, but that's not bad, and yes, CNN failed to identify the town by name so it might as well have been Peabody Junction or Grovers Corners or Big Butt, Wisconsin, but nevertheless.

Not so shabby for a town of 2,182 out in the hinterlands. Central Minnesota: hardly a focal point of American culture. Hog farms, soybeans, long Lutheran sermons, hard winters, and a steady exodus of young people heading south and southwest. Only time you ever see Minnesota on national TV is if people perish in a blizzard or if a very polite young man goes off and murders six old schoolteachers in a van. You would think that the smart fellow who can get millions of people to look at Lake Wobegon on a festive day in summer, his colleagues on the Fourth of July Committee would say, "You have exceeded our every expectation, Clint. You have brought glory to our town. The children of Lake Wobegon bless you."

Fourteen speaking invitations from community groups in Osakis, Melrose, Little Falls, Brainerd, etc., etc. *Fourteen!* People who recognized his achievement.

It was a coup. You'd think maybe they would've put his name on a bronze plaque or name a sandwich after him or give him a trophy with seraphim holding up a golden harp, or something. In Paris, Karachi, Berlin, Mumbai, Kyoto, Moscow, Swaziland, Rio, Jakarta, Jerusalem, Madrid, Acapulco, and Abu Dhabi, images of the Sons of Knute and the statue of the Unknown Norwegian and Ralph's Pretty Good Grocery and Mayor Eloise Krebsbach saying, "The Fourth of July is a time when we all come together as one community."

Ha! What a joke. What it did was tear people apart.

Success was the problem. You bring forth a triumph and people (1) resent you for it, (2) expect you to do it again, except better, (3) watch for signs of pride on your part, and (4) await your debacle with cheerful anticipation.

About one third of the town thought—Hey, great. Fifty-seven million people. You put us on the map. Congratulations to all who worked so hard and let's build on their success and do even better next year.

And a third said—It was okay. It could've been worse. But it could've been done for half the cost and without alienating so many people by excluding them from participation. Let's make a Fourth that we can all take part in.

And the third third said—The Fourth of July has gotten completely out of control. National TV exposure has gone to our heads. In our lust for the spotlight, we have forgotten who we are and we are attracting to this community an element of people who you've got no idea who they are. We never used to lock our doors at night and now we do. They could come in here late at night with pliers and a screwdriver and take anything they want.

And at the very next Committee meeting, Viola Tors lit into him and said, "Why did CNN not identify our town? Nobody said 'Lake Wobegon.' No name on the screen. Who dropped the ball there? And why did they not refer to Delivery Day? And why was the four-minute silence completely overlooked?"*

* The Fourth of July was known to some older residents as Delivery Day, commemorating Lake Wobegon's miraculous survival of the Great Tornado of July 4, 1965—to the north and west, several towns got whacked hard, water towers and grain elevators leveled, trailers blown away, but Lake Wobegon emerged with little damage. It was a sunny day in town—the storms were fifty miles to the northwest—but debris was carried by high-altitude winds from the storm front, and out of a clear blue sky a barn door came flying in, whirling like a top, and sliced off the attic of the Irv Peterson house as the family sat in the dining room, eating rhubarb crumble. A 1957 Chevrolet the tornado picked up from behind Helen's Hi-Top Lounge in Fergus Falls fell to earth in the garden of the Earl Dickmeiers, missing their house crowded with grandchildren, by inches, judging by the fact that the TV antenna from the roof was found impaled in the car's left rear tire. The spot in the garden where the car hit was the rhubarb patch. And a wooden crate containing thirty-six bowling balls lifted off from the Breckenridge train depot, flew for miles, split open, and rained bowling balls down on Lake Wobegon—some splintered, some embedded

She looked straight at Clint as she said it. He replied that he was not the TV director and that probably they didn't call it Delivery Day because it'd take too long to explain about the bowling balls falling from the sky like artillery shells and in the end people wouldn't believe it anyway so what's the point? She just harrumphed and said that he ought to listen to his own speech about taking care of details. That was Viola. A killjoy. She had a terrier who was just like her, a headache of a dog who liked to hector other dogs. Every yard was Booji's territory and he bristled at the very existence of other dogs. He was a barker from the word go. Like him, Viola had discovered the usefulness of belligerence. In this town, people tend to back down if you bristle at them. They don't want to tussle.

She tapped a pencil on her big front teeth and shook her little curly head and rolled her blue eyes as if he were the dumbest boy in the third grade. She wanted more community involvement, public hearings, more transparency, a poll, an environ-

---

themselves in soft ground, one bounced on the loading dock behind Ralph's Grocery, flew a hundred feet in the air, bounced on Main Street, and landed on the roof of the Sidetrack Tap—there was no warning at all, just small objects in the sky suddenly getting larger, and none of them touched a soul, though the town was packed with people. And so every year, the Catholic Knights of the Golden Nimbus marched under a banner

UNITED TOGETHER
BY GOD'S MERCY
JULY 4, 1965

and carried the hood of that 1957 Chevrolet and a green bowling ball, and people stood in silence as they passed. And then at the time of the bombardment, 4:36 p.m., the entire town observed four minutes of silence in gratitude for God's mercy.

mental impact study—"You go around with all these wonderful ideas in your head—how about sharing with the rest of us?" she told him, which sounded reasonable unless you knew Viola. She was a killer of wonderful ideas and like so many murderers she used procedure as a weapon. File your wonderful idea with me and in seven (7) days I will show you ten (10) reasons why it can't be done.

"I should think you'd've at least made sure they mentioned Delivery Day," she said. "You can't let these people run roughshod over you just because they're from New York. You have to speak up. Have a little gumption. If you can't handle these details, maybe we need to get you some help." She had been steamed at him for a year and three months. It was a Friday afternoon, he remembered it well. He walked into her office, her back was to the door, and she was saying, "Oh, pussy willow, I can't wait to see you. Three hours. I'm counting the minutes, pussy love." And the floorboard squeaked and she jumped and hung up the phone and said, "Why are you spying on me?" She'd been pissed ever since.

2. LEADERSHIP

ast year's Fourth of July (Delivery Day) was so glorious because he, Clint Bunsen, had taken charge and moved forward. If the Fourth had been run democratically by committee, it would have taken place in November and been the same old boring cortege as in olden days, a procession of whoever was available. The Committee was a coffee-club social: After all was said and done, a lot was said and not much done. Somebody has to tell people what to do. Set up the stage here and not over there. Just do it—no discussion, thank you very much. Some guys like to dither, weigh false alternatives, kid around, recall how it was done in 1982—God help us, just get the thing done, put the stage there, and get rid of those silly Roman candles, set off the big rockets, that's what people love, the big bang in the sky. Don't tell me about the fireworks display you saw in Boston the time you visited your nephew who was thinking of attending Emerson College but then went to Winona State instead and majored in elementary education and taught school for a while in Williston and then fell in love with a girl whose dad was in the oil business and he sent Curt to Bahrain and they're quite content there, he and Melissa have three children—now what are their names?—let's just do what needs to be done, spare me the storytelling.

He had led. He dared to step on toes and get rid of deadwood. He wanted the thing to be *eventful—exuberant—sumptuous*. Of course you couldn't use the word "sumptuous" here—people would think "Who does he think he is?"—but why go halfway? Why not try to create Glee among these dour people. Exuberance. Rejuvenation. He hired jugglers and a couple of magicians to work the crowd—a little bonus for the folks: You come expecting queens and marching bands and here's a man who creates a beautiful arc of six yellow tennis balls in the air and here is another who removes a fifty-cent piece from your nose. He nixed the dog parade, which alienated plenty of people, and he cancelled Cowpie Bingo—you pay ten bucks for a number, 1 to 50, and two well-fed cows are let out onto a fenced-off section of Main Street on which fifty numbered squares have been painted and if a cow wanders onto your numbered square you whoop and yell and if she drops a cowpie on it, you win a hundred dollars. Clint thought it was stupid. Yokel stuff. Also the cowpie throw. "It's like painting a sign on your back that says, 'Hick,'" he said. He dared tell the Sons of Knute they could no longer march. Too old, too pokey. Wizened oldsters in musty capes and plumed hats, swords, sashes, badges, stepping down the street, turning left and right, and sort of curtsying, in what supposedly was an ancient Viking warrior dance but it looked like old men searching for their car keys. They had marched in the parade forever and now their marching days were done. "Ride on a float. Make it easy on yourselves," Clint said. "But put away the big Norwegian flag. It's the Fourth of July. It's not Syttende Mai." The Knutes were hurt, and in true Lake Wobegon style they picked up their marbles and went home and sulked. And told people that Clint had kicked them out of the parade. Not true. And he told the Ladies Sextette they would no longer ride the fire truck and shriek "It's A Grand Old Flag" through megaphones. The Sextette had sung in the parade since Jesus was in the third grade, but no more. They sang sharp. He told them that. "Sharp?" Yes, sharp. Painfully sharp. "I can't tell you," Lucille told him, "how many people have told us how much our music meant to them and how wounded we are by your cruel remarks." "I am doing you a favor," said Clint. "Let's have people remember you at your best." So the Sextette put an ad in the *Herald Star.*

Due to an artistic disagreement with Delivery Day management, the Ladies Sextette (founded 1924) has withdrawn from participation this year. We regret this and wish the Committee a great success, which has been our goal all along. And thanks to all of our friends for their encouragement at this very painful time. You have meant so much to us. "There is no such thing as defeat when one still has loyal friends and true."

And then last year Clint killed off the reading of the Declaration of Independence. Mr. Detmer had done the reading for thirty-odd years, standing on the steps of the Central Building, paper in hand, four feet away from the microphone, reading into his shirt front in a flat, droney voice and if you tried to move the microphone closer, he jumped back as if it were a snake. Five years ago he lost his place two-thirds of the way through and started again from the beginning. Pure torture. People hated it. But nobody dared say so. They said, "Isn't it remarkable that he's been doing this for thirty-three years? The man sure is dedicated." (Yes, and so are mosquitoes.) The man had become a visible symbol of pure idiocy, reading slowly and incomprehensibly something nobody wanted to hear. It might as well have been in Urdu, but a little crowd stood like dumb cattle and listened to it, with as much pleasure as if you watched a man mow his lawn, and since the Fourth was about pleasure, Clint took him aside three years ago and suggested that the Declaration be edited down and the long list of grievances against King George III be dropped.

"But that's part of the Declaration," Mr. Detmer said.

"I know, but the king is dead and the British are gone and we're all over it now."

"It's history. We need to know these things."

"It's in the library if anybody needs to go read it, but we don't have to listen to it every year, do we."

The old man shook his head and said that rather than reading an inaccurate version of the Declaration, he'd prefer to not read at all.

"Fine. Then we'll do that," said Clint. "Let's give the Declaration a vacation."

Well, Mrs. Detmer had a fit, and she got a posse together and there were secret meetings that were no secret to anybody and the next Sunday a flyer appeared, anonymous, under windshield wipers of cars parked at Lake Wobegon Lutheran and Our Lady of Perpetual Responsibility.

We think it's pretty self-evident that all men are created more or less equal, considering, that they are endowed by their Creator with enough basic intelligence to know what they want, and whenever Tyrants come along who Abuse and Usurp, it is our Duty to throw them out. The present Chairman of the Fourth of July has established an absolute Tyranny over our Community. Let Facts be submitted to a candid world.

He has refused to allow Long-Time Residents to participate in the Parade, though they have as much right to do so as anybody else.

He has forbidden our Performers to sing the Numbers they have performed for lo these many years.

He has refused to allow Families to drive their Pickups or Threshers or Tractors and Hay Wagons in the Parade, unless they conform to his Unreasonable Demands which are fatiguing and expensive.

He has endeavored to introduce Outsiders to our Lake Wobegon Independence Day Observance so that it scarcely represents us anymore.

He has made Decisions without our consent and harassed with ridicule those who dare to speak against him or question his Edicts, which have plundered our treasury, ravaged our spirits, burnt bridges, and destroyed the goodwill of our people.

Now, therefore, we the Citizens of Lake Wobegon solemnly publish and declare, That henceforth we shall observe the Glorious Fourth exactly as we wish, regardless of who attempts to restrict us, as a matter of Sacred Honor.

What a kick in the shins! It really burned his bacon. People you've known all your life can be meaner than skunks and total strangers can be sweet as can be. Elsewhere he was practically a celebrity.

Fourteen speaking invitations in the past year!—to come give his Glorious Fourth speech, "Dare To Make A Difference"— about why the Fourth was important. "You need to keep sticking your neck out and making Large Occasions, otherwise you sink down into the drift and debris of life," he said. "You have to think big because the future doesn't arrive ready-made. You have to welcome it." In Lake Wobegon he was just a guy who fixed your brakes, but if he drove thirty miles in any direction his reputation rose and people lined up to shake his hand. (They knew what he'd accomplished with the Glorious Fourth in Lake Wobegon. People in Lake Wobegon might think he was a tyrant, but outsiders admired him for it.) And when he was introduced to speak, the master of ceremonies always pointed out that *everywhere the Fourth is in decline, but over in Lake Wobegon it's a major success and the reason is Leadership, my friends—Leadership—and that's why it gives me great pleasure*, etc.—and Clint stood up and walked to the lectern and people applauded and applauded and he spoke. He said, "Politics today is all complaining. People moaning about how the big guys are picking on the little guys, and the family farm is no more, and the schools are rotten, and Wal-Mart is destroying Main Street, and I just want to say, it's a great country. Let's love it for a change. (APPLAUSE.) So things change. Deal with it. Okay, so Wal-Mart comes in and some stores on Main Street have to close. People like to get stuff cheap. When was it any different? You don't like it, pass a law against human nature. But stop bad-mouthing our country. Government isn't going to solve all these problems, believe me. So let's have one day in the year when we can stop hammering on each other and just stand and wave the flag and sing the national anthem and be proud of who we are."

A standing ovation at the end. Always a standing ovation. People leaped to their feet, their eyes shining, and whooped and whistled. In Lake Wobegon he wouldn't get a standing ovation if he set the seats on fire. But in Brainerd and Willmar and Sauk Center and St. Cloud and Little Falls he was recognized as a guy who had dared to step on toes and spend some cash and make something truly illustrious. He hadn't gone to New York to learn that, he had learned it at Lake Wobegon High School. Helen Story, his 11th-grade English teacher, who gave her class a talk about daring to be smart, even if people made fun of you, and she wrote on the blackboard, "Keep away from people who belittle your ambition. Small people always do that, but the really great make you feel that you, too, can become great." And under it, MARK TWAIN. The belittlers were everywhere to be found, and what a price they paid—it became more and more clear the older they got. To see Berge, his old classmate, a good fullback, a promising student, turn into a crank and then the town drunk. His face blasted by drink, you'd think cougars had been chewing on him, and walking around like he had a load in his pants, which maybe he did, you didn't want to ask. Tragic and also a big bore. "Aim high," Miss Story said. And the lesson stuck with him. So he had tried to do. *"Ad astra per aspera."*

But in this town you got not much credit at all except the grudging admission that, yes, you were a good worker and you showed up on time and got the job done. Nobody was awestruck by anything you did, no matter how awesome. **Michelangelo:** he worked hard on that chapel ceiling and he cleaned up after himself too. Bach: he got that *St. Matthew Passion* done on time and the copies were very clean, very readable. *War and Peace*: no mispellings, no grammatical mistakes. Living in Lake Wobegon was like being stuck in a bad marriage. Which Clint knew something about. It had taken him years to figure it out, but he and Irene just plain didn't mesh. "Marriage is the truest test of character," wrote Dr. Biggs in his best-selling *Reviving the Romance*, and Clint thought maybe he'd like to take the test over with somebody else. "To make a life with your best critic is tough, no doubt about it. You have many critics but your spouse is by far the best-informed of all of them," wrote Dr. Biggs. Okay, but sometimes a critic is operating on old information.

It was like the Herdsmen, the Lake Wobegon Lutheran ushers who flew to California and won the National Church Ushers Competition in Santa Barbara, sponsored by the National Church Assistants & Acolytes Association, the NC-Triple-A, and brought home the first-runner-up trophy, even though it was a rough trip out there and the little plane from L.A. to Santa Barbara bounced like a trampoline, steam gushing from the vents, the wings flapping, and the flight attendants in back were saying the Lord's Prayer out loud, and the plane landed so hard on the tarmac that oxygen masks dropped from the ceiling, and the Herdsmen had to rush to the auditorium to compete and it was a four-aisle venue, which they're not used to, and a motley crowd of Unitarians and blind people and 140 kids from St. Vitus's School for children with ADD—it was like herding fruit bats and water buffalo, and there were only 20 stalls at the Communion rail but the Herdsmen got the job done and divided the people into a slow line and an express line, the sippers and the dippers—won first runner-up, came home, marched into the Chatterbox Cafe, and set the trophy down on the counter.

"What's that, a bowling trophy?" Dorothy said.

"We won first runner-up in the national ushers competition."

She looked at them as if they had geraniums growing out of their foreheads. "Well, aren't you special."

You got no credit for accomplishment in this town. You could be awarded the Nobel Peace Prize and they'd say, "Peas! The man never grew peas in his life! Wouldn't know peas from lentils!"

His own son Chad, a good 4-H'er who stood up and pledged his head to clearer thinking, his heart to greater loyalty, his hands to larger service, his health to better living for his family, his club, his community, his country, and his world, was taken over by aliens and got video games and malt liquor. Went to college and sat in his room watching movies on a computer. Dropped out, talked about bartending school, talked about going into the moving business, talked about what he might do one of these days and never did it.

"Leave him alone," said Irene, so Clint did, ignoring the marijuana fumes from the basement. And then Irene discovered the pornography in the computer. "Out!" she cried. The boy wept and promised to do better. "Do better somewhere else!" she said. "Out!" And now he had a job delivering plants and lived in a basement apartment with four high-school buddies, not an achiever in the bunch.

His cheerful, capable boy had turned into a slacker and a

whiner, slouched in a beanbag chair, sucking smoke, hypnotized by images of violence and degradation, and for this, Clint blamed the Democrats. They were the party who encouraged two-thirds of the country to imagine they were oppressed by the other third, their chances cut off, their gas siphoned from the tank, pure paranoia, the fear of radon coming up from the ground or growth hormones in milk or secret cabals spreading the AIDS virus, low-frequency sound from high-tension powerlines—everyone a victim of the big drug companies, the big HMOs, Wall Street bankers—ignoring the simple facts of life. It is filled with risk. There is no free ride, people. This is how much health care costs and somebody must pay it, probably you. To do that, you'll have to buckle down in school and do the work so you can get a decent job and maybe forego spiderweb tattoos on your neck. Simple. Chad chose to fritter away his life. His choice. Nothing to be done about it. The responsibility did not lie with the public schools and the lack of nurturing programs for kids like him. He did it to himself, so let him deal with it. Let him experience the dawning of reality. The helping hand is at the end of your own arm. Use it.

3. INGRATITUDE

The accusation of tyranny stung him. He tried to ignore it, but it hurt. His brother said, "Look at it this way. People resent you because you're the mechanic. You know how much they don't know about cars. That takes away a little piece of their manhood. They resent you for that. You drive the wrecker and haul them out of the ditch in the winter. A guy can't start his car on a cold morning, you come out and hook up jumper cables and bang, she starts right up. He's embarrassed. He resents you for it. That's what this is about."

"Pay no attention to it," said Irene. "A handful of soreheads. You've got that type of person in any community. Don't judge the town by what a few barflies think. Ignore it and it will all pass over."

It was more than a handful though. It was the bitter chip-on-a-shoulder German Catholics who clung to a sense of being oppressed, going back to the anti-Hun propaganda of World War I—Oh just get over it! And dark Lutherans who believe that life is misery and if it doesn't seem so now, just be patient, and if you are lacking misery, they can supply you with all you need. If they had been at the Sermon on the Mount when Jesus brought forth the miracle of the loaves and fishes, they would've thought: "Did he wash his hands? Where are the napkins? How long was that fish cooked?" Lighten up, people! Life is short enough—why spend it in the shadows?

In June came the revolution. The Committee had gone along with Clint for years, murmured their Yeas, shook their heads when asked for objections, but they got their backs up over the issue of an official Hospitality Suite. Viola Tors's idea. She sat opposite him at the long table, sharp-nosed, frizzy-haired Viola in a little pink knitted number, tapping a pencil on her spreadsheets, sending deadly vexation waves his way. She was the treasurer, ex officio as Lake Wobegon town clerk—the town council demanded that as a condition of its support. But why was she making a big issue of this Hospitality Suite? There never had been one in the past, but she had a bug up her butt and browbeat the Committee into voting 5–1 a month before the Fourth to create one with a wine bar, espresso machine, fresh fruit, and frozen yogurt, since the governor had indicated he would be attending and so (they hoped) would the national press and maybe other celebrities. Viola was beating the bushes for celebrities left and right, TV weathermen, retired sports figures, even authors. "If they come, and I hope they will, we need a place where they can relax, out of the spotlight," she said. "You can't expect these people to stand in line at a Port-A-Potty."

"Why not?" said Clint, the lone No vote. "Afraid someone might sneak a peek?"

Viola made a face at him. "Don't be nasty. The bottom line is that at the end of the day, when all is said and done, anybody who puts on a function and expects celebrities is going to provide a Hospitality Suite and that is just the simple truth." All of her favorite phrases in one sentence plus the word "function," which she liked, too. And this is how she wrote it up in the Committee minutes:

> TORS moved that the Committee create a Hospitality Suite to be staffed by volunteers to offer the usual courtesies to visiting dignitaries and disseminate accurate information to the media about our town, its history, and the tradition of Delivery Day as distinct from the Fourth of July. Motion was discussed and adopted, 5–1.

No reference to his objections—"You create a roped-off area for the big shots and then you have to decide which of the little pissers get to be there and you're going to have hard feelings," he said, and she glared at him and said, "Well, we're no strangers to hard feelings now, are we." A reference to Clint's plain-spoken style.

"Who is upset now?" he said.

"You know perfectly well." She sniffed and looked around the room for support. Father Wilmer looked like he might jump up and run, as he always did at any hint of disagreement. (*Don't wimp out on me, pal*, Clint thought. *She won't bite you.*) But Diener was in Viola's corner now. He said, "We've been a little rough on farmers, just to name one. One group, that is."

True, Clint had told several people in the past few weeks that they couldn't drive their tractors in the parade. Not even antiques, unless they were pre-1950. And no pickups either. Sorry. Not even brand-new ones. It's a parade, not a procession.

A parade demands a little dazzle. He was anti-dinge, anti-drag. The St. Cloud Shriners Precision Rider Mower Unit was okay because the Shriners wore showy fezzes and Arab shoes with curly toes. Fat men in overalls on John Deeres, no thank you.

Viola asked what he had against tractors.

"You let one tractor in and you'll have a hundred. A festival of farm implements. Boring."

"But who are we to impose our standards of boring?" said Ingrid. She was new to the Committee, she taught middle school English, she was a swing vote. "Isn't the issue one of personal freedom?"

"Freedom doesn't mean aimlessness. We can't just sleepwalk through life. I'm sure you teach your seventh-graders that. Freedom demands structure. It's our job to put on a parade, not pander to everybody's little whims and predilections. A parade is supposed to be spectacular! Phenomenal!" Viola rolled her eyes. "Okay, but you need money for that," she said. "Leland is not donating money this year. That's five hundred dollars we don't get to spend."

"Leland wanted his gun safety class to march. All thirty-five of them. Just walk along, carrying shotguns. Said it would be a nice recognition of all the work they'd put in. So I said, 'How about you put them in uniforms?' No, he didn't want uniforms. 'How about they ride on a float or something?' He suggested they ride on a schoolbus. Cheaper than making a float. I said, 'If cheap is our guideline, then why bother to put on a parade? If mediocrity is the purpose here, then people can do that at home.'"

"You're saying you think that his gun safety class is mediocre?" said Mr. Hoppe, ever the literalist.

"Let's not start cutting corners on standards a few months before the parade," said Clint. "You just create confusion. If you want to go back to how it used to be when anybody was in the parade who wanted to be, you can do that next year."

"I liked that old parade," said Mr. Hoppe. "Remember? We used to go around twice, so people who watched it the first time around could be in it the second time. And vice-versa. It was very sociable."

Ingrid said she thought that sounded wonderful.

"Take it from me, it wasn't," said Clint. "It was a lot of people milling around in the street and people on the sidewalk watching them do it."

"A lot of people have told me how much they miss the old parade," said Diener.

"Fine. You want that, I'll resign effective July 5, you can do what you want." And he stood up and walked down the hall to the men's room.

The next week Viola's minutes read:

BUNSEN announced that, effective July 5, he will resign as Chair. TORS moved to accept his resignation and to express the Committee's appreciation for his service. Approved unanimously.

What? Resigned? Not on your life. Okay, he had occasionally complained to the Old Regulars about the aggravations, but he had never considered resigning. Daddy had been Chairman of the Fourth of July back in 1965 when the tornado struck. His quick action getting people indoors under cover in the minute after the first bowling ball struck, before the other thirty-five rained down, was credited with saving lives. Daddy was, in fact, the Delivery Man of Delivery Day. He loved the Fourth and Clint loved his dad. The thought of giving up the Fourth was painful. But here Viola Tors had apparently ousted him in the minutes, printed in the *Herald Star*.

He said nothing. He thought of calling her and telling her off but decided to be cool. Ignore it. At the next meeting she was sitting in his place.

"Are you sitting there, Viola?" he asked.

"Did you want to sit here?" she said, accusingly.

"I don't care where I sit. It isn't important."

"Then why make an issue of it?"

So he sat down in her old place. She called the meeting to order. When she called for old business, he said, "I see by the minutes of the last meeting that I turned in my resignation. Which comes as a surprise to me. But if that's what all of you want, fine. It's been a wonderful experience working with all of you and maybe it's time I turned it over to someone else. I don't want to but if that's what you want, okay by me."

He expected Mr. Hoppe or Father Wilmer to rise to his defense, but no. A great cloud of silence filled the room. Quiet breathing. A foot tapping.

"I clearly understood that you resigned," said Viola. "You said so and you got up and left the room."

"I went to the restroom."

"Well, whatever. We all understood that you were resigning."

"If that's what you want, just say so."

"Well, it's hard to undo what's been done," said Viola. "Personally my only interest is the Fourth of July. I want to see it done right. That's the bottom line." She went on to enumerate his sins without referring to him personally or looking him in the eye—the wounded Knutes, the weeping Sextette, the people who loved Cowpie Bingo, the dog owners, etc., etc.—and her frizzy hair shook and her skinny fist popped the table. Viola had thrown tantrums as a child and now she was in the grip of another one.

"So you want me to resign?" he said.

"That's how we voted," she said. "It was unanimous."

Nobody said a word. An awkward few seconds. Father Wilmer looked thoughtfully up at the ceiling and Mr. Hoppe stared at the table and Mr. Diener scratched his nose as if about to poke into a nostril and do some excavating. Clint thought maybe he should reminisce about his dad and the old days, make everyone smile, spread oil on troubled waters. What he wanted to say was, *After a few months of Viola, you are going to miss me a lot. But you won't get me back because I am seriously thinking about running for Congress, unbelievable as that may seem to you. I am about 65 percent decided. I may announce on the Fourth. I plan to win the election and when I do, I am out of here and you are going to wish you hadn't done this.* And then Viola cleared her throat and said, "Any other old business?" and that was that. The moment was over. Six years as chairman. Done. He was deposed because he had to pee. Evidently they were as sick of him as he was of them. He hoped there would not be a recognition ceremony after the parade and the presentation of some big chunk of Lucite for meritorious service. He guessed not.

4. ART

So they decided on Art's Baits & Night O' Rest Motel for the official Hospitality Suite instead of the rectory of Our Lady of Perpetual Responsibility (offered by Father Wilmer). Insanity. Pure insanity. Art was the least hospitable person in town, his motel hadn't had paying guests for several years, the No Vacancy sign was permanent—Art Grundtvig was 78. He was a mental case. For years Clint had expected to find Art on the front page of the Minneapolis *Star Tribune*. RURAL MAN SHOOTS FAMILY OF SIX: "THEY JUST GOT ON MY NERVES." He had inherited the motel from a jovial uncle who loved to serenade his guests with "Oh What A Beautiful Morning" in a booming baritone, whanging on a tenor banjo, but Art was a prickly bachelor and a proud member of the Freedom Fighter Movement, sworn in blood to defend the Constitution against its enemies, including leftist judges, the media, and the electric company, which sent its agents onto private property to install listening devices. He posted warning signs outside the cabins, hand-lettered on plywood, such as NO METER READERS ON THE PREMISES. THIS MEANS YOU. TRESPASSES BY GAS OR ELECTRIC EMPLOYEES WILL RESULT IN DRASTIC

ACTION. NO IFS, ANDS, OR BUTS. DON'T SAY YOU WEREN'T WARNED. THAT IS AN OUTRIGHT LIE!!!! The casual visitor, seeing the big neon Motel sign, pulled into a yard with an old silver bus parked in tall weeds which Art was fixing up as a getaway vehicle and a string of six cabins sheathed in pale blue plastic siding and picnic tables nearby and big signs beside the doors: NO FLAG DESECRATION ON THE PREMISES. YOU WANT TO TEST ME, GO RIGHT AHEAD—IT WILL BE YOUR LAST TIME. ANY DISRESPECT TO OLD GLORY BY WORD OR DEED WILL RESULT IN IMMEDIATE EXPULSION AND CONFISCATION OF PERSONAL PROPERTY. NO EXCEPTIONS. NO BOO-HOOING THAT YOU "DIDN'T REALIZE" IT WAS DISRESPECT—HA!!!! I'VE HEARD THAT ONE BEFORE AND AM NOT FALLING FOR IT. IF YOU ARE NOT A 100% LOYAL AMERICAN, YOU ARE NOT WANTED HERE. There were other warnings posted on the grounds, NO HONKING, NO PARKING, NO HUNTING, NO PEDDLERS, and on the side of the garage a big sign, GOOD MEN GAVE THEIR LIVES FOR THIS COUNTRY. I WILL TOO. DON'T PUSH ME. And if, despite the prickliness in the air, you should decide that you wanted to rent a cabin and you went to the main house and the door marked Office, you saw a sign there: BEFORE KNOCKING, READ FOLLOWING: DO NOT ASK TO BORROW (1) MATCHES, (2) TOILET PAPER, (3) CONDIMENTS OF ANY KIND, OR ASK TO USE THE TELEPHONE OR TO WATCH TELEVISION. I DO NOT HAVE TIME TO CHITCHAT WITH GUESTS. I AM A CITIZEN SOLDIER ON ACTIVE DUTY IN DEFENSE OF THE GREATEST COUNTRY ON EARTH AND DON'T YOU FORGET IT.

THE MANAGEMENT

And if you knocked on the door, you met a skinny old coot with tusks of nose hair an inch long and enormous foreboding eyebrows and a ponytail and his khakis hitched up under his armpits and an unmistakeable Smith & Wesson revolver in his belt and he told you that the motel was shut down for remodeling, and he closed the door in your face.

But Viola felt sorry for Art. She said he'd suffered a concussion when a dog jumped out of a tree on him, a dog he was training to hunt squirrels. She proposed paying him $500 for use of the motel for two days. "Why two?" said Clint. Because it'd take a day to clean it. Clint pointed out the fact that Art was armed and dangerous, Viola just pooh-poohed him. "I've spoken to Art and he is going to be in Montana visiting his niece, and he's happy for us to use it."

"Art is insane. He calls himself the Resistance. He stores boxes of rations up there. Tents, ammunition. He thinks the power company is going to blow him up in his sleep. He thinks the government is getting ready to take over the country."

But the Committee was feeling their oats. They had deposed the Tyrant and now they voted to dwell in the House of the Lunatic, 3–2 in favor (Father Wilmer had left the room to smoke a cigarette) and there it was. And Viola looked around and said, "All in favor of adjournment sina die?" and there was a murmur of Ayes and she said, "Meeting adjourned."

"Viola," he said. "I'm still chairman until July 5 and it's the chairman who adjourns the meeting. Not the treasurer."

"If you want to sit here and talk to yourself, fine," she said, rising. "The rest of us are going home."

5. DADDY

Viola was a vexatious person. He had known her all her life and he didn't need to tap her knee with a mallet or give her the Rorschach test, she was screwed up, just like everybody else. You learn that in a small town. There is no normal. Viola's daddy ran away with Viola's teacher when Viola was 11. He was parked outside school when Viola came out the front door and then Mrs. Samuelson came out with a cardboard suitcase and got in his car and Viola never saw either of them again. She never got over it. People never get over things. And then the pussywillow incident pushed her over the edge.

So he was ousted. That was the thanks you got for six years of hard work as Chairman. Years of worrying about the damn Living Flag, the picnic, the fireworks, and liability insurance. You sat around a cold linoleum-top table and tried to fend off Mr. Hoppe who wanted to bring in a chainsaw-sculpture contest and a motorcycle rally, and you stiff-armed Father Wilmer who wanted a sunrise ecumenical service by the lake, and you parried Viola who had a dozen picky questions about procedure. And then somebody wanted their nephew's band The Atomic Tree

Toads to play in the stage show and somebody whose old uncle could recite from memory the 87 counties of Minnesota in 25 seconds.

In Clint's childhood, the Fourth was big and brassy with precision marching bands and troops of horses with riders in gaudy headdresses holding banners and plenty of flash and sparkle. Daddy was the impresario. Daddy hired Dave the Diver who plunged thirty feet onto a wet sponge, and brought in the Hooper Bros. Carnival with the Ferris wheel and the Spinner that pinned the riders flat to the rim as it spun and flattened their faces so they saw stars, he loved the roar and the rumble, the hoopla, loved jazz—"coon music," he called it, and Clint had to tell him not to use that word—Jelly Glass Mortenson and His Hot Pickles— "The Mud Room Stomp," "The Slow Dog Drag," big hits. Daddy was a showman at heart and he loved carnival rides, fire-eaters and pole-sitters, the Wild Man from Borneo, chickens who parachuted from a tower, a man who played guitar hanging by his heels and could talk backward and belch the entire alphabet in one expulsion of gas. Daddy exhibited Donald and David, the Minnesota Twins conjoined at the hip, famous for the fact that they hadn't spoken to each other in twenty-three years—people paid 50 cents admission in hopes of persuading the men to make up—"Come on! Just look at him! Put your arm around him!"— but the men, who were short, thick-necked, dark-browed, thin-lipped, just glowered at the customers and told them to mind their own business. Daddy exhibited Herman the Human Lightning Rod, struck seven times by lightning. He was a large man, slow on his feet, but nonetheless—seven times? What was the message there? The Human Lightning Rod had not lost his faith in a beneficent God: in fact, he had gospel tracts printed up, "Struck By Lightning—Still Praising The Lord." On the other hand, he sold the tracts for 35 cents apiece. And there were the Ancient Aztec Midgets, four small brown persons who sat solemnly, blinking, as a swarthy man lectured on their ancient culture. Clint hung around and absorbed it all, saw the sadness of the razzle-dazzle, how thin the gaiety was, the empty faces of the clowns, the loneliness of the drum major, and once saw Daddy kiss the contortionist, a slender bun-headed Mexican woman in gaudy oriental pantaloons, kissed her on the mouth hard, then slipped between the tent flaps with her. Clint had seen her perform. She worked on a table, lean and brown, in trousers and a very skimpy bra that you kept hoping would come off. She could tie her legs in a knot behind her neck and do the same with her arms and after demonstrating these grotesque entanglements, she brought out a glass jar that appeared to be about one-third her size and she simply folded herself into it and an assistant rolled it around for your inspection and then she popped out and took a bow, the bra still on. Clint was 14. He imagined Daddy on a table and the Mexican woman entwining herself around him. The thought almost burst inside of him and he cried himself to sleep that night. He knew it was wrong but he kept Daddy's secret.

It was the first enormous secret of his life, Daddy's love for Bonita. He knew he should tell but he did not tell.

Daddy had wanted to bring in a hoochie-kooch show called "Puss 'N' Boots," two girls who strutted around in their underwear. "Some people want to see that type of thing, so why not?" he said. But the town got wind of it and Daddy had to lie and say he had no knowledge of the nature of the thing—he thought it was a kiddie show. "It's only human nature to want to see a couple fine young women dance," he said, "but some people are opposed to human nature."

Grandpa started the Ford dealership in 1919 and Daddy took it over though he knew nothing about cars whatsoever, he was a snappy dresser and favored seersucker suits and red bow ties and hats with brims. A big white straw hat and a big gold-toothed grin. He liked to pretend to pull his thumb off and then hold out his little finger and when you pulled, he let out a fart. He loved the Sunday comics, *Jiggs and Maggie*, *Little Iodine*, *Gasoline Alley*, and he smoked a pipe like the dads in comic strips and had a mustache too. Daddy was a deacon of the Lutheran church but he was no more Lutheran than Ramon Navarro was. He used Jergens hand lotion and Swank cologne. He came home from church on Sunday and sang "It Ain't Necessarily So" to irritate Mom and fixed himself a gin martini and a plate of Ritz crackers with deviled ham and put Frank Sinatra on the turntable and got a dreamy look in his eye. He was thinking about his Mexican contortionist Bonita. When Clarence took over the Fourth of July he found payments to Bonita of $300 a year for ten years, the only performer to get that kind of dough—twenty bucks was more like it—and he asked Clint, "What gives?" Clint said, "Bonita was a charity case. Six kids and her husband was a trombonist. Dad took pity on her." Which wasn't true. She was Dad's sweetie. He kept a picture of her in his desk drawer, among the Ford brochures. She wore leopard-skin tights and was doing the splits.

After Daddy died, the Fourth took a dive. It was Open House for anybody who wanted to trudge four blocks with a flag in hand. No more bands and circus wagons. Too expensive. Clarence ran the show and Clarence was unable to say no. Clint said it easily. No. That's all there was to it. No. And then they said, Oh, and then they went away. But Clarence was too good-natured to tell people to please dress up, it's a Parade for God's sake, so the parade went on as a motley procession of snot-faced kids in paper tricornered hats waving sticks, anybody with a pickup truck, maybe with a couple elderly dogs and a sullen teenager holding a small flag. Ridiculous. When Clint took over, he cleared out the dogs and raised the money to bring in quality parade units and culled the geezer honor guards and the minor royalty (Miss Particle Board, Miss Rutabaga Days, Miss Nut Goodie, Princess Louise of Processed Cheese) and the Science Fair winners and the kazoo band and the 4-H'ers leading their heifers. It was the Festival of the Dullards, the Procession of Geeks and Nerds, but nobody wanted to say anything, so Clint did the dirty work, because it was his job to, and now they were all mad at him.

6. DNA

O n April 11th, the day Clint Bunsen turned sixty, two months before he was overthrown as Chairman of the Fourth of July, he peed blood in the toilet and without a word to Irene went off to a urologist in St. Paul to find out why. The doctor was a tall young man with thinning hair and a restless leg who seemed very enthused about urology. He had Clint drop his drawers and grab hold of a brass pole and bend over for a digital examination of the prostate that seemed to include the kidneys and pancreas and perhaps the lower half of the left lung. Clint could feel that left leg jiggle as the finger in the rubber glove probed his innards and the doc murmured and said, "Steady now" and "Almost done" and "You'll feel a little pressure now" and "Don't jump, hold steady" and "Take a deep breath and hold it" and "Cough" and "Okay, just about done now" and finally it was over. While Clint caught his breath, the doc said, "We're discovering that the key to all of this is heredity" and he recommended that Clint have his DNA checked. He gave him an article from *Genealogy Today* about DNA testing and how a woman in New Jersey had found she was a descendant of Henry

Thoreau. You just sent a swab of saliva to a lab in Phoenix along with a check for $140. The doctor had a swab available. So Clint paid up and the lab report came back the next week, saying he was less than half Norwegian, some Finnish, some Welsh, and almost half Spanish.

It was the same week that he met Angelica Pflame.

It was a shock to Clint—all his life he had been 100 percent pure Norwegian, and now he was down a few quarts. So Grandpa had lied about coming over from Bergen during the great herring famine of 1893 and seeing the Statue of Liberty in New York harbor and feeling welcome in the New World. A big lie. Clint went online and searched for "Ancestor Alarm" and "Shocking DNA Results" and "Loss of Heritage" and discovered a website, Heritage Is Destiny, which was run by Miss Pflame who said—

> Where you come from tells you where you are going. Mystics have always known this. Heritage is Destiny. Let me help you find your personal truth and escape the stereotypes that have held you back. You are NOT THE PERSON THEY SAY YOU ARE. And a true psychic trained in genealogical psychology can read your future by interpreting your past. Give me a call and let's journey into your future together. My rates are reasonable and I can work by phone or e-mail, though in-person sessions are preferred.

There were a few pages of glowing recommendations ("I was horrified to discover that Grandpa had done prison time for embezzlement but Angelica showed me how this dark family secret actually pointed toward a career in business. She was a turning

point in my life. S.B. Minneapolis") and a photograph of a tall
red-haired woman, grinning, standing beside a black horse,
mountains in the background ("Me in Santa Barbara, January
23"). Clint had once, many years ago, planned to live in Santa
Barbara. Ding-dong. He e-mailed her. and found out that she
lived in St. Cloud, the big town south of Lake Wobegon. "I
marched in the Fourth of July parade in your town," she said.
"A friend of mine was supposed to dress up as the Statue of
Liberty and at the last moment she couldn't make it and I took
her place. It was great except her gown was way too long and I
had to walk along carrying my own train and it was hot but I got
to march in front of ten thousand people. And then a very nice
man fixed the thermostat on my car and he wouldn't accept a
dime."

"So that was you."

"You were the guy?"

"I remember it well."

And so in his mind, the discovery of his Hispanic roots and
his meeting Angelica, and his entry into old age, were all bound
up in a circle.

He sent Angelica a picture of Grandpa in his Norwegian knee
pants and frock coat for Syttende Mai, holding one strand of the
May Pole, and she wrote back her vision:

*Grandpa was a sailor from Barcelona who got in a really bad fight
with the first mate who threatened to whip him and so he jumped
ship in New York harbor and there stood Señorita Libertad holding her torch high and telling him to be true to his dream and be
whoever he wanted to be. He came up with the name Bunsen in*

honor of Barcelona and boarded a train to Florida to pick oranges
and by mistake wound up in Minnesota and his English was, like
really bad, so he couldn't tell them he was lost, so he settled in, got
a job on a hog farm. It was October, cold and rainy. His Latin blood
was thin, he felt like really really bad, and then it was November.
Snow fell. That's what I'm seeing. You finish it.

Grandma was the farmer's daughter. She was 31, tall, homely, and she got him through that first winter, and in August, Daddy was born. Grandpa never quite got a grip on English, but he was, according to family legend, a great lover who sometimes, in his eagerness to get his wife into bed, left the car at the curb, lights on, engine running, and who, at age 85, buying a new mattress, made sure it was not too firm. "You need a soft mattress so your knees don't slip," he explained to Clint's older brother Clarence, who didn't understand. "You got to get a good purchase with your knees," said the old man.

Clint didn't feel Spanish necessarily, not in the sense of feeling the urge to put on pointy-toed shoes and dancing with his arms up over his head and crying out "*Caramba!*" and "*Ajua!*" He was a plugger, head mechanic at Bunsen Motors, (soon-to-be-former) Chairman of the Fourth, husband of Irene, father of Tiffany, Chad, and Kira, member of the board of Lake Wobegon Lutheran—but in fact, as he got to thinking about it, he had always felt like an outsider, silent at basketball games, dark and brooding at Christmas, a non-fisherman, depressed by winter, not like Irene who got all happy when it snowed and put on a Norwegian ski sweater and whomped up a cheesy hotdish and put on a CD of Christmas favorites and made hot mulled wine.

When snow fell, Clint's heart sank and he pulled on his long johns and insulated boots and felt a powerful homing urge to head south and keep going. Runaway Mechanic Spotted In New Mexico. He didn't belong here. Winter depressed him, the cloudy days especially. He craved sunlight. How did he miss these early warning signs? He was not one of these people. They were stoics and he was a romantic. He had married the wrong woman and thereby missed out on his destiny, which lay to the Southwest. In Austin, Texas, people were eating outdoors in March, barbecue sandwiches and beer, dancing in the parking lots to a Mexican band, and in Minnesota they were huddled in their kitchens, gaunt survivors, gnawing on the leg traps.

God, with His fine sense of humor, had dropped him here among the Lutherans, a Spaniard by the waters of Lake Wobegon—*a las aguas del lago Wobegon*. That day he got the news, he bought a guitar, sent away for a catalog of flamenco wear, and sent Angelica a picture of himself and a note—"I may be out of line here but I will be bold and say: I need some personal guidance— what to read, etc. Could we meet for a glass of wine?"

She wrote back that she had a vision of the two of them in a dark room, undressing, music playing. Or maybe not music. And maybe there was a lamp or something. Or a cat. She wasn't sure.

7. CONVERSATION

he was about to turn his world upside down. He gazed at her picture thirty-seven times a day, searched for her online at night.

She introduced him to a chat room called ZipZone, an amazement. You went to the website and selected from a menu

ADULT

FAMILY

LIFESTYLE

POLITICS

RELIGION

SPORTS

TRAVEL

WORKPLACE

and typed in your ZIP code and—alakazam! Your screen name (OLD BUNS) popped up in a box to the side of a dialogue window where people nearby were rapping out lines of chatter and you could join in the chatter or you click on a name in the list and chat privately.

It was a miracle. Deliverance from a world of repression. Pure freedom of speech. Nobody in Lake Wobegon would dare to say what people put out there in ZipZone.

CHUCKLES: Today I saw my mother out back weeding the irises and felt a sudden urge to shoot her. I am 38. Is this normal?

BOBBI: That's why I don't keep guns at home.

CHUCKLES: She has been riding my ass since I was ten. Nothing I do is good enough for her.

DR NO: U married?

CHUCKLES: Was.

DR NO: Why not move away?

CHUCKLES: Easier said than done. She watches my kids when I'm at work.

BOBBI: Better not shoot her then.

Lifestyle and Travel were rather tranquil, but in Religion people raged against the Lutheran church.

BUNKY: Read about the serial killer in Wichita? The Lutheran deacon?

TODO: Weird.

BUNKY: The control freak who could not stand to see unkempt lawns.

TODO: Right.

BUNKY: So he went around killing people with dandelions in their yards. Or people who didn't rake up clippings. For 21 years. He broke into their homes when they were alone and tied them up and tortured them with shears and decapitated them with a Weed Whacker.

TODO: I know the type.

BUNKY: He killed 38 people.

TODO: He had a job to do and he did it.

BUNKY: At the trial he sat there expressionless. No remorse. No feeling.

TODO: My God. I know people like that.

Skeptics held court. Lapsed Catholics. Dissenting Unitarians. Former fundamentalists in therapy.

FUNDY: Thunder and lightning terrify me so that I have to take four Paxil and go to the basement. It's fear of the Second Coming. Sometimes I haul out a hymnal and sing "Just As I Am" or "Lord, I'm Coming Home" and bawl like a baby. Once I called up my cousin to make sure she hadn't been Raptured. She used to be such a believer. Turned out she's Buddhist now and happy as a clam.

And these weren't New Yorkers or Angelenos, not even Minneapolitans—with ZipZone you went into chat rooms with people in central Minnesota. People from Avon and Albany and St. Cloud and Holdingford. People who said, "What's the deal with that?" and "Oh for crying out loud!" People who would tell you not to be so persnickety. "Oh sheesh," they said. "Go figure. Anyhoo." People you might very well see at the Lake Wobegon Fourth of July. But here they weren't talking about the weather; they were saying what's on their mind.

RIP: I love to walk naked through a cornfield and feel the long tassels brush against my skin which I find terribly arousing.

RED: Well, don't you have a vivid imagination, you big corndog you.

RIP: There is a full moon out tonight. I would be happy to meet a woman in a cornfield around 11 p.m.

RED: You big corndog you.

RIP: Age and weight unimportant. Tell me which crossroads and I will be there.

RED: I'd like to but we're going into town.

DOTTY: Is anyone else out there into tickling? I am sort of new to this but would like to explore it with a more experienced person (M or F) who is willing to respect boundaries.

TROT: Oh Jeeze, how do ya think of those things?

FLO: I can't believe I am saying what I am about to say but I would like to meet up with someone who is willing to let me talk very very dirty to them while they sit in a chair and listen. No touching, just talk. No reciprocation expected. I am a Lutheran and must be extremely discreet.

BOB: Flo?

FLO: What?

BOB: Is your name really Flo?

FLO: No.

BOB: Okay. Forget it then.

Irene was scornful of the Internet and thought it "impersonal," but Clint saw that it was the door to everything he'd missed out on by living in Lake Wobegon.

It released you from the terrible pained politeness, the extreme reticence. The Internet sprang the lock and you left your prison cell and walked out onto the great meadow of freedom.

> DUPER: Me: 50, pharmacist, a little chunky but good-
> looking. Married. You, 34, married, three kids, very hot, living
> next door. I've watched you mowing your lawn in short shorts
> and tank top and now I see on your clothesline six bras and six
> pairs of panties in various pastels. I know you have a clothes
> dryer, so I'm wondering if this is a signal. You seemed flirtatious
> yesterday. If this is you, please know that I would love to meet
> you anytime at a place of your choosing. I have a green van with
> a camping bed. We could park and make out for a while. I know of
> good places. If this interests you, let me know by hanging your
> husband's coveralls on the line upside down and however many
> clothespins you use—7, 8, 10—is the time I'll pull up behind your
> garage and wait to pick you up. I have condoms.

The reality was that he was starved for conversation. Which, around Lake Wobegon, was formal, almost liturgical—*Looks like rain.* Yep. *But I guess we could use some.* You can say that again. *So what you been up to?* Oh, not much—You might've been studying the molecular structure of Jell-O or writing passionate sonnets in French to a penpal in Lyon or planning a trip to Nepal, but you'd never say so—"Oh, not much" was the right thing to say, because if you told about the amazing thing you were doing, nobody in Lake Wobegon would ever say, *Wow, that is great!!!!!!!* It wouldn't happen. Nobody ever said that something was great. They were not an exclamatory people.

You sat in the Chatterbox Cafe and got an earful of complaint about kids, lower-back pain, taxes, Congress, the general downward trend of things—all of it ritualistic, nothing earnest or original. Nobody ever said what was on their mind, such as, *I always used to worry that I'd wind up just like my father and by George that is exactly what happened. Why am I wasting my life? Why, when they ask me to coach girls' softball again next year, do I say yes? I don't want to yell at a bunch of 13-year-olds to hustle and pay attention. I want to live.*

ZipZone offered conversation wild and free, as much as you wanted, on any subject, any hour of day or night—and whatever the prevailing tide of opinion was, you could count on plenty of devil's advocates. It reminded him of an old radio adventure show called *The Invisible Boy* in which Greg Pritzer who had saved an old man in a blizzard was given a bottle of blue pills that made him invisible. Greg promised that the pills would be used only to solve crime and not to spy on people, but one day Greg solved the crime in a few minutes and had a couple hours left over until the drug wore off and he walked into people's houses and saw what they were like when they thought nobody was looking. They were sadder, for one thing, and they talked to themselves and they said very strange things.

He talked to Angelica almost every night in ZipZone—clicked on her screen name and there she was, whispering to him in a little box.

MISS VALIANT: How is it being Hispanic? Is it fun?

OLD BUNS: It's not bad. I'm still Republican though.

MISS VALIANT: LOL. When are you going to sing your songs to me?

OLD BUNS: Just say the word, Angel.

MISS VALIANT: I never made love to a Republican. Interesting.

OLD BUNS: Republicans take more than a minute. We can go for an hour. You don't know what you're missing.

MISS VALIANT: What do you think about Bush?

OLD BUNS: What about him? He's a few bricks shy of a load, but so what?

MISS VALIANT: You support him?

OLD BUNS: Voted for him.

MISS VALIANT: Feel good about that?

OLD BUNS: I'm not a Republican because I love Bush. I love my country and I get tired of people running it down. Democrats don't like individualism and that's the problem with them. They believe in One Size Fits All and social management and it just plain doesn't work here. They want to make things fair. But life isn't fair. Only a child would think it should be.

MISS VALIANT: Want to have a child with me?

OLD BUNS: It's the Republican party that holds to the idea that each individual is complicated and mysterious and has a lot of meanness which is programmed into us and can't be wished away. And so we have an army and police force and they carry real guns and not bouquets of chrysanthemums.

MISS VALIANT: Can I say something?

OLD BUNS: Democrats are all about Identity Groups and that's bullshit.

MISS VALIANT: I take it you are not one of the Christian crusaders who

OLD BUNS: NO. NO NO NO. The party is about individualism. You're a woman, I'm a white guy in a small town, but we may

have more in common than we would with others in our group.
We don't have to be enemies.

MISS VALIANT: are out to banish gay

OLD BUNS: I fix cars. But I hate the term "blue collar," it does not
sum me up at all. But that's how Democrats think of people.

MISS VALIANT: We could talk about this in bed.

OLD BUNS: You want to?

MISS VALIANT: My nipples are getting hard for some reason.

OLD BUNS: What are you wearing?

MISS VALIANT: brb

She got him steamed up. He sat in his green shorts and Golden
Gophers jersey and heartily lusted after her. The power of words
on a bright screen.

MISS VALIANT: You're turning me on.

OLD BUNS: Likewise, kid.

MISS VALIANT: How'd you get stuck in a pothole like Lake
Wobegon?

OLD BUNS: Born here.

MISS VALIANT: So? Ever think about busting out?

OLD BUNS: All the time.

MISS VALIANT: So you're not really conservative.

OLD BUNS: Nope. More libertarian.

MISS VALIANT: Spent your whole life in Lake Wobegon?

OLD BUNS: Not yet.

MISS VALIANT: lol

OLD BUNS: Spent three years in California. Navy. Came back here and got ambushed and before I knew it I was married and in debt and had a child with the croup.

MISS VALIANT: You still married?

OLD BUNS: I guess so. Last I checked.

MISS VALIANT: Hmmm. And hmm.

OLD BUNS: I loved it in San Diego. You could swim most of the year. I lived off-base in an apartment on Vallejo and on weekends I'd go out surfing. I was so proud of myself for becoming a Californian that I had to come home and tell everybody and they made me feel like a criminal and so I stayed. Make sense? Anyway, the answer to your question is yes. You still there?

MISS VALIANT: I want to move back there. More to do. Surfing, skiing, hiking, climbing—people don't sit around and brood like people here. I went to school in Pomona. Came back to take care of my mother. My family sits around all winter, pissing and moaning and worrying about what's going to happen to them.

OLD BUNS: Great minds think alike. Let's go.

MISS VALIANT: Where?

OLD BUNS: San Francisco.

MISS VALIANT: That is so weird. I was just thinking the same exact thing. Let's go.

OLD BUNS: Let's.

MISS VALIANT: You're joking.

OLD BUNS: Am I?

MISS VALIANT: Only one way to find out.

OLD BUNS: Go for it.

8. THE NAKED MOMENT

He spoke to the Boy Scout troop the next day about the Fourth of July but it was Angelica on his mind. He told them the Fourth is special because it's the day we honor our country and it's important to do this right and not just roast some weenies and blow off bottle rockets. This is our country and it's worth it—and meanwhile he was imagining the country of Angelica's body, the ridge of collarbone, the beautiful mounds, the ribs, the meadow of her belly, and the sweet valley beyond.

He asked for questions and one boy asked if they were tall enough to be in the Living Flag (yes) and another if there really had been a naked lady in the Fourth of July parade last year. "Some people thought so," he said. "But no."

No, the naked lady was not naked in the parade, she was naked in his imagination. He called her that night from Clarence's office at the garage. He told Irene he was going for a walk. ("When did you start taking walks?" she said. "Since you told me I ought to." *Badonkadonk*.) It was the third week of April. Angelica sounded happy. So he got right to the point.

"I want to meet you," he said.

On the phone she spoke so fast, words tumbling down the line and stutter phrases like *like you know* and *so she goes like* and *I go like* and *we were like*, that she was like almost incomprehensible though he picked up references to lemonade and Gemini and Christmas in Miami (or isthmus of Panama?), her voice was more like water running than actual language but he said, "Aha" and "Interesting" and "Maybe so" and that was like good enough.

She said something about conflict.

"Well, yes. Of course. I've been conflicted since I was ten."

"I don't believe in, like, forcing these things. When it's right, it's right, and until it's right, you're, like, just a fly or something beating its wings on the window glass."

"I'm a fly who's been pounding glass for a long time."

They talked for almost an hour. She was 28. She grew up in Oregon with hippie parents, he thought she said, and had worked with puppets, and now she supported herself by modeling, teaching yoga, counseling, and "selling stuff." The website was a sideline. She danced three nights a week at a club. Topless. Her contract ran through the end of June. She'd be moving on then. Being psychic, she knew this.

It was a gift she'd had since she was seven years old when she had clearly visualized her mother falling down the stairs.

"What happened?"

"She sprained an ankle."

"Did you warn her?"

"No, I did not. I wasn't aware of it as a gift. I thought it was a dream."

"And you still have it?"

"Sort of. Like, glimmers. It takes a lot of discipline, though. Sometimes I lose it and after awhile it comes back. It goes, like, in cycles."

She told him he was calling from an office, he was standing and not sitting, and there was a brand-new car nearby. Bingo.

"What am I wearing?" he said.

"If I were there, you wouldn't be wearing anything."

He laughed. "Great minds think alike." But he was thrilled. A lusty young woman. "I'm sixty, you know," he said. "I like older men," she said. "They're not so goal-oriented." *Hmmmm.* And then she said something about condominiums, it sounded like.

He stood there in the garage at Daddy's old high desk with a shelf of old account books below and arranged to meet her in St. Cloud for lunch the next day. Across the street, the Mercantile, the battered manikins in their antique sport clothes, and after Angelica said, "Good-bye. I love you," and they hung up, he thought about calling her back and canceling the whole thing He could imagine her looking him over and getting that wooden expression women get when you don't measure up. That flicker of the eyelids and then they look beyond you. He got that a lot around here. People look at you and think, *Auto mechanic,* and they glance around for someone more worthy of attention, a movie actor maybe or an interesting criminal. It's a good job though, fixing cars. People can get along without the Christian faith, and by God people have, but they can't get along without a car. That's a fact, son. You change air filters and tune up engines and install mufflers and your mind can roam and you don't have to suck up to anybody. Your mind is free, unlike, say,

Pastor Ingqvist's which is toiling day and night to uphold ortho-
doxy and rationalize the Resurrection and frame up a sermon on
the parable of the unjust steward and maybe figure out what to
tell Clint about marital infidelity. To be pastor of Lake Wobegon
Lutheran is rather prestigious compared to the modest task of
replacing sparkplugs. And yet—and yet—your mind is wonder-
fully free to recall girls whom you parked with in your old '56
Ford with the bench seat. Both of them, Irene and Maggie. He
married Irene. Maggie went to San Francisco. She was a permanent memory. Tall, strong legs and shoulders, and when she
kissed she nibbled at his mouth and she was a very good girl and
yet she welcomed his advances and when he reached down to
touch her she opened her legs and sighed so beautifully, long
sweet sighs.

You couldn't work up a sermon on the unjust steward and
think about Maggie at the same time, and there was one advantage of auto mechanics—it permitted freedom of thought.

He did not cancel. He went to St. Cloud the next morning and
promptly at 1 p.m. she walked into O'Connell's and sat down in
the booth opposite him and smiled an enormous smile. She was
tall, long reddish hair pulled back in a yellow clip, jeans, sandals,
a spangly T-shirt, and that brilliant smile. Absolutely stunning.
Shockingly beautiful. She smelled sweet and rich, like lima
beans.

"You're still conflicted about knowing me," she said, "but I
have to let you worry about that. How are you?"

"Thrilled." He'd worn his blue blazer, jeans, a black T-shirt,
hoping to blur his identity as a mechanic, though she knew that
about him already. She knew a lot, some that he'd told her, other

things she intuited. "You're mulling over a big decision that could take you away from here," she said. "And it's dangerous, but, like really really exciting."

He had the shepherd's pie, she had a salad, which she barely touched. She sat holding a pendant on a chain, watching it, then looking him straight in the eye. She was reading his chakras, the meridians of energy emanating from his polarities, trying to align them psychically.

She took his right hand between her palms and closed her eyes. She said, "I see engines. A water sprinkler. I see horses pulling a large red and yellow wagon. I see flowers, like a whole lot of them. There is a woman you've known for many years and this relationship is in a state of change. I see a heavyset bald man in a suit. I smell burning coffee."

"My brother Clarence."

"Thank you. I was going to say Charles. Clarence—"

"Charles was the name of my parents' first child."

"He died."

"Yes, he did. He was premature. They put him in a cigar box and set it on the oven door to incubate him. He only lived a few days."

It was rather astonishing, her intuition. She was way off the mark on some things—him being deeply religious (not even close), him playing the stock market (never), his son being a musician (ha!)—but when she hit the mark, she hit it straight on. His wife Irene was a grower of champion tomatoes and had a caustic tongue, and his brother Clarence was sentimental and sometimes walked through his house at night touching things and weeping, and Clint was worried about his daughter Kira's sexual orientation, and he had come in for a lot of flak about the Fourth of July—one fact after another, she ticked them off. And then she said, "You're not going to run for Congress. It's not going to happen."

"You're right about that."

"Right. Totally. And I see you and me going to a motel."

A delicious thought, being in a dark room with the fragrant Angelica, and he carried it home with him and took it to work and thought the thought over and over as he pulled Mr. Berge's engine and dropped in a new one—thought of a 60-year-old man, a 28-year-old woman—whispering and nuzzling, clinging to each other, and the loosening of clothing and slipping your hands underneath. The unclasping, unbuttoning. The great anticipation. And lie naked, the whole front of him pressed against her flank and his hands roaming, spreading goodwill. His lifetime of failure behind him—all of those casual friendships that failed to satisfy, the afternoons of longing among the pretty lawns and shady boulevards, dreaming of upstairs rooms with shades pulled—now this naked moment when, entwined with her, he could become a nameless animal with no story, obeying a simple urge to couple in the dark—a beautiful urge whether you are president of the United States or a wheat farmer in Nebraska, the same exaltation. The intimate dark, the whispering, the skin on your skin—you search for the naked moment at great risk of embarrassment. Oh my God. Bill Clinton endured waves of public humiliation and thousands of hours closeted with lawyers trying to fend off the great hairy hand of history, and all for a little lovely intimacy—the screwing he got was not worth the screwing he got—and yet what a simple urge. And what can you say about those who resist it in order to protect their careers? To deny the animal within so as not to jeopardize cash flow. Irene was furious at Bill Clinton for bogging the country down in a year and a half of controversy. Sat and read the paper and fumed. Clint listened in silence. He objected to plenty about Clinton but surely a man who sends men off to shoot and be shot at can be forgiven for allowing a lovely young woman to unzip his pants. And the moment Angelica mentioned a motel, he looked forward to the day. Or night. Anytime, darling. I'll be there.

9. GARDENS OF AVON

Angelica, Angelica, light of his life, a breath of light-heartedness in his metric life, a haven of tenderness on the frozen tundra of monogamy. She was telephathic and moved with his moods, lifting him up, leveling him out. How small and pitiful is a man, crying out for the mere touch of a woman's hand, someone who is glad to see him—and there she was! "I'll be giving a speech at the Kiwanis in St. Cloud on Monday," he said. "I'll come see it," she said. She came and he went all out and made a good speech, all about daring to be better than what people expect of you. Aspiring to greatness. Defying the force of mediocrity, the curse of the prairie, that old egalitarianism turned in on itself like a cancer, eating its own seed—"Why can't Minnesota produce genius? Genius awakes in each of us every morning"—oh they loved that line and didn't know whether to laugh or weep. "There is an opening for genius in every work given to us to do," he cried. "And when I took over the Fourth of July parade in Lake Wobegon, I decided I wanted to make it *phenomenal.*"

The word stunned them. *Phenomenal.* In Lake Wobegon??

The very name brought visions of sad-sack football teams getting chewed up and mashed into the grass by lopsided scores and those pitiful Whippets motoring around in the asthmatic orange bus, stumbling onto the field and serving up gopher balls and getting hammered, and the 1941 grain elevator explosion (caused by a dimwit who switched off a ventilator, thinking it was the light in the toilet), and the 1965 tornado that dumped bowling balls on the town.

And yet the town had been seen by millions on CNN. A heck of an accomplishment.

She hung around afterward and waited for his admirers to disperse.

She was tall. Slim, with strong shoulders. Big legs. She wore a dress the color of dawn, she smelled like young corn, buttered. Red hair pulled back in a yellow clip, a good strong nose, green eyes. Pale freckled skin. Hands behind her back and she bounced on her toes. "How about coffee?" she said. They sat at the counter and he turned toward her, his knee pressed against her leg, and she did not flinch or pull away.

"You don't think people are going to resent you for saying all that? About mediocrity?"

"People know it's true. People in Lake Wobegon love this big parade—they hate to give me credit for it, they resent the hell out of me for making them happy, but they love it—because they remember how grim that holiday used to be. Standing around eating burnt weenies with your old relatives who've had nothing to say for forty years—it was torture. Cue the orchestra. Bring in the elephants."

Angelica was talking about California. Her father had married a woman from Santa Barbara, and in their late seventies they ran up mountains and practiced tantric sex and were learning Arabic for the fun of it. Every day was a new day in California. You woke up and even if you had lost your shirt the night before or contracted dysentery or been convicted of manslaughter, nonetheless you had big new ideas and a goal for yourself and something exciting to look forward to.

And two days later he met her at a supper club in Avon. In the bar, a skinny kid with a shock of blond hair curled himself around an old Gibson Archtop and played a sweet choppy version of "If I Had You." Angelica wore green warm-up pants and a salmon tank top. He took one look at her and his heart sank from the weight of feeling. God, she had the walk, she had the rocking motion in the hips, she had the sweet talk, and she wanted to be loved and there he was. Ready, willing, happy to be of service. She said, "I knew the moment I met you online that I wanted to know you." Her skin glowed, her eyes shone. She believed that what delights us expands us and loosens the living spark buried under our studied complacency. We embolden each other, she said, we give each other courage. He was emboldened to turn on the stool so that his knee pressed lightly against her flank. She pressed back. He pressed harder against her and he leaned in close to hear her over the music—the guitarist was deep into "I Got Rhythm" now—and then he put his hand lightly on her shoulder—for emphasis—when he told her the joke about the grasshopper who walked into the bar and the bartender said, "Hey, we've got a drink named after you," and the grasshopper said, "Why would anyone name a drink Bob?" She laughed hard. She'd never heard that one. Oh, he had a lot more like that one. A lot more.

"I can't hear you with the music so loud," she said. "Let's go back outside."

They walked across the parking lot to Lake Watab glimmering in the moonlight and sat down on a picnic table. He pulled out a cigarette. "I'm quitting," he said. "Slow motion. I let myself have six a day. This is my fourth." That was a lie, it was actually his tenth. He lit it and took a drag. "What do you hope for in life?" he said.

"I hope for what I already have. Adventure. I can't live without it. That's why I'm leaving for California. And what do you hope for?"

"I hope for courage."

"Courage to do what?"

"To kiss you."

She smiled and touched his arm. "I'm leaving soon so there's no point in playing hard-to-get," she said. She kissed him lightly and didn't pull away. She stayed and he parted his lips and her tongue flicked against his tongue and her arms were around him and then she was kissing him hard.

She put her head on his shoulder. She told him she adored him. She had adored him for two weeks now. It eased his heart. Astonishing, how this lovely young mammal could make him forget the languors of marriage and the troubles with the Committee and the problems of Bunsen Motors, all of that stuff, gone. She murmured something about finding a place to kiss some more and he led her over to his pickup and drove her to the Gardens of Avon motel and ten minutes later they walked into Room 6, and as soon as the door was shut, she was unbuttoning his shirt and unzipping his pants, her lips locked to his, and the tank top was on the floor and then the green pants, and she sprang up on the bed in an advanced state of nudity and bounced up and down and jumped into his arms. He was naked, it was his skin and her skin, and onto the bed they unfolded and she wrapped herself around him and whispered in his ear something about gladness. Oh what a fine body. Her flat, firm abdomen between the expanse of womanly hips and the fine bush of dark hair and the tender lips so delicately pursed and folded and the sweet-salty taste of her and she sang and whimpered and cried out and moaned—her pleasure was so generous and elaborate, as if he were the world's greatest lover, which he wasn't, except maybe right at this moment to a woman of combustible imagination—he'd never known a woman who enjoyed being made love to so much—Irene was mostly quiet and businesslike in bed, same as in the kitchen, making pie crust—you didn't moan and whimper as you did it or cry out, "More flour! Flour! Flour!" And the two other women he'd been with in the course of his marriage were each so stunned by guilt and remorse that they lay flat and inert and then wept afterward—but Angelica was a great enthusiast. She went to town. She had decided to have sex and so, by George, she was going to have all of it and not leave anything out. Man on top, woman on top, woman on top reversed, man from behind on bed, man from behind standing at the window, over and over, up and down, in and out, and meanwhile her scat singing which thrilled him, her *Oh yes yes yes Oh my God yes yes yes Oh Jesus God yes like that Oh yes Oh yes* and then there was a faint ripping sound and the smell of stale gas. "Was that you?" she said. "Or me?" "It's okay," he said. And then she needed a drink of water and she tiptoed to the bathroom leading him behind her, her hand grasping his tool, and then she sat on the bathroom counter and opened herself and they did it there, and then back to bed—a long, careening rush down miles of steep slope until he finally burst the bonds of earth and briefly flew and they lay quietly together, breathing hard, and he asked her, "Was that nice?" and she said, "Was what nice?" "Making love," he said. "I liked it a lot," she said. "Couldn't you tell?" "I thought you did," he said. He heard music from next door. The man in the next room had turned up his radio to drown out their lovemaking and it was a band playing "In The Mood"—

Oh, baby, was it good for you?
You drove me wild, doing the things
  you do.
I'll never forget the night we screwed.
So mahvelous—guess we were In The Mood.

So lovely, so lovely. All the rigmarole of marriage dispensed with. Just two creatures lying intertwined, breathing, him spooned behind her, his arms clasped around her middle, kissing her shoulders. After she left the motel, he lay awake in the tumultuous sheets smelling of her and thought that maybe he wasn't a Lutheran after all. No guilt. None. She had opened a door and he walked in. It didn't seem like a Lutheran thing to do. Lutherans were bred for monogamy, it was programmed into them. But maybe the whole God thing was just a big hoax and people needed to believe in it because it made them feel more important than they actually are. Much more dramatic, committing adultery and risking hellfire and everything. Whereas all he was was just an old dude who after a circumspect middle age suddenly got entwined with a young woman. An ancient cliché. A goat-footed hairy-legged brute chasing maidens through the forest. *Whoopee.* Mr. Brains-In-His-Pants. A character unwelcome in any decent American home, and yet a man no different from the others. A little naked furtive guy dithering in the mishmash, scared, your id throbbing. You see a smiling face across a crowded room. The piano plays and there are drinks. She touches your hand. *Hello.* You rise when the rooster crows and roll around in the sack and blow your wad and then she goes home. A joyful time is had by all. Thank you, very much.

10. THE CHAIRMAN SINGS

They looked down their noses at the old auto mechanic, the old grease monkey, like they looked down on plumbers or farmers, though it was pure stupidity on their part. *They didn't know a damn thing about cars.* Diener and Val Tollefson and all of them. Take a look at a repair manual now. It's all about computers. You don't take things apart and clean the armature or put new bearings in—you pull the whole component and re-place it. The old Ford V8 engine, any teenage boy could fiddle with it, but it's a whole new ball game now. You've got ten miles of wires and sensors running your butt heater, your climate con-trol, your A/C, your airbag, the GPS, the cruise control, and you've got to be able to read the service manual which is written in its own language, not English.

Nuts to them. He was done with them now. Clintonio and his old Duotone guitar, *mi amor, mi bella dama,* he would sing you a *canción dulce*—about moonlit nights—*luz de las noches del luna—el aroma de los pinos*—he once was Norwegian but now he was free. He sat in his porch and strummed a C chord and sang

He was only an auto mechanic with grease on his face
  and hands
But while he worked in the pit he longed for a great
  romance.
As he lubricated the Universal Joint with his big grease gun,
He could hear her crying out, "Oh yes yes my darling one,
Now darling pick up that gun and thrill me again,
You are the best ever, my love, you are a perfect ten."

His songs were not the sort people around here would appreciate. They preferred the smooth old ballads or inspirational folk-rock about morning dew and dreams come true me and you, and his were more in the Spanish style—

Love me, my lady, for soon I must die.
Perhaps this evening death will come by
And call my name and open his cold steel gate.
Come, let us eat the best oranges now and not wait.
Let us make love this very afternoon.
I hear the creaking of wagon wheels. He will be here soon.

Nobody knew he wrote songs except Irene who had found some written on bank deposit slips and she made no comment—odd, for her—but she was occupied with her garden, nursing her prize tomatoes toward the annual sweepstakes at the Mist County Fair in August. She was worrying about Kira in California whose roommate was a six-foot hairy-legged lesbian in hiking boots—was Kira safe?

Sometimes he sang in the basement, next to the old monster furnace and sometimes in the car. He'd drive south past the Farmer's Union grain elevator and Art's Baits & Night O' Rest Motel and sing—

Oh these tedious summer days, going in circles,
    going nowhere—
How I long to kiss you, dark lady, and touch your hair
And nibble your sweet lips and your tender breasts
And escape these suspicious streets and meaningless
    contests.

All his troubles seemed to vanish when he picked up a guitar and sang, especially if he sang about his troubles.

I walk down the street and I can feel them stare.
I hear them whisper, "He has a girlfriend somewhere"
And I want to tell them, "Yes, there is one for whom I
    yearn
And when I go away with her, I don't expect ever to return."

As a Norwegian he hadn't sung—what would people think?— but now that he wasn't anymore, he could sing in high, tender tones without fear and he hoped someone would overhear him and think, "Clint in love! What's the deal there? And does this mean my car won't be ready on Friday?"

I am a prisoner, he thought. *I am married to a waspish to-mato grower who has been sort of pissed off at me for years. I*

am a Hispanic American who labored for years under the bur-
den of Norwegianness and now I am reconsidering the whole
deal. Sixty years old: last chance to have a life.

Years have passed and I still miss my daddy coming home.
I'm older than him now and I am waiting all alone,
Thinking of a girl I love and what my life could have been.
How did I wind up in this army of disappointed men?

One nice thing about songs—Irene couldn't interrupt him
and say, "What do you mean, you're 'waiting all alone'? Hello?
I'm here." She was relentless, a corrector, a finisher of sentences.
He'd say, "Well, if you ask me—" and pause and she filled in the
blank. He pointed this out to her once and she said, "Oh, it's all
my fault, isn't it. It's all about me. I ruined your life. I'm a terrible person." And got in the car and didn't come back until almost midnight. It was a Rasmussen trait, a dogged devotion to
your own point of view. Before he married her, he should've
paid more attention to heredity. Every apple comes from a
tree. Look around, it's not far away. Tiffany inherited Irene's
relentlessness—pushing, pushing, pushing. When she was 17
she pushed him to buy her a car and she beat him up over it for
two months, every day some new argument, single-minded, a
little teenage Stalinist. Kira was more like him, easygoing, take
it as it comes and let go when it's done. The day-by-day plan. Do
your best and then give it a rest. But now his laid-backness had
turned around and bit him in the butt—had he pissed his life
away, one pointless day after another, and now he was winding
up the backstretch and did he have anything to show for it? A

few friends, a dogged marriage, a tenuous perch in hometown society—the thing that really distinguished him was the fact that Angelica was in love with him. Or was sort of in love with him. That he had enough spark left in him to make a young woman cry out for him? That he was still Alive. Was it not?

11. THE CHAIRMAN BROODS

I t was 8 p.m. on Fourth of July Eve. A Sabbath calm lay over the town though the Chairman's phone was hot. Mr. Hoppe called to report overhearing three Norwegian bachelor farmers talk about driving in the parade with a truckload of pig manure. "They've been talking about that for years," said Clint. The Betsy Ross people had canceled, a big blow—she'd been a hit last year. The Leaping Lutherans Parachute Team had canceled out for tomorrow—mechanical problems with the jump plane—and the Busy Biffy people had delivered 100 portable toilets instead of 150 and would that be okay?—and Art of Art's Baits & Night O' Rest Motel had changed his mind about letting the motel be used as a Hospitality Suite unless the Committee posted a bond guaranteeing that no card-carrying liberals would be welcomed there. The high school choir director Miss Falconer called to ask if he had received her letter, hand-delivered yesterday. Yes, he had. "And what do you think?" He thought it would give him a heart attack to have forty high school kids singing on the roof of the Central Building as the parade passed below. "How about thirty?" Miss Falconer was desperate to get her choir on

TV. "I understand," he said. "Let me see what I can do." And Mr. Diener called to say he was holding firm in his resolve to have six men impersonate dead soldiers on the American Legion float ("Our Men Make The Ultimate Sacrifice While Self-Appointed Critics Slam The War Effort: Whose Side Are You On?").

Clint said, "Couldn't we please keep politics out of the parade" and Diener said, "It's not politics, it's patriotism."

"Do we need to have bloody corpses?"

"Men died for our freedoms," said Diener. "Let's not forget that. It wasn't teachers and trial lawyers who got the job done."

He'd known Diener since third grade when his nickname was Diener the Wiener because he had lice and brown liquid was painted on his shaved head and he had suffered God knows what blow to his self-esteem and had been a jerk ever since.

On the other hand, his fund-raising ability was well known. He had a knack that most decent people do not, for confronting a man and asking him face-to-face to donate an astonishing sum of money. He was a terrier. He'd soft-soap you and tell you how wonderful your family was and then come in for the kill and ask for a leadership donation of five thousand dollars. You blanched at this figure, your eyes twitched, your arm jerked. *Five thousand dollars is a lot of money.* You were hoping to get by with a hundred bucks but the man was looking you in the eye, no joke. You wanted to say, "Roger, let me think about it, right now my house is on fire and my children are gone"—but the man will not be put off. He wants a check. If you don't give him one now, he will come back tomorrow. The man is not to be denied. He is facing you down.

The Fourth was paid for with a few big contributions from the

Farmers Co-op, Mist County Power & Light, the Boosters Club, plus the Liberty Lottery in February, $10 for a chance at a brand-new Ford from Bunsen Motors, which raked in the dough from neighboring towns. Last year, almost ten thousand tickets were sold, a hundred grand, two-thirds of it pure profit. But Mr. Diener's sheepdog doggedness was crucial to the effort.

If he wanted dead bodies, he was going to have dead bodies.

Clint walked out the front door of his stucco house on McKinley Street and down the steps, his gray shirt loose on him and his gray pants hitched up with a belt: He'd lost twenty pounds since that night at the Gardens of Avon Motel. He hadn't seen Angelica since then. She'd gone to California for a few weeks, sent him a letter ("What a perfect night! How can one repeat perfection? I adore adore adore you.") and they had chatted online. The night in Avon inspired him to go on the No White Food & Eat Only When You're Hungry Diet. He hoped there would be another night in Avon but he didn't want to beg. His plan tonight was to soak in a hot bath, take two Amnezine, hit the sack by 9:30, and arise bright and early at 5 a.m. to take command of his final Fourth of July and bring it home in triumph. He'd saved two tablets from the twenty Dr. DeHaven prescribed in February. DeHaven had done a U-turn on pharmaceuticals since he put himself on Felicitate and nowadays you ran into more and more residents of Lake Wobegon who seemed mellower, more laid-back, even semivacant, who used to be cranky and waspish and ready to bite your head off and now they smiled and told you to have a nice day and follow your star. Amnezine was a beautiful drug that induced short-term amnesia and he had used it for some painful meetings of the Fourth of July

Committee back in April when Mr. Diener was being a pain in the neck. He'd come home bruised from the hostilities, take a pill, wipe the slate clean.

He saw his wife Irene barefoot in green walking shorts and white blouse watering the hydrangeas in front. They dropped from their wad of blossoms, beads of water on the leaves. Her black hair streaked with gray pulled back with a French comb. The sound of water flowing out of the hose made him think he'd better go pee. He had already peed twice since supper, a thin trickle each time, and still gallons were left in the tank. DeHaven had put him on a pill called DynaFlo to shrink the prostate and give him a stream like a thoroughbred's but unfortunately among its side effects, listed on the bottle, was diminution of libido. Clint saw that and took himself off DynaFlo promptly—his libido was small enough as it was—and his stream dwindled to a trickle, sometimes a drip. But he thought he might make love to Irene tonight, if she didn't stay up too late. It had been several weeks. Maybe five. Or six. A long time. The woman surely was entitled to some amorous attention. Assuming that's what she wanted. Hard to tell. Lake Wobegon women didn't go in for seduction, considering it beneath them. Flirtation was immature and any sort of playfulness between men and women was dangerous: You could get a Reputation. So a professional chill prevailed. Irene had been sort of sweet before the wedding and very amorous afterward because she wanted a baby but as soon as she had three of them, a full clutch, she bared her teeth when he came near. Maybe a primitive form of birth control. Snapping and snarling about the garage, the lawn, the basement, the minister's sermon last Sunday, low water pressure, the president's foreign policy. Once he overheard her telling her sister on the phone how uncommunicative he was, so he wrote her a note—"The reason I don't talk is that you wouldn't like what I have to say." And then tore it up. But now Irene had a Latin lover. A macho man. He would have plenty to tell her. But not quite yet.

The forecast for the Fourth was for a high of 78 and for the sun to shine. He announced this to Irene. "At least you have a good day for it," said Irene.

"What do you mean, 'at least'?"

She grinned. She despised the Fourth, always had. A day of banging as if someone took a pipe wrench and beat on the radiators for the sheer delight of it. Her brother Irv used to compete in the pie-eating contest back before they changed the rules to disqualify contestants who vomited. Irv was able to eat and throw up more or less simultaneously. The memory of it was still vivid to her. A day of male hooting and woofing and girlish squeals and the booming of brass bands, mobs of people moving slowly, dazed by sunlight, weeping children—not so much difference between a big civic festival and, say, the evacuation of a city about to be bombed. Not that she could see.

"Pretty good summer so far," he said.

"Oh?"

"You don't think so?"

"Could use more rain."

"Well, that is for sure, but it rains now and your mosquito population is going to go through the roof. So it all balances out."

"I guess."

Irene wasn't easy to talk to. She worried all the time about

81

the kids. He'd given up worrying, what good did it do? Their eldest, Tiffany, was in Atlanta, perishing in the heat, where she'd gone to be with her boyfriend who tattooed IDs on the groins of dogs and cats, and then he left her for a country singer named Misty Rivers on whose left tit he had tattooed a rose, leaving Tiffany with a pillowful of tears and a year-long lease on a mildewy apartment. Irene sent her money every week. Sometimes Tiff talked about coming back home "to get her life together." A boomerang child. Their son, Chad, was employed in St. Cloud, a 30-year-old delivery boy, and was indulging his obsession with a video game called *Unbalanced* in which you burst into college classrooms and gun people down. Six loans to Chad had disappeared, like aircraft lost at sea. And Kira, the youngest, was in Monterey, California, managing Papa Bob's Lobster Pot restaurant. She was Clint's darling, his sweetie, his Baby Bumps, his Bumpster. Twenty-two and gone, gone, gone. It was for her that Clint carried a cell phone in his pocket, in case she should fall among bad companions and need him to tell her what to do.

A blue-green hummingbird hovered, blurred, by a honeysuckle vine. A contrail hung in the sky, a jet on the Detroit–Beijing run. She asked how everything was going. He said everything was fine. He had been lying to her without much success for a long time but he wasn't ready to give up yet.

"What's wrong?" she said. "Nothing," he said. "Well, something is," she said.

He was devastated, sort of, was what was wrong. His heart was torn to shreds by an e-mail Angelica sent him on Wednesday which he read a couple dozen times:

My darling,

I thought you should know that I am dating a man I met at a meet-up in Minneapolis called People of Spirit which is people curious about psychic phenomena, mysticism, prophecy, etc. He is a sweet man and I think he could be a good partner so we are exploring that and we plan to head for California in a week or two to attend the Oxnard Institute. Is this weird that I'm telling you this? Well, you said you wanted to know everything so now you know. I love you but you are (1) married, (2) a lot older, (3) not interested in having kids and (4) not a spiritual person and I really really need that dimension in my life. That's the truth. The truth shall make you free. I'd like to see the Fourth of July one more time and be Miss Liberty again and if you want to meet Kevin, he'll be with me then. He was a radiologist and then his wife died and he dropped everything and became a surfer bum until he found a source of light in the poetry of Dumi. More later.

As ever,

Angelica

"As ever"? He and Angelica had been lovers. He was counting on a return engagement. She was the most amazing lover he'd ever known—a select group, to be sure, but nevertheless— she was a shot of adrenaline, a big updraft, and when he suggested dinner, a drive in the country, a visit to Avon, she (psychic that she was) parried, said, "Not so fast." Said she needed time to think, and then she didn't answer his e-mails, and now this.

And now her long, luxurious body and searching lips, her strong swimmer's arms and shoulders, her delicate breasts with the delicious nipples, her bush and cleft, were the domain of another. And Clint was supposed to say that he understood and wished her well, and in fact it made him crazy. He thought of driving to St. Cloud and challenging the guy. Bump chests with him. Or maybe wire some explosives to his ignition. Easily done.

Irene was studying him and asking him again what was wrong.

"Oh," he said. "This is my last year doing this, and I ought to have fun, but suddenly I start to think maybe we'll have runaway horses, maybe the fireworks truck will blow up, maybe some yahoo in a burnoose'll run a truck loaded with homemade explosives into the Living Flag and blow it to Kingdom Come."

"You've been worrying about all that for years."

"This time it could be for real." He plopped down on the steps. "Last year we had—I donno—twenty thousand people. What if each of them came back and brought two other people. Sixty thousand. Maybe more. I'm short on toilets. Short on water. What if we get temperatures in the nineties and people start keeling over and we're short on emergency personnel and people die in the street. It happens. Six years of running the show and I go out on a note of death. Criminal neglect. The county attorney decides that I should've done the math and had six gallons of drinkable water per attendee and one doctor per thousand, and in September I'm sitting in a courtroom listening to people talk about me like I was the Unabomber."

"I doubt that they can get a trial going that fast. Probably you'd have until March or April."

He looked down the hill to the Central Building on Main Street where Lyle Janske's decoration committee was hanging bunting from the cornice and yes it looked to be old man Magendanz on the roof who suffers dizzy spells and also, Clint thinks, is taking Coumadin along with his usual dosage of bourbon but there he was waving his arms and yelling down at someone in the street. Clint looked away (LOCAL MAN, 75, DIES IN FALL, WAS HANGING FLAG FOR JULY 4 FESTIVITIES; DA ACCUSES SPONSORS OF "THOUGHTLESS DISREGARD"—VOWS TO BRING CHARGES.) and wished he were flying to Beijing with Angelica. They'd be coming around with drinks about now and warm cashews and she would have her hand in his lap.

It was still bright out at eight o'clock. A boy walked down the sidewalk bouncing a basketball and you could hear his happiness in the rhythm of it. Out on the lake the soft buzz of a distant outboard. It felt good, the sun and the mist from the hose. "Got people pissed off at me from one end of town to the other. Feel like an old wounded buffalo in a blizzard and the wolves circling for a clear shot at my butt."

"The problem," she said, "is that it's hard to repeat success. As you ought to know by now."

"I feel hated," he said. "Seriously. That's why they shit-canned me." "Nonsense," she said.

He followed her as she moved around to the side to water the irises and climbing roses. From uptown near the old depot came the clanging of the fire bell. The fire department was about to put a torch to the annual bonfire. Two old chicken coops had been trucked in and the remains of a one-room schoolhouse, piled on gasoline-soaked beams and a mountain of dry brush and debris. It was the firemen's party and they were pissed at Clint so he didn't attend. Probably Viola was there, assuring everybody that next year they could be in charge of fireworks again. Looking at his house, he thought, *I might go to Washington and never return and nobody knows this except me. People are going to look at this house and say, Bunsen lived there. A man of mystery. Used to fix my car. Now he's in Congress. Who knew?*

It was a new idea. It hit him seeing the idiot incumbent Jack S. Olson one night on the news. Verbose and pompous and a voice like a coffee grinder. *I could beat this jerk. Why not?*

The Bunsen house was still known as the Huber house to older Wobegonians, having been owned by former Mist County sheriff Walt Huber who ran for Congress in 1958, a Democrat, and he lost after it was revealed he once vacationed in Paris with his wife Lavonne. She went off her rocker after he died (self-inflicted shotgun wound in the cranium, referred to publicly as a hunting accident) and kept calling the sheriff's office to report a deadly snake in her basement and a deputy had to be dispatched to calm her down. And then, a year before she died, the snake got out and ate a neighbor's dog, a miniature cocker spaniel, and choked on it and was shot. (The dog revived but suffered from anxiety attacks—the flushing of a toilet threw it into spasms of terror—and it was banished to the outdoors and subsequently run over by a gravel truck.) The snake was sixteen feet long and thirty-seven inches in circumference. Evidently it had fallen off a snake truck en route to a reptile garden and taken refuge in the basement, slipping in and out through a dryer vent. So Lavonne Huber was vindicated. People still thought she was crazy but for other reasons. When Clint and Irene bought the house they discovered snakeskin boots in a closet and copies of an agnostic magazine, *Not So*. She had sold the house to them for a song—"I always liked you," she whispered to Clint, still a big flirt at 82.

It was one of the few brick houses in Lake Wobegon—one of four, to be precise, and the only one owned by a Lutheran, the others being the Wilfred Kotzes, the Hugo Hattendorfs, and the Larry Lugers, all German Catholics.

His mind collected odd facts such as that—Year That Babe Ruth Came To Town On Sorbitol Barnstorming Tour: 1934, and he walloped a home run against the Lake Wobegon Schroeders, a long ball that never was found. Smartest Graduate of L.W.H.S., probably Phil Johnson, who became a physicist and performed science experiments in the Ringling Brothers Circus. Most Beautiful Girl, probably Eunice Tollefson, who was Miss Sixth Congressional District of 1978 or perhaps Marnie Montaine, who changed her name from Barb Diener and went to Hollywood and was strangled in a movie called *The Dark Under the Bed* and then changed her name to something else and nobody ever heard a word about her again, she was swallowed by Hollywood. Year That Alhambra Ballroom Burned Down: 1955. Year that Sanctified Brethren (18 members) split into the Consecrated Sanctified Brethren (11 members) and the Faithful Remnant of Sanctified Brethren (5 members): 1947. (Two became Lutherans.)

He cherished facts. Since he was a boy, he had pored over the *World Almanac*, soaking up information. For example, there are 100 billion more suns as big as this one in the Milky Way galaxy alone and here we sit, a dust speck in a galaxy which itself is only one of 100 billion galaxies, so far as we on the dust speck are aware. We, in turn, each contain 50 trillion cells, each of which has a coil of DNA that, uncoiled, would extend six feet long, so each of us consists of an invisible coil stretching 950 million miles, all the way to the sun and ten times beyond. Each of us is insignificant and each is vast and complicated, and this includes his wife, trudging barefooted in the grass, watering her flowers.

The sun is ten thousand times the size of the earth and contains 99.8 percent of all the mass in our solar system (and Jupiter contains most of the rest) and it shines on rich and poor alike, on male and female, on Democrat and Republican. He was a Republican. Irene was a Democrat, bless her heart, a good liberal, tolerant to a fault except where her husband was concerned. A good woman. Mom was right about that. But Irene was hard to open your heart to. You could pour out your innermost thoughts and she'd likely say, "I don't know where you come up with that stuff." Which was true, she didn't. And now he knew why: She was Norwegian, he was Spanish. He craved tenderness. Lake Wobegon women were brought up to be no-nonsense, and it wasn't in them to put their head on a man's shoulder, an arm around his waist, murmur *"Muy bien, mi amor."* They were more likely to say, "Aren't those the pants you wore yesterday? Why not put on clean clothes? I do your laundry, why not use it?"

He sat on his front steps in the gathering twilight and imagined his other life, the one he could've had if he'd found out who he was back when he was young enough to do something about it—he'd have settled in the California hills, in the coastal village of San Margarita Maria, in a cottage covered with grape vines looking out at the big ocean waves thwamming against the rocks, and a big-hipped olive-skinned woman with dark hair hanging down her back sitting next to him, sharing a cold beer, a plate of salsa and chips, savoring the conversation of sighs and caresses that is preliminary to the ceremony of love. Love in Lake Wobegon was a complex maneuver, like organizing a softball game— you had to get a lot of pieces in place before it happened.

He stood up. Time to crack down. He had to order more toilets and make sure the football field was ready for the arrival of the horses and wagons and check with the fireworks people. So he forgot about the Amnezine and tried to focus on the task at hand. He called the Betsy Ross people. How hard is it to be inert and let people throw you in the air? The lady said, "A Betsy has to undergo twenty hours of training. We have a backup Betsy but she's in a production of *Mary Poppins*."

"How about you toss a Minuteman?"

"Then it wouldn't be a Betsy Ross Blanket Toss."

He had booked the Betsy through Asher Variety & Theatrical in the Lumber Exchange in Minneapolis, an agent named Murray who tried to sell him on a troupe of tumbling chickens— "They could wear star-spangled capes, no problem, I know somebody who can sew"—and a strongman who lifts cars—"You could put people in it in costume, light people"—and also Brazilian clog dancers. "I didn't know there were clog dancers in Brazil," said Clint. "On the coast there are some," said Murray. Clint nixed the dancers and the chickens but he was delighted to get Wally the Human Pinwheel who could do cartwheels nonstop for up to a mile at a time. A great addition to any parade. And only $50.

12. FREEDOM

And there was a voice-mail message. Angelica said, "I am coming tomorrow, Bunny. I am sensing that you're under a great deal of stress and I want to be there. And you need a Statue of Liberty. And then I'm going to California. I finally decided. Thanks for the encouragement. You're right, I need to make a new life. I think about you a lot."

California was where he'd left his freedom behind: in San Diego. He was mustered out of the Navy, 23, good-looking, able to run up and down stairs two at a time and put away a 32-oz. porterhouse and baked potato and banana cream pie and go to sleep with no regrets. He had applied to St. Joseph School of Art in Santa Barbara to study wood sculpture. He had decided to move to California. That was the plan. And he was in California at the time so he could've just stayed (Duh) but he drove a thousand miles back to Minnesota to say good-bye to Mom and Dad and in no time they made him feel guilty and wretched for wanting to abandon them so he stayed in the frozen North and married the high school sweetheart who he'd tried to leave behind. People expected him to marry Irene so he did. As if he were in a play written by someone who didn't like him. And then Daddy's mechanic Bud lost a finger to a circular saw and Clint got sucked into the family business—became the mechanic because he had the brains—Clarence had the warmth, which is all a salesman needs, a grin and a backslap and peppermints for the kiddies, but a mechanic has to know his business—and now he was 60, the business was tanking, he was tired of the dipstick, the tire gauge, the battery tester, thinking he'd like to try dry goods, shirts, ties, and he finds out he's a Spanish swan among the Norwegian geese.

The Clint Bunsen Story, doggone it. He'd gone back to that wrong-way odyssey in his own mind, back to Durango, Colorado, sitting at the wheel of the red '64 Mustang, a Navy vet, driving back home to Minnesota against his better judgment. Should've turned that puppy around, made the tires squeal on the Colorado asphalt. It's a free country. He'd done well in the Navy. Gunnery mate. Fat and sassy. The chaplain saw him whittling little farmer and fisherman figures and asked him to carve a cross, and he did, and then a standing Christ, and then a Mother and Child. So he wanted to matriculate in art school in Santa Barbara. He should have hunkered down, unplugged the phone, let the mail go unopened. He loved California, the balmy climate, the surfers, the tall women playing volleyball on the beach. Why did he drive away from what he wanted? Daddy sent a postcard: "I am counting the days until you come back to us. Nothing has been right since you left."

And now the wrong turn was 37 years back down the road. He sat with the Old Regulars in the corner booth at the Chatterbox and a still, small voice said, "Gather those rosebuds, pal, and all the pleasures prove because the flower that smiles today will be dying tomorrow. Nothing can bring back the hour of splendor in the grass, boyo. Seize the day! Hit the road!" He no longer believed in the efficacy of hard work—all of his had only dug him in deeper and subjected him to a long list of deprivations. He'd worked a six-day week for years until Irene put a stop to it. The point is: Life is short, dang it. Daddy had gone down hard to colon cancer at the age of 60, still in the traces. It was on Clint's mind as the cake was brought in with a conflagration of candles and his friends sang in their ancient ruined voices.

Don't die in Lake Wobegon, don't do it, don't do it. Don't let them drop you down into this cold ground. Die under the palm trees, suddenly, with several sweet tall women in swimsuits sitting at your side, holding your hands.

And then a second message from Angelica: "Bunny, did I mention that Kevin will be with me on the Fourth? Is that okay? Please don't feel bad. You are one of the important people in my life and you always will be. I love you."

Turning 60 ought to make you mellow and warm and chuckly, but not him. He only felt panic. Sixty-five was on the horizon and then the short, sudden decline into dementia and death. Shuffling around the Good Shepherd Home in pee-stained pants, trying to remember the route to his room, trying to keep his sphincter clamped shut. Mourning for all the beautiful girls he knew who were beautiful no more and all the dances he'd passed up. Regretting his long life of indentured service to family and community. Then some tossing and turning and then the merciful descent of night and then they stuff you into the blue suit you used to wear to other people's funerals and you lie in the funeral parlor smelling of roses and Windex and your kids come and blink back their tears—his darling Kira, now beyond his love and care, oh my God—and then one night a woman stands at your coffin and sobs her eyes out—but who is she? It's too dim to tell. She weeps bitterly and then goes away and does not come to your funeral, your farce of a funeral, and people orating about his fidelity and goodness who never had a kind word for him in life and spinning heartwarming tales about things that never happened. And the short ride up the hill and you're thinking, "Oh geeze. My last car ride. I remember that drive from San Diego to Lake Wobegon. Sixty-four Mustang. Sweet little car. Four on the floor. Nice pickup, handled well on the highway. I installed that speaker on the roof behind the driver's seat. Beautiful sound. Loved that car." And then the hearse stops and you think, "Well, here we are. That's that. Good-bye highway." And the pallbearers carry you jouncing over rough ground and set you on a brass frame and old Ingqvist reads a prayer and the survivors sing "Children of the Heavenly Father" without much conviction and your kids stand around snuffling and nobody throws herself on your coffin and cries out, "Oh Daddy, our darling Daddy, don't leave us! We can't bear it!" They all walk away except for some guys on the cemetery committee who discuss drainage problems and then the undertaker folds up the plastic grass and drives away and the gravediggers come and one of them says, "That sumbitch Clint Bunsen sold me a Ford Falcon years ago, man that was the shittiest car I ever had. What a jerk." And the hum of the pulleys lowering you into the vault and a hard bump and the thud of the concrete lid. You lie there for a few minutes and say, "Okay, I'm ready now." And God says, "For what?" "For the gardens of heaven. The place with no tears. Singing all the time. Where we'll all be young and beautiful forever." And God says, "Let me check on that and get back to you." And there you lie for a hundred years waiting patiently in your nice blue suit, tie knotted, hands folded, and every so often you think, "Damn, I should've turned around in Durango."

That Standard Oil station in Durango: the petroleum-soaked red dirt around the twin pumps, the dark-eyed Indian kid with the leather necklace who pumped the gas, not a word out of him, and the old brick storefronts across the street and the Stockmen's Bar, door open, Lefty Frizzell singing "That's The Way Love Goes," the dark mountains in the bright blue sky, and the payphone inside the garage where he dropped in the quarters and called Mom to tell her he was not coming home and he put the coins in before he got his story worked out in his own mind. He was going to say, "Guess what! I got this great job as a desk clerk at a hotel called The Inn of the Spanish Gardens and I promised I would start work on Monday." Mom believed in keeping your promise. But the story wasn't true and when she said, "Clinton! Where are you?" he decided not to lie. He said, "Colorado. But I was thinking maybe I'd come home for Christmas instead." A pitiful thing to say. Asking your mom for permission to run away from home. Mom said, "But we haven't laid eyes on you for almost a year, Clint. We want you right here, honey. Daddy needs you. He's having heart pains. Irene misses you so much. She keeps asking about you. Honey, you have to come home. We'd just plain die if you didn't."

So he continued north and then in Lincoln he stopped at the Cornhusker Hotel and woke up at 3 a.m. hearing fate tell him to turn around and go back to California, go back, go back, and he called home to tell them he had changed his mind and nobody was home. The phone rang and rang. No answering machines in those days where you could leave your message—"I ain't coming. Forget about it"—and that would be that. For lack of voice-mail, he was doomed to go home and spend his life in Lake Wobegon. Simple as that. He got home and Daddy was worn out and needed a mechanic and the next day Clint started work.

And nobody in Lake Wobegon cared about The Clint Bunsen Story, because here, you don't entertain regrets. Everybody has them so don't try to unravel the twisted cords of history, because there's no end to it. Put it behind you and wake up with a smile and make this day the best it can be.

He pulled out a cigarette, the last of his day's ration, and stuck it in his mouth unlit. He felt light-headed, Don Clintonio, the old lover. His heart fluttered in an interesting way. *Courage*. The wolves were out to bring him down, and eventually they would. And his carcass would fertilize the grass and life would go on. That was what it was all about, the Committee dumping him— his townsmen were only fulfilling nature's mission. Push the old guy out and let somebody new come in. Cull the herd, prune the roses. Throw the old lover off the balcony and make the bed for a new one. Oh well. At least he wouldn't have to run the Fourth of July again. Safe at last. No more meetings where he said,

"Let's try to make this work, okay?" Nobody was going to put a clipboard in his cold, petrified fingers. He had lost twenty pounds and he would look good at the end and people would be a little surprised when he kicked the bucket. And tonight he intended to make love to his wife. He had bought a bottle of red wine for $25, a Tempranillo from Barcelona in the province of Tarragona, a pound of garlic olives, and a dozen jumbo shrimp and horseradish. He had heard that red wine and shellfish was definitely a help.

13. THE CHAIRMAN AWAKENS

Six a.m. on the Fourth of July and the Chairman of the day had gotten two phone calls already and had smoked one of his ten allotted smokes and was about to light the second. Todd, the governor's flunky, had called from the capitol to say the governor might be a couple hours late and Lyle called to say he was having a nervous breakdown. A text message from Angelica: "Adoro a usted, senor. I am mighty loco for you." Clint sat on the front steps, the smell of coffee and flowers in the air. He had made love to his indifferent wife the night before and he'd done a good job of it and made her cry out his name and say a vulgar word over and over that she seldom ever said and that was an accomplishment, and now he sat on his front steps, in his pajamas, cigarette and coffee in hand, studying the sky, a few high wisps of cloud to the north like patches of oatmeal in a blue bowl. He waited for the boom of the cannon, which should've gone off at six. Berge was the cannon man. Maybe he'd overslept.

He hadn't slept well at all. He worried about the Fourth and then thought about Angelica and about Kevin who was kissing her, holding her in his arms, unbuttoning her blouse, and Clint wanted to go get a shotgun and blow the man's head off. Clean. A bloody stump of neck, the brains glittering on the sidewalk. The scalp lying in the street. It was the Spanish in him. Around midnight he turned to his old wife and snaked his foot over and touched hers, and she said, "What?" He said, "You're very lovely, you know that?" She sighed a weary sigh ("Not that again . . ."), but he persevered, and stroked her hair, kissed her freckled shoulders and breasts, touched all the switches, it was like starting a car on a cold morning, and in the end she was on her hands and knees thrusting her bare rump at him and crying, "Do it! Do it!"—how refreshing to hear it from the matron of the church kitchen, she who was so caustic about pornography and wondered what anybody saw in it—sharp-tongued Irene of the Rhubarb Patch, crying out, "O Christ!" as he dashed steaming around third base toward home and the crowd rose to its feet, and in he came he came he came sailing into home and she whinnied with joy and he collapsed on her and they lay there exhaling for a few minutes. She got up out of bed, her great white haunches naked in the moonlight, and tiptoed into the bathroom and closed the door and peed quietly, musically, and then slipped back into bed.

"It's been a long time," she murmured. She kissed him on the neck. "Put your arm around me," she said. He did.

"What are you thinking?"

"Thinking about you."

"Not about your girlfriend?"

"No." And he wasn't. Not until she mentioned it. And then

he remembered Angelica and her new lover and wondered what they might be up to tonight, imagined their clothing mingled on her bedroom floor.

"Do you still love me?" He said that indeed he did.

"Do you really? Are you sure?" Yes, he said, he really was. Though he wasn't completely sure, now that she asked. But what could he say? *Maybe. Let me think about it?* And make her feel bad, and then she'd have you in counseling and you'd lose your Wednesday nights for a while and face a long, grim drive together to St. Cloud and back. No, making love was the right thing. Go on the offensive, secure the beachhead, and short-circuit those questions women drive you nuts with—*Do you love me? Do you think we have a good marriage? Why don't we spend more time together?*

So he took care of that, and she rolled over and started snoring and he lay awake, looking at the ceiling, thinking about his heart. He slept for a while until raccoons woke him up at 2 a.m., two big males rolling the garbage can down the driveway like patrons at a buffet, and he ran them off and then spotted Miss Simpson across the alley up in her bathroom, God help us, taking a shower, the window half open, her bare back quite visible in the mist, and he stood, pondering whether to warn her that her window was open and any yahoo could observe her, and then she turned toward the window to rinse her back, and he decided not to. We all have to take our chances in this life.

Then after lusting after the flat chest of a math teacher, he listened to *Party Line* on WDUL and T.J. was yakking about spiders and how the average person eats thirteen spiders in a lifetime. More if you snore. They tiptoe along your lips in the night, attracted to drool, and if you snore, the intake will suck them in, and as you swallow them they empty their bowels which is that bitter taste you wake up with in the morning. Spider turds. A proven fact. That's why men drink whiskey for breakfast, and also to kill off spider toxins that can trigger hormonal changes in men. The poisons a spider kills houseflies with may take the lead out of your pencil. "I maybe shouldn't be saying this," said a caller, "but I gotta wonder if homosexuality may not be caused by spiders." T.J. pooh-poohed that but another caller said, "No, my brother-in-law had an infestation of spiders one spring and within weeks he was dating a man named Sean. A very nice man, don't get me wrong, but nevertheless—"

"I think that your brother-in-law probably always was gay and just didn't know it," said T.J. "That's about what I'd expect a liberal like yourself to say," said the caller and was about to say more and then T.J. cut to a commercial for asphalt delivered hot to your home.

After that there was no sleep for Clint. He watched three and four o'clock click over on the digital clock radio, and he heard the voice of his old dad say, *Look out. A beautiful summer day may turn out badly. Someone could drown. It happens.* Clint drifted off to sleep and dreamed he heard women screaming, a child had been trampled by a horse. The team comes wheeling around the corner by the Sons of Knute temple and a child dashes in front of the beasts! He disappears under the mighty hooves. The mother screams and crawls into the mass of horseflesh as the teamster hauls on the reins and she emerges with a small bloody bundle, the face cruelly torn—a siren approaches . . .

Clint sat up in bed, sweat trickling down his forehead, salt burning his eyes. It was 4:15 and the curtains stirred in the breeze and a sound like water trickling from a faucet. He got up to check. Pulled on his pants and a sweatshirt and went downstairs. Actually it was something flapping, like leaves against a window, or scissors cutting construction paper. He half-expected to find Kira, 10 years old, in the kitchen pasting together the walls of a little house in which tiny paper people—Mom, Dad, Chad, Tiff, Me—sat glued to a table eating food scrawled on round circles. No, it was a bird chirping on a branch outside the kitchen window. A low chirp of bird trepidation. "Not good," it said. "Not good at all." He stepped out into the dark yard, faint rays of light from beyond the lake. And there was a message from Angelica: "Darling, I can't sleep because I'm thinking about you and worrying. I have a vision of you in agony. Is that true? I am sorry if I'm the cause of it. If you want to call me, please do."

He walked to the end of the yard and into Irene's garden. Pole beans, tomatoes, the cucumber vines, peppers, radishes. A tribe of crows had taken lodging in a red oak tree behind the Lutheran church who were starting to murmur now, like old men stirring in their sleep. He thought he could hear Daddy's voice and then Uncle Jack's. Daddy was telling his Mexican paramour how much he loved her, and Jack was complaining—"Jeeze, Clinty. I was only fifty-four. What kind of deal is that? Got divorced from Dot and looked forward to a new life and, wham, liver cancer.

Me. Mr. Eagle Scout. I never drank. Wasted years, Clinty. Wasted years. Damn it to hell, when I think of the hours I spent watching golf on TV. Jesus. Help me. I'm not done yet. I want to come back. Please. Pray for my return to earth. Being a crow is a lousy way to end up. Tell God I deserve better."

Jack sat in the tree muttering and Clint went back indoors.

14. CONGRESS

The kitchen smelled of citron. He turned on the coffeemaker. He made a list on an index card:

1. STAGE
2. TOILETS
3. GOVERNOR
4. WHEN CNN?
5. FIRST AID (DEHYDRATION)
6. FALCONER
7. ART
8. MORE FLAGS
9. PERCH. (VISIT)
10.

He took the card and a cup of coffee out on the porch and sat on the front steps waiting for the cannon to go off and was about to call up Berge when he heard Irene's bare feet on the floorboards behind him. She stood behind him, her knees grazing the back of his head. Little croakers in the grass and a redwing black-bird in the bushes.

"That was rather lovely last night. And completely unexpected," she said. "I guess we ought to have red wine more often."

"You okay?" she said.

"I'm fine."

"What are you thinking?" She eased herself down on the step beside him, as if she expected a cogent answer. What was he thinking?—it would take the rest of his life to tell her.

"I'm trying not to think."

"I can hear the wheels in your head going around." She put a hand on his knee. "What's the big news? Out with it."

"I'm thinking about running for Congress. I'm not going to do it but I'm thinking about it."

"Not such a bad idea," she said. "After we've had an idiot for a president—who's to say what's crazy?"

"I don't know—there's this guy—" A man in St. Cloud, a very well-connected man named Griswold, was pushing him to do it. The man had seen Clint give a speech at the Kiwanis in Little Falls and thought it was great. And the time was now.

A week ago the Honorable John "Smilin' Jack" S. Olson had sidled up to a man standing at a urinal in a men's room at the Minneapolis–St. Paul airport and asked him to dance. "Let's you and me and your puppy dog boogie," he said, according to men at nearby urinals. Olson then cried, "Wheeeee!" and grabbed the man by the wrists and attempted to twirl him. He made lascivious thrusting movements with his pelvis. A bystander captured the scene on his cell phone. The congressman was arrested for lewd behavior. His office claimed he was suffering from a mood swing caused by the use of the steroid prednisone, and he flew to New Zealand on a fact-finding mission to the kiwi industry. A week later, after other urinal incidents had come to light, all involving an offer to dance, he tearfully resigned.

Irene shook her head. "So you just came up with this since all that happened to Olson?"

No, not really. Though the toilet dancing was what opened the door. Last year's Fourth of July/Delivery Day had gotten a lot of press. All year, in the wake of the CNN exposure, Clint had been giving a speech, "Dare To Make A Difference," which had gone over well at Kiwanis and Jaycee groups, and Griswold said, "That speech can take you to Congress, my friend. I kid you not." He was a wiry little guy with a fixed grin and he grabbed both of Clint's elbows and got up close to him and said, "Lack of experience is not the disability it once was. Voters want fresh faces. The fact that you are an auto mechanic and get grease on your hands is only to your advantage, being a Republican."

A right-wing nut named Georgia Brickhouse had already filed for the primary September 8, a fundamentalist dame who had gotten a command direct from the Lord to run. A loony.

"So that's what I'm thinking," he said. Irene laughed. "You want to go to Washington, you go alone," she said. "I'm a small-town girl. I have to have a garden."

Griswold was already talking about an ad campaign showing Clint in his coveralls next to a car: "I've been fixing things all my life and now it's time to do an overhaul in Washington. . . ." Another showing Clint pointing with a clipboard, directing last year's parade: "Big cities have canceled their Fourth of July parades but Lake Wobegon's got bigger and better, thanks to a man who dared to dream—last year 57 million people saw it on CNN—and now you can send this heroic dreamer to work for you in Washington. . . ."

But now he wasn't sure. There was the Angelica business, a complication of a high order. Gossip about him playing footsie with a young woman would hurt him in this town, no doubt about it. In this town adultery was considered not only immoral but grotesque, like pouring whiskey on your cornflakes or having a spider tattooed on your face—Why? What was the point? **REPUB-LICAN HOPEFUL ADMITS "INDISCRETION"—TEARFUL BUNSEN: "I WAS WRONG. I GET IT NOW. PLEASE FORGIVE ME."** And now the governor was coming up from St. Paul for the Fourth and Griswold was pushing Clint to announce his candidacy, ask the governor for his blessing, get the show on the road. And Clarence was pushing him to take over the business so he and Arlene could go to Florida this winter.

Too much going on.

The Living Flag was scheduled for 11:30 so the sun would be high for an overhead photo with no shadows and the parade was at 2 o'clock and the Honor America Program at 3:30 but the governor was running late and there was no word from CNN so the schedule might need to be juggled and Father Wilmer the Living Flag chairman had turned things over to Constable Gary because Father was having an anxiety attack about riding in a convertible as Parade Grand Marshal though he'd known about it for weeks—Gary was half out of his mind, having been taken off one medication and put on another—and Lyle, ordinarily Mr. Reliable, had gotten dithery since his marriage was on the rocks and he was in charge of the stage show, meanwhile, Mr.

Berge the parade chairman had fallen off the wagon and was liable to spend the day in bed.

Todd suggested that the governor might like to make a speech after the parade. In olden days there had been a Fourth of July speech by a noted orator but the noted orators all died off, Gene McCarthy that old spellbinder had come in 1958, Clint remembered, and held the crowd in the palm of his hand, crying out against injustice and the exploitation of labor, and in 1963 his rival Hubert Humphrey stood on a haywagon in the middle of Main Street and raised his voice and five thousand people jammed in tight, on tiptoe, necks craning, to see the man, his shirtsleeves rolled up, big perspiration stains on his back and under his arms, but then those old champions who could stand up and belt out a speech died off and then one year the speaker didn't show up— he got the date wrong—and nobody seemed to miss it, and that was the end of it.

"It could be a short speech," said Todd. "Ten or fifteen minutes."

"How about he gets up and gives a greeting?"

"How long is a greeting?"

"A hundred words or less."

"How about two hundred?"

"Okay, how about just a grin and a wave?"

Todd pretended to be offended. "You're saying he can't speak? This is the governor of Minnesota, not some yahoo."

"People don't come to hear speeches anymore."

"Who says?"

Clint had been dealing with Todd for two months. He liked to get in your face.

15. DRESSING UP

Viola Tors called to say that she'd heard that Clint was upset and hoped it wasn't true. She was afraid they might draw too may people—80,000 would be a disaster. Maybe they needed to hire more security. She said Art had left for Montana yesterday. She had put him on the bus in St. Cloud with a dozen cheese Danish and a bottle of Jim Beam and he was happy. He was carrying a pistol in a leg holster but she wasn't going to worry about that. Probably he passed out and would sleep right through to Billings. She had the keys to the motel, and she and four ladies from church were going to clean out two cabins, one for CNN and one for the governor, and Dorothy was whomping up a nice buffet of cold shrimp, smoked venison sausage, four kinds of pickles, a cheese platter, smoked whitefish, deluxe olives, and a selection of canned beverages. She was hoping Clint could assign someone to keep Mr. Berge under control. He wandered into the Chatterbox at 6:30 in the morning jabbering about chiggers. "I will speak to him," said Clint.

Berge went on drinking binges whenever he thought he was

dying. Something—a heart palpitation, blurred vision, irregular bowel habits—convinced him that the end was near and he felt the inferno and he hit the bottle again. Berge was a student of his own bowel movements and he was happy to share his findings with you. Once, in the Sidetrack Tap, he stuck his head out of the men's can and yelled to Wally, "Come here! I want you to take a look at something!" Wally told him to flush the toilet.

"Can you call CNN and make sure they're coming?" she said.

He reminded her that his term as Chairman was almost up. "I'm going to have fun for once. Leave the worries to the rest of you."

"I was afraid of that," she said. She was sorry for any hurt feelings. She hadn't meant it personally. "Please don't leave us hanging," she said. Her voice got soft and trembly. "We need you, Clint. We're counting on you."

And then he went upstairs to get dressed. He had sent for the costume through a website called Muchacho Allegre in Las Cruces, white pants with gold buttons shaped like figure-8s down the pantlegs and slit at the cuffs, a white waist-jacket embroidered with vines and flowers, a silk shirt with pearl buttons and roses embroidered across the yoke. A broad-brimmed sombrero, made of felt, and a golden belt with a silver buckle, and a big yellow bow tie. And black sandals. He had never worn sandals before except in San Diego, during his Navy years, flip-flops for the beach. In Lake Wobegon, a man wore shoes or boots.

He struck a pose in front of the mirror. It was a different look, that was for sure. Maybe too different. He put the sombrero back in the closet, and the jacket. The pants were tight, but oh well.

He put the jacket back on. Took it off. It's okay to dress up but you don't want people to think you've lost your marbles. He took off the shirt, put on a white T-shirt. That was better. Easy does it. And then he took off the T-shirt and put on the flowered one. What the hell. He pinned a button to one of the roses, it said LIBERTY.

Irene looked in the door and clicked her tongue. "Sort of goofy but I like it. Is this the new you?" She rolled her eyes. "Could be fun."

His brother Clarence was loitering on the front porch when Clint came out the door to go downtown. "Didn't know it was Halloween," he said. Clint pointed at his Liberty button and Clarence grimaced. "Whatever you say. Not sure people are going to want Zorro to fix their mufflers, though." Clarence was on a blood thinner and it affected his sense of humor.

Clint told him about the DNA test, done at a lab in Phoenix. "We are Hispanic. Norwegian no longer. We can give up eating lutefisk. We never need to listen to that stupid 'Helsa dem der Hjemme' anymore. Ja, hey. Guess what? We're free, *compadre*. Is that a good deal or what?"

"Is this a joke?"

"I don't know. But you and I are about fifty-eight percent Spanish. If that isn't nice, I don't know what is. We are Hispanic Americans, brothers to the Jimenezes and the Garcias. We don't need to go to Syttende Mai and wear those dumb knee pants. No more pickled herring. We can eat food that tastes like something. We can laugh, we can cry, we can dance—"

"Maybe you need to go to a doctor and have your brains looked at," said Clarence.

"Let's have him look at Art first and then Berge and Viola and I'll wait my turn in line."

Clarence blanched. "Somebody ought to lock Art up. For his own sake. He's been a lunatic lately. Running around shooting squirrels. I found three squirrel corpses in our garden. Heads blown off. I think the guy is using a silencer."

"Art took a bus to Montana," said Clint.

"And what about you? People say you're planning to leave town. I get asked about it every day."

"People have big imaginations."

"Well, I'm sorry you resigned. You're leaving big shoes to fill. You did a great job." He sat down in the big white lawn chair that had been Dad's.

"Did I?"

"Of course you did."

"Then why didn't anybody ever say so?"

Clarence shrugged.

What Clint wanted to tell his brother was, *Tell your wife not to count her chickens. So you want to retire. Fine. Go right ahead. God bless you. But the dinero is gone. Lost. Perdido. Don't imagine I'm going to buy out your half at the ridiculous price you mentioned back in April. You're dreaming. The net worth of Bunsen Motors is nowhere near that. You can get as mad as you like but I will not take out a mortgage so I can pay you a fortune for a dealership that is going to go belly-up in a few years, meanwhile you and Arlene are collecting seashells on Sanibel Island and I am busting my hump trying to raise the Titanic. Our faithful old customers are abandoning the big dealerships with the pennants and balloons and the free hot dogs so they can save a few hundred bucks.*

They are cutting our throats. People we sit next to in church, the parents of our kids' best friends. Maybe they know we're Spanish, we're not of their northern tribe.

Clarence looked away, embarrassed. "Not sure I should tell you, but people've been talking about you. Not sure you know that." *Well, I hope it was interesting.* "Somebody said you're having an affair with a young woman in St. Cloud." *This is true.* "Does Irene know?" *Irene knows everything, of course.* "So what's the story?" *I'm in love with her and she's found someone else. So it's all over.* "So you're sure it's over?" *Pretty sure. I wish it weren't but probably it is. I'll find out more today.* "Just don't blow up your life so you can have sex with somebody. Okay?" *Already had the sex, and it was wonderful of course, now I'm trying to figure out what to do with my life. Same as everybody else.* "Have you spoken to David Ingqvist about this? I think you should." *He's got enough on his mind without me adding to it.*

Anyway. How's the pyrotechnics?

16. EXPLOSIVES

larence brightened up. Fireworks was his big love, after Arlene. "It's going to be spectacular. With eighty-five grand in the budget. We never had that kind of dough before. How'd you ever get money from the Department of Homeland Security?"

"Well, they wanted to give us a bomb disposal unit, which we didn't need, so we asked for rockets instead. We saved them about fifty thousand dollars. They're not called fireworks, by the way; they are 'aerial diversion devices.' A-D-D. Ten-inch diameter shells that go up fifteen hundred feet."

"Yeah, but this hits the headlines and you and me are gonna be getting our pictures in the paper, coming out of the courthouse holding hats over our faces."

Clint stood up and adjusted his pants. "The war on terror is a real war and a big part of any war is morale. This is a war without a front line. We're all in it and we all need morale builders lest we give up and just hunker down and wait for Islamic extremists to come in and blow up the water tower. People need to remain vigilant and vigilance is the hardest thing there is. To be on the lookout for strangers wanting to give you odd packages. Strange cars circling through town at night. Women with backpacks. Olive-skinned men who inquire about landing areas. We need people to be on the lookout. So we're building community spirit so people will be watchful for suspicious activities."

"Where did you learn to bullshit like this?"

"All I know is what I see on television," he said.

Clarence pulled a diagram out of his pocket. "I ordered that Vesuvius Curtain from China. A hundred feet long. You set it up on a steel mesh and it spells out 'Lake Wobegon' in letters ten feet high, it's a regular curtain of fire." The Vesuvius Curtain would be hung between two pontoon boats that would race across the lake as the ADDs went up from the ballpark. Very deluxe. But the emphasis was going to be on rockets, four-footers that blast up in the air and burst in clusters two hundred feet across—silver, gold, blue, white, red—ten solid minutes of flaming thunder! And one rocket that would spell out *CNN* in flaming letters. They could set up a camera at the end of the dock at Art's Baits & Night O' Rest Motel. A panoramic view.

The fireworks used to be the province of the Volunteer Fire Department but they had proven unreliable. The Fourth of July was a big party for them, and two years ago the weight of the firemen on the firing raft changed the trajectory so that forty-five shells headed, one after the other, straight at the crowd on shore—like the British bombardment of Fort McHenry, and the firemen dove into the water and swam for shore as the crowd panicked and ran, bombs bursting in air and also skittering along the grass and blowing up at people's heels as families fled for their lives. A year after, children still awoke screaming from bad dreams. The firemen blamed the mishap on a change of wind direction. "Bullshit," said Clint. What was worse, one of the firemen, in his extreme humiliation, swam in the dark to shore and crept home and hid in the basement, and so the lake had to be dragged for his body and men with long poles walked the shore, lanterns in hand, and his weeping wife and children huddled in the Chatterbox Cafe at 3 a.m., missing their sweet daddy, who, when he resurrected himself around noon the next day and appeared in the flesh to Gary and LeRoy who'd gone to the home to inform the family that one of Daddy's shoes had been found, was not greeted warmly as you might expect a dead man would be. They stuffed him in the backseat of the cruiser and yelled at him and took him down to the basement of the town hall and stuck him in the town's only cell, an 8-×-5-×-8-foot cage next to the old coal furnace, and toted up the expense of the search, and made him sign a promissory note. You do not put people to that sort of trouble unless you are actually drowned—personal humiliation is not a good enough reason.

So Clint proposed that the Committee hire a company called Aerial Display to do the fireworks last year. "I have the greatest respect for firemen," he said at a Committee meeting attended by thirty firemen, "but there have been advances in pyrotechnics now that you can put a microchip in the payload, such as the Umbrella of Fire." He showed a slide of the Umbrella of Fire. Spectacular.

Mr. Diener took it upon himself to defend the firemen. He said, "Well, maybe we had a bad year but one swallow doesn't make a summer and I say, don't fix it if it ain't broke." The crowd cheered.

Clint said, "The point is: We can do better. Really light up the sky. There's one called the Sky Writer. It's a cluster of rockets, radio-controlled from a computer. You program the software, detonate the fuse, up it goes, and it writes up to forty-five characters across the sky—'We hold these truths to be self-evident, that all men are created equal' or 'O say does that star-spangled banner still wave o'er the land of the free and the home of the brave' or whatever you want—all of it surrounded by a High Sky Fountain followed by three Aerial Cannon Volleys. They set it off once in Texas and people were so moved they burst into tears and went home and wrote out checks to the IRS for everything they'd cheated Uncle Sam out of for the past ten years."

"How much does that cost?" said Viola Tors.

"It's expensive. But not that expensive."

"Well," Diener said, "I don't see the need for some newfangled gizmo with all that firepower, especially not with children around—your computer could be off by one decimal point, and we'd have death and destruction on a scale this town has never seen before, and a mass funeral, tiny white coffins on the gymnasium floor. Do whatever you think best. Maybe I'm in the minority here. So be it. But I just pray to God it doesn't wind up in some horrible tragedy. Of course it's a slap in the face to our firemen who, year after year after year, have given selflessly of themselves, with no pay, holding benefit dances and bake sales to pay for their equipment, in order to defend this town against fire and to provide emergency lifesaving services. All of you are getting older, and if the day comes, God forbid, you're crossing Main Street and feel chest pains and you grab hold of a light pole and you fall down and lie there, your face on the cold concrete, hardly able to draw a breath, I hope to God someone is going to come running and administer CPR, one of the volunteer firemen who you are telling, 'You're good enough to save my life but you're not good enough to set off fireworks in this town.' But he will do his professional best to save your life so that you can see many more Fourth of Julys because that's just the kind of people we are."

And he rose majestically from the Committee table, tears glittering in his eyes, and brushed the strands of hair across his bald head and strode from the room to great applause and commotion. A great performance. And then the discussion dragged on. Some firemen left. And Diener returned with a long strand of toilet paper stuck to his shoe. It was about ten feet long. "You have toilet paper on your shoe," said Viola, trying to be helpful. "Let's take a vote and get this over," he said. Father Wilmer knelt and removed the paper and Diener said, "Who put that there?" And Aerial Display was hired to do the show and the firemen were put on standby alert and the show was spectacular. It did what a fireworks show should do—it gives the vicarious pleasure of nearby destructive power and the crowd watches with joy and terror as the whamming and blamming get bigger and louder and the heavens are riven with flaming pods that burst into suns and the apocalypse is near and the earth shakes and the air is aflame and then one ultimate cataclysmic earth-shattering BOOMBOOMBOOM echoes in the cosmos and after it a sea of silence and everyone cheers from sheer relief and goes home, peaceful and satisfied, and all the anger is gone from them, and amity and harmony reign supreme for at least a day or two.

17. ANGELICA ARRIVES

The Bunsen brothers hiked toward Main Street and ran into Carl Krebsbach who was looking for Clint. "Lyle is fried," he said.

Lyle was parked in a golf cart in front of Pop's Barber Shop ("Ask him about Lano-Phyll hair stimulant for men") and his eyes were closed. He'd put decal letters on the cart, gold with glitter, L-Y-L-E, and a bumper sticker, HONK IF YOU WANT TO SEE MY FINGER.

"Don't talk to me," he said. "Whoever you are. I need ten minutes to collect myself." His head ached. He had chest pains. He had been on the run since midnight. The truck with the bleachers had wound up in Freeport the night before and he and Carl had to drive down there to deal with the driver who demanded a 10 percent delivery surcharge, but by 7 a.m. Lyle and his crew had set up the two sections of 12-row bleachers at the north end of Main Street, a reviewing stand—across the street, a hundred feet of curb was barricaded, with signs, RESERVED FOR CNN—IMPORTANT—NO PARKING UNDER ANY CIRCUMSTANCES—YES, THIS

MEANS YOU, and then they'd gone to work on the stage for the big Honor America show.

The stage was a flatbed truck with wings for the sides and the roof and it had to be backed over the curb between two lightpoles and maneuvered into position next to a tree and then four hydraulic legs extended and placed on plywood sheets and one of the hydraulics was leaking.

"Don't tell me everything," said Clint. "I haven't had breakfast yet." And then Lyle noticed his fancy pants. "When does the rodeo start?" he said. "And which event are you? Sheeproping?"

The high schoolers who were going to paint scenery had simply vanished so Lyle had hung four big painter's dropcloths for a back curtain, which actually looked nice, with splotches of green and white and pale blue, and he laid a big square of red carpeting on the stage, which was splintery and rather disgusting. The last occupants of this stage were a Christian slash band from Detroit called The Castaway Demons who had, in Fergus Falls two nights ago, slaughtered a lamb on the stage and the planking stank of blood though the crew had soaped and sanded it and sprayed it with lacquer.

And there were no overhead lights. "It came without the truss," said Carl. "The Castaway Demons evidently broke it when they swung from it. So there's nothing to hang lights from."

Lyle was not sure the stage was strong enough to hold the Happy Hoppers square dancers, sixteen hefty folks in matching bib overalls and red-checked shirts, if they got to stomping in rhythm, the load per square foot could bring the whole thing crashing down.

"Call Viola and ask **her** what to do," Clint said. "I'm not really Chairman anymore. I'm only a figurehead."

Lyle looked up and blinked. "Come on. Get serious."

"I'm serious. I'm done trying to figure out this stuff."

"You're not done until it's done."

"Play it by ear," said Clint.

Lyle shrugged. "I don't get it—this is your parade and you're just walking away from it? Just because that crazy Viola is on your tail. You going to let her and Diener scrub the floor with you? What kind of a deal is that? Tell 'em to take a leap."

"Don't get all unraveled," said Clint. "Not worth it."

Lyle made a face. "Anyway, we gotta get us some power cables long enough to run them out of the back door of the Mercantile. And where are the microphones?"

"Not my department," said Clint. He put a friendly hand on his shoulder: "Your barn door's open."

"I don't care," said Lyle. "Been up all night trying to figure out this stage, and right now, I'd say, let's burn it."

His whole stage crew was beat. It had taken thirteen tries to get the roof up and now they weren't sure the pins were placed properly. So Clint told Lyle to take it down and do it again. Obviously. You don't want to spend all day thinking about it, imagining a thousand pounds of roof crashing down on the third-graders singing "This Is My Country"—so? Do it. The crew groaned. But they went back to work. That's a leader's job:

tell people to do what they don't want to know they have to do, but they have to do it. They really do.

"We gotta brace that up where the hydraulic's leaking," said Carl. "It's simple."

"You're crazy," said Lyle. "First of all, you push that flatbed up over the curb, you're liable to bust it and then the rental company takes us to the cleaners. Why not just put the stage down at the ballpark like we always used to?"

Clint pointed out that the ballpark was in use: The fireworks were set up there.

"It's not that complicated," said Carl. "Go get the John Deere and we'll hook it up and I'll show you."

"You want to bust the stage, do it. We can torch the sucker later. I'm going to get some Pepto-Bismol."

A horn honked and a truck rolled up with four brass cannons on a trailer—Civil War replicas—and a van full of Civil War troopers. No wonder the cannons hadn't boomed that morning—Berge never told them when to arrive. Clint waved them toward the hill up behind the high school. His phone was ringing. Todd said the governor might make it by three. Irene said she'd heard Angelica might be coming and she hoped it wasn't true. "Have a little respect," she said. The head wrangler called to say the caravan of horse trailers was on its way. No problem. Angelica left a message: Where could she change into her costume?

Clint walked toward the café and lit a smoke. He had quit smoking three years ago but he resumed this spring, what with Angelica and the Fourth of July. He took a deep drag and he could feel eyes fixed on him. A Smoker. One of the last to hang on to the filthy habit. The look in those eyes said, *Don't you know the statistics?* Yes, of course, but life isn't about statistics, it's about adventure. He was Hispanic and his people knew about these things. In Granada old grizzled men sat under the olive trees and enjoyed a smoke in the afternoon and a glass of tequila. The world isn't a hospital. We are stronger than we think. Smoke irritates the lungs and we thrive on irritation, it stimulates the blood. He smoked his cigarette wishing one of those Boy Scouts would walk over and say, "You shouldn't be doing that, Mr. Bunsen." And he would say, "Well, I am a man who does things I shouldn't and that's why I'm happy. Maybe you'll figure this out someday, kid. Sin boldly. Don't let kindergarten ruin your life. Run in the halls."

He walked down the middle of the street, cigarette in hand, clipboard in the other, white pants with gold buttons down the sides, a flowered shirt.

Hispanic. *Soy un hombre. Un hombre valiente.* The Nordic mists lift, a path appears in the shining wood, the path that leads away from the snowdrifts and blighted faces and scraggly trees to the moist green headlands and delta and rainforest valleys. My brown-skinned people, *mi glorioso amigos,* where are you? Welcome your lost brother kidnapped by the fierce northern tribes, sold into slavery by the lies of his own grandpapa. Bring him a wineskin, a good robust *vino,* not the pale cosseted Burgundies or the effeminate Pinot Noirs but something with teeth and hair, a Rioja. To hell with AA and the self-righteous in recovery and long live the reprobate! *Viva banditos!*

And then he heard Lyle say, "Lordy, Lordy, feast your eyes on that." And turned and saw her walking slowly up the street, tall and lithe and lovely in her long green pants and a loose silk blouse, walking hand in hand with a smiley-faced man in khaki shorts, glasses on a chain around his neck, a Red Sox cap, a T-shirt with some dumb thing written on it which you couldn't read unless you got up close to him and why would you want to? They were strolling along, killing time, pretending not to know they were being observed. She stops to look in the window of the hardware store and a display of hammers on a pegboard. She puts on her dark glasses and turns, brushing her hair back from her face.

"She's not from around here, is she?" said Lyle.

"That's the woman who carried the torch in the parade last year. The Statue of Liberty," said Carl.

Angelica, the goddess of liberty, and a dork in shorts—Clint's heart burned, tears came to his eyes. Jealousy. Yellow jealousy. She had told him she was coming with Kevin but it hadn't dawned on him until right now that she liked somebody else better than she liked him. Him in the ridiculous mariachi outfit. God help us.

18. THE PEOPLE, YES

Nine a.m. and firecrackers were popping all over town. Signs were up: PARADE POSTPONED UNTIL 4. "LIVING FLAG" AT 2:30. PLEASE TAKE PART—THANK YOU FOR COMING. The Boy Scout brigade was out, red flags flapping, directing traffic streaming into town from the south. The Scouts looked like androids. Cars swish-swashed by and a string of motorcycles revving and rumbling, carrying fat old men with ponytails—PRAIRIE PORKERS stitched on their leather vests. The Scouts waved them up the hill to the high school and then to the fields around the grain elevator and to Mr. Hansen's pasture north of town where Holsteins once grazed, chewing thoughtfully, thinking back on the wrong turns they'd made that led them to a life in the dairy business. They were gone now. Mr. Hansen gave up dairy farming after a failed suicide attempt. He jumped from a silo, hoping to hit the barbed wire fence and slice himself in half, but landed in a pool of manure instead. What others had thought was Mr. Hansen's strong character turned out to be depression, and one month after Dr. DeHaven put him on Lucitol the clouds opened and Mr. Hansen sold the cows for hamburger and let his hair grow long and spent his days watching interview shows on TV, hoping to sharpen his conversational skills which had dwindled to murmurs over the years. He was watching *The Bob Roberts Show* this morning on Fox whose guest was a movie starlet just out of detox who felt her life was just starting anew. So was Mr. Hansen's. He was learning to converse. And he called Clint on the phone.

"It's a new life, Clint. I'm all done grumping about the dairy business and I'm seeing the beauty of the everyday. Like flowers and stuff. What you up to?"

Clint was on his way from where the Civil War cannoneers were setting up their sandbagged emplacement on the sledding hill behind the high school and heading down to see the Percheron horses arriving at the football field, ten big trailers of them and four more on the way. He did not want to hear about Hansen's renaissance or whatever it was—he had skipped an emergency meeting of the Committee to go and visit the horses—Viola was worried about security issues, since some unknown persons had been spotted on Elm Street ducking behind things and she wanted Clint to ask the governor to call out a unit of the National Guard. Instead he swung around to Leonards Field where the teamsters were guiding a great gray Percheron out of a trailer and down a long ramp to join four others who stood quietly, skin rippling with pleasure, heads up, sniffing the air, ears up, alert.

Hansen: "I just need to share this with someone. You ever have moments like this? When you think, 'Aha! Now I get it.'? You ever thave those *Aha* moments?"

Clint: "I don't think so."

The Percherons gave an air of majesty to this grassy plain and he wouldn't have been surprised if a procession of bishops and dukes arrived in crimson and lapis, followed by a king and a pope or two. The horse descending had white markings on his forehead and fetlocks and a short stump of tail. He placed his feet carefully on the hard rubber tread, his powerful thigh muscles easing him down. There was no skittishness—he had negotiated this ramp before—and his great calm eyes took in the entire scene and noted Clint's approach and the dignified look in his eye was that of a duke awaiting a serf. Once a warhorse bred to keep his head in the clangor of battle, now consigned to pulling wagons, the great beast heaved a deep horsely sigh and chuffed in a welcoming way as Clint reached up and touched the tender black nose and the solemn forehead.

Daddy was fearful of horses but fascinated nonetheless, and once, chatting with the cowboy star Rex Ryder, Grand Marshal of the 1956 parade, seated atop his horse Blazing Star, Daddy coolly raised his barker's cane and stroked the horse's underside, and the animal's penis emerged as long as your arm, brown and speckled. There were children around and they gaped and snickered and boys punched each other's shoulders and girls turned away in disgust, but there it was, the unspeakable thing out in the open for the whole town to see.

The voice of Hansen was in his ear, talking about how free he was to travel now and do as he liked, but the man did not sound free at all. He'd gotten out of prison but he was sitting with his back against the gray stone walls and what was the difference?

The teamsters kept to their work, and Clint walked along the line of horses tethered to a long rope stretched between posts pounded into the running track. Two girls on stepstools braided a horse's mane. A man poured molasses into a bucket of mash. Little bands of horse admirers straggled along the line, fathers and their broods, old codgers in snap-brim hats, couples in shorts and sneakers, cameras popping, pinprick flashes. No locals. Lake Wobegon wasn't horse country. Horses were something rich people did, or teenage girls. Nothing for serious people. *Too much trouble.*

The horses stood under canvas tarps strung taut to shade them from the sun, plastic buckets of water at each place and the horse's name on a wooden shingle hung from the tarp, a long line of proud stalwarts—Ira, Soupy, Good Son, Robin, Eric, Aristotle, Hudson, Royal Bill, Irv, Jack, Lancelot, Quentin, Trinity, Leo, Pharaoh, Oscar, Leeds, Cochise, Cougar, Daniel, Aramis, Thomas, Merlin, Chester, and Calvin Bud, who raised his great head thoughtfully as if he could speak and chose not to at this particular time. "I am not from here," Clint said. "I am Spanish. My people brought horses to North America. They were poets at heart, singers, wanderers, so they valued their mobility. They were civilized people who knew when society gets stale. I may be leaving, who knows when, perhaps tonight. I am tired of sarcasm. I'm looking for a more merciful way of living." The horse listened to his confession with supreme gravity, though chewing corn. He licked the white froth from his lips and waited for Clint to say more.

"The firemen are all mad at me because I said there was no need to blast the siren every time there's an emergency call. The firemen all have pagers and that works just fine. They love the siren for the drama and everybody gets excited and sees them hustling off to whatever it is and it makes them look like heroes.

But it's a pain in the butt. So I said so, and those guys are never going to forgive me for it. Damn it, you pay a high price for speaking your mind in this town."

The horse regarded him with sympathy and Clint stroked the long forehead and scratched up around the forelock. He wanted to put his arms around the horse and feel its head next to his own. "I did all I could do here. Married, raised kids, buried both my parents, fixed thousands of cars and started cars on cold mornings, flooded the ice rink and got up early in the morning to coach peewee hockey, shoveled old people's sidewalks, cleaned the church, gave money to some who needed it, bought rounds of beer when it was my turn, ate dinner at people's houses and tried to make conversation though I didn't care that much for them, was president of the Boosters Club, and for the past six years I ran the Fourth of July. And now I need to do something for myself." The horse seemed to understand.

"You from the Parade Committee?" He jumped. One of the teamsters stood behind him. A big man with a gray ponytail and a big honker of a nose. "Right," said Clint. "What can I do for you?"

"We were told there would be hot meals."

"I'll take care of it right away." He got on the walkie-talkie to Donnie Krebsbach who patched him through to Dorothy at the café. "Fourteen egg sandwiches with bacon. And coffee. And hash browns. Have Carl or whoever bring it up to the football field. Make it two dozen. And some apples for the horses."

"Just want you to know—you run a great parade," the man said. "I know, I've been in enough of 'em. These things are dying off, like everything else. People blame it on the kids, I blame it on us. Slacking off. Not doing things the way they need to be done. But this one is. And I want to thank you." And he put his calloused hand in Clint's own and they shook, gravely. "Like the pants too," he said. The man turned away and then turned back—"You don't remember me but I served with you in the Navy. Payne's the name. Art Payne. We took a course at the Presidio together. San Francisco. I remember you specifically because I saw you coming into Cheyenne's house as I was going out. Chinese woman. You remember. She was quite a girl, wasn't she. I wonder what became of her. Guess she got old like the rest of us, huh?"

He didn't want to look at the man. "I don't know any Cheyenne," he said. "Sorry."

"Well, you did back then. She was on Lincoln Avenue up above a dry cleaner's. Little room with beaded curtains and a little ivory Buddha and incense burning and a red bedspread. Bought a red bedspread for my wife a few years back with gold dragons embroidered on it. Made a difference, if you know what I mean."

"I was only there for a few months," Clint said apropos of nothing whatsoever.

"She was quite a girl. Such beautiful hands. She had so much love in her. You can't fake that stuff. I never forgot her. Sorry you did."

Old fat man with a ponytail and earrings, somebody's grandpa, too old to be thinking about his rutting days. But it was nice to think about Cheyenne again.

* * *

The four circus wagons had arrived from Baraboo the night before. Men were hosing the dust off them and wiping them down and waxing them—the gaudy red and gold, the mirrors, the gilt, the silver tassels, and the giddy carvings of exotic beasts, pyramids, Indians, Indian sultans, a chariot, an acrobat with pencil-thin legs, a bald eagle, statuesque ladies with bosoms like shelves, lions and elephants, a racehorse named Dan Patch, Aztecs, dolphins, Old Glory, goddesses, wizards and swamis, dragons, Greek temples, and half-naked beauties, and down deep he felt dazzled by the lavish foolishness of it, this wild concoction of color and mythology swirling by—how irresistible when he was a boy and the Cole Brothers rolled into town on a Saturday in August—*Come away from the cornfields, boys, and duck into the big tent for just two bits, the fourth part of a dollar, and see things You Had Not Dared To Dream—They Will Appear Before Your Very Eyes!!* He was trudging off to mow the neighbor's lawn and then a 4-H softball game which he hated because he was no good at third base and then he detoured toward the train depot in hopes of seeing the wagons and there they were and then suddenly the day had a high point. And now here he was, years later, all sorts of pleasures available, and yet sorrow seems almost permanent, life impenetrable. And the circus wagons irresistible. Just as they had been to Daddy. The great wagons rumbling along, sunburst wheels turning, drawn by the Percherons in gilt trappings, the teamsters in silk cracking their big whips, and the band atop blasting away, or a calliope wailing and steam billowing from the stack.

★ ★ ★

He called up to Art's and got Viola Tors who said Irene was busy swamping out the bathrooms. "Tell her it's her husband," said Clint.

"She knows it's her husband. She wants to know what you want."

"I want to talk to her."

"About what?"

"Never mind." He'd only wanted her to come look at the horses. Two more long trailers had just pulled up and Leonards Field was a scene of medieval glory.

The camera crew from CNN had not shown up so far, said Viola, though LeRoy had posted signs on the state highway— LAKE WOBEGON—WELCOME CNN!!!! Still no sign of them nor any other members of the press. "I guess we're not news anymore," said Viola. "We were news last year and not this year. That's how it works. Unless somebody goes berserk with an automatic weapon and shoots fifteen or twenty people."

"Art's gone to Montana," said Clint. Viola laughed. "I don't think Art could knock off more than two or three. He'd lose interest."

He wished people wouldn't make jokes like that. You say a dark thought out loud and it floats away on the breeze and it can be inhaled by some loner living in his camper at an abandoned farmsite who suffered some humiliation years before—maybe he missed a crucial free throw against Lake Wobegon and was jeered by the Leonards fans and had been chewing on it ever since, replaying the game over and over in his mind, and finally decided to load up his AK-47 and hang two bandoliers over his shoulders to make a big X on his chest and hook some smoke grenades to his belt and blacken his face and head over to Lake Wobegon and see how much collateral damage he can visit on the civilian population before he is eliminated.

And then he smelled her smell, a sort of cucumber-based aroma, and turned and she was running toward him, shopping bag in hand. She whooped and took his hands in hers and twirled him, against his will, in a circle, her head thrown back, laughing. "Oh Bunny, I'm so glad I found you, how are you?" She kissed him on the lips. "I adore you. You rock my world. Do you know that? I think about you all the time."

"Could we go somewhere private?" he said. "Where's what's-his-name?"

"Oh, screw 'em. I can kiss you if I want to."

She said Kevin had gone off somewhere to park his camper. *Good,* Clint thought. *Maybe he'll knock the manifold loose and carbon monoxide will give him the peace he's looking for.*

"What is this stupid paper somebody gave me?" she said. She waved a blue paper at him. It was a warranty "to be signed by all parade participants . . . affirming under penalty of all future rights and privileges whatsoever, that the signer is not participating for any purpose other than patriotic and is obligated to uphold all local rules and regulations, and that nudity is strictly prohibited at all times, and the Parade Committee hereinafter reserves the right to reject and or eject any person who violates this understanding in whole or in part." It was signed by Mr. Diener, Chairman of the Security Committee.

"This little weasel with the swept-back hairdo sidled up to me and told me to sign it," she said. "You asking all the tuba players to sign? Is Miss Pork going to have to sign? Or just me?"

"I will look into it," said Clint.

He started to explain about northern European people, then thought, *I am not one of them. Soy de España. Mi sangre es el español. Soy del pueblo español. I am of the Spanish people.* He put his hand on her shoulder and it slid along the wing of her back and down her spine, and came to rest on Angelica's lower back. The Boy Scouts across the street turned and looked. Myrtle and Florian stood on the corner, gazing his way. *Hands off her, Bunsen!* Mr. Berge was behind them, dazed from drink, staring over their shoulder. Cliff stood in the doorway of the Mercantile, talking to Ralph, both of them watching Clint. Thought balloons rose over their heads: *There is the man who said in Adult Bible Study Class that he did not believe that God condemns His children and there is no hell, and look at him, he has a girlfriend.* The Magendanz family cruised by in their green Chevy van, all eyes on Clint with his hand on the back of the red-haired woman. Blue geese overhead put on the brakes and dove down for a look, squirrels paused in their labors, a fish jumped and looked his way.

"Oh," she said. She fished in her purse.

Clint removed his arm from around Angelica's lower back.

"I brought you something"—she handed him a newspaper clipping—"Thought you should see this."

DNA LAB FINED FOR FALSIFYING REPORTS

The owner of the Phoenix Heredity Institute pleaded guilty to mail fraud yesterday for having falsely informed 152 clients in northern states that they were Hispanic.

U.S. District Judge Stephanie Cervantes ordered the PHI to pay fines totaling fifty thousand dollars and to refund the victims' money.

Arturo Georgio, owner of the company, said that night-shift lab workers, as a prank, had decided to make purebred Scandinavian and German clients into Hispanics. "Those employees have all re-signed," he said.

"We are all in favor of diversity," said Judge Cervantes, "but this is not the way to achieve it."

I am an ordinary old white man of the soybean-raising north.
I ran many races and never finished higher than third or fourth
I thought I had sprung from the olive orchards of Spain
No, I am a Great Lover lost on this vast frozen plain.

And then Gary and LeRoy pulled up in the cruiser.

Gary and LeRoy climbed out of the car, which took more effort than it should for law-enforcement officers—a hand on the roof of the car for lift and a big heave and a sincere grunt—and he wondered if he should've hired some skinny security men, who could give chase on foot should the need arise. Gary stood by the car and LeRoy approached. "Ma'am," he nodded to Angelica, then stepped in close to Clint. "Somebody saw Art down by the lake, sleeping in that big culvert. We checked and he isn't there, but somebody was. Also had reports of shouting in the woods beyond the motel."

"Viola said she put him on a bus to Montana."

"We spoke to Greyhound and according to their records he disembarked in Alexandria."

"Problem is," said LeRoy, "we can't arrest him unless he's made threats. Has he?"

"Art's been making threats for years. Threat is the meaning of Art's life, are you kidding?"

"I mean, has he made specific threats?"

"Who is Art?" said Angelica.

"He is a lunatic who's been living here for so long we all got used to him," said LeRoy. *Un loco,* thought Clint.

Today I shall die at the hands of a crazy man with a gun
I shall die for una bella dama, you my beautiful someone
Shots ring out and my chest hurts, I fall in great surprise
O God before I leave this earth let me look once more into
  her green eyes.

19. IN THE CHATTERBOX

Flags flew all over town, bright new flags on housefronts, in the steel flag-holders the Sons of Knute had sold door-to-door ("Installation, free!!"), and red geraniums sat in pots on front steps or hung from porch ceilings. Yard after yard burgeoned with petunias, pansies, geraniums, delphiniums, phlox, and roses in full bloom. And firecrackers were going off, strings of them in the alleys, firecrackers in garbage cans, and on a sidewalk in front of a little stucco bungalow a little girl in blue tights waved a sparkler and danced in a circle. Clint walked past her, heading downtown, realizing he had put on the wrong socks, an old pair that were falling down. He was Spanish no longer. Or rather—he had decided this—he would decide his ancestry for himself. He would be Hispanic some days when he was up for it and otherwise be whatever he happened to be.

He saw black curly marks on the sidewalk where boys had lit snakes. Two boys were about to light a cherry bomb and drop it in a garbage can. He yelled at them and they did him the courtesy of waiting for him to pass before they set it off. A boy carried a brown paper bag full of torpedoes and every ten feet or so

141

he threw one at the sidewalk and it banged. Two Knutes were straightening the Liberty Pole in front of the statue of the Unknown Norwegian. Hawks soared in the clear blue sky and a woman fussed at a little girl about sunscreen—"You're going to turn red as a lobster." The little girl didn't know about lobsters. He stopped to talk to Chuck who was wheeling a freezer unit onto the sidewalk in front of Skoglund's Five & Dime to sell ice cream cones, Chocolate Mint and Butter Pecan, the big seller, and Strawberry-Rhubarb, which nobody likes. And Lake Wobegon postcards for sale, including one of three men in a boat hauling in a fish the size of a two-bedroom rambler (Home of the "Big Ones"). "Remember Willie the Walleye?" said Chuck. "Largest talking fish replica in the country," said Clint. "The lower jaw moved and two fins and the eyes. Quite an attraction at one time. Willie used to do it, work the levers, talk into the microphone, say hi to the kids, sing 'Happy Birthday,' and then after the war his son Dave took it over and he wasn't so patient and sometimes the walleye would yell at kids, and tell them to quit poking around that little door in his tail or he'd shit on them, and that was the end of it. What happened to the fish, I wonder." Chuck wondered the same thing. "I suppose somebody came and busted it up." Clint shook his head. No idea.

A girl in a teeny teeny red bikini top and a translucent wrap around her legs and her teeny teeny bikini bottom crossed the street, trailed by three boys in green nylon jackets with CENTRAL written on the back. They were wearing dark glasses, so you couldn't see their eyes bulging. "My cousin's girl," said Chuck. "Fourteen. They start early now."

* * *

The Chatterbox Cafe was packed, the regulars crowded into the back booths by a host of newcomers. Eleven a.m. and it was almost time for lunch. Or "dinner," some people called it. Three old widows in one booth with two of their sisters and six burly farmers in another, eating sticky buns the size of softballs. They were the special that morning along with the three-egg omelets with sausage and green pepper and onion. A thin man in a suit and tie stood by the cash register, obviously a stranger. His hair was treated with some sort of pomade that made it stick up in little tufts. *Why would anyone do that?* thought Darlene the waitress, moving around with a carafe of coffee, filling up cups, swinging her big boobs under the white blouse. She had taken the time to put on lipstick, eye shadow, mascara, toning cream, and her uniform was nicely starched. She had hurt herself when a pot of coffee burned in the kitchen and she opened the back door to air the place out and Bruno the fishing dog walked in, smelling like death, and Darlene, chasing him out, slipped and sprained her ankle. She sat down and put her foot in a bucket of ice and lit a cigarette. "I thought there was no smoking in here," said Leland. "There is now," she said and she pretended to slap him.

"You gonna be on TV, Darlene? Guess you think so."

"If our Darlene gets on TV, she'll be out of here before you can say Jack Robinson," said Mr. Hoppe. "Somebody in New Delhi will take one look and say, 'That is the girl for me,' and that's the last we'll see of her."

"I don't know anybody in New Delhi," said Darlene.

Florian and Myrtle Krebsbach came traipsing in, Myrtle with a whoop and a cry and she struck a pose like a majorette, one knee up high, arms out. She was all dolled up in shiny green pants and a pink top and a headband that held a red-white-and-blue umbrella over her head. She sashayed up to Clint and put her old face down close to his and said, "I saw you slip your arm around that little doxy out there—what is going on with you as if I didn't know? You old dog you. Hormones finally kicking in, huh?" She glanced back over her shoulder. "If you're looking for action, buddy boy, why go for a novice? Why not find a woman who's been around the block and knows what's what?" She winked and pinched his shoulder. Hard. "That girl is barely old enough to ride a bike. I could show you a thing or two. You don't think so, come around sometime." She winked again as Florian said, "Hey Clint—" and she said, loudly, "I heard there was a chance of rain in the afternoon. That's how come the umbrella. I just got my hair done yesterday."

"You heard wrong," said Clint. He was just tucking into his breakfast, two sunny-side up on hash browns, sausage on the side.

"Darlene here is hoping to get on TV this year," said Hoppe. "I was telling her she oughta be taking singing lessons from that Albanian guy so when the offers start rolling in, she's all ready to go."

"I have no idea what you're talking about," she said. "Though I will say those TV people last year were nice people. A lot nicer than what you meet as a waitress sometimes, I'd have to say. One of them gave me his business card and said to look him up if I was ever in Chicago."

"Don't forget where you got your start, Darlene. Don't forget who your true friends are," said Hoppe.

Myrtle sashayed toward the men at the counter like she was in a conga line. Her hair dyed jet-black and her old wrinkly face under the umbrella hat. "I hope those TV people aren't counting on me to ride a float or anything. I've got delicate skin, I've gotta stay out of the sun."

"I thought you were going to be the longevity queen," said Hoppe.

She put her arm over his shoulders. "Don't talk to me about sex unless you mean it, mister."

"I don't know what you're talking about," he said.

"I was afraid of that." She gave Clint a big wink. "Anyway, I got my cap set for Mr. Bunsen there. He's a man who knows how to please a lady. That's what I hear. I saw Irene watering her plants this morning and whistling to herself and I said to myself, Now there is a woman who has been very well loved. Oh my yes. I can tell. She's a woman whose toaster's been busy." And she cackled and moved off to join her sister Margaret in the corner. Margaret the quiet one. Myrtle was the wild card in the family.

He sat and ate his breakfast and listened to the chatter in the room, like water going over rocks, and his ear tuned to the grumblers in the far corner booth under the Great Northern Railway poster, a mountain goat on a rocky crag against a blue sky. All the old goats sat piled into that booth, the ones who had succeeded in defeating almost every intelligent and hopeful initiative to move Lake Wobegon forward in the past forty years. Their motto: What Do We Need That For? We've Gotten Along Without It So Far, Why Change Now? These guys could've stopped Pythagoras dead in his tracks and shot Galileo and prevented Mr. Jenner from inoculating that boy for smallpox. They had resented and resisted the celebration of the Fourth of July, preferring the old parade of pickups and tractors, the Sextette warbling like crazed geese, Mr. Detmer mumbling the Declaration of Independence, the firemen on the pontoon boat setting off a few Roman candles. They were in a jovial mood this morning. They knew Clint was leaving office and soon would come the Restoration of Cowpie Bingo and all the rest.

"I see they're setting up fireworks at the ballpark," said Mr. Diener. "I hope to God they don't burn the place down. The money we're spending on rockets—we could replace the warming house with that. Instead we're just blowing it up into the sky. I don't get it."

Clint wanted to get up and march over and tell them: *Next year at this time I will be in the Congress of the United States and you dopes will be reading about me in the newspaper. I will be participating in decisions that will affect the history of the world for years to come and I will be working for peace and justice and prosperity but now and then I might pick up a phone and have somebody at the IRS check your tax returns with a fine-tooth comb just to make sure your deductions are all in order.*

And now Mr. Detmer had joined them.

"I'm going to miss you reading the Declaration this year," said Val loudly. "That always was one of the high points for me." Others murmured in agreement. "I don't know how one man can decide for everybody else how we get to observe the Fourth of July." He was talking loud for Clint's benefit and Clint thought of turning around and throwing a cinnamon roll at him.

Or walking over and upturning the table and all the coffee and saying something good and sharp. *I am the best goddamn mechanic you've got in this little tank town and when I clear out and leave you drunks and losers behind, you'll have to drive to Little Falls to get your work done, except you know what? Your cars won't make it that far. So Little Falls will have to send a wrecker. That's gonna cost you. You won't be heading to Florida next March because Little Falls is going to charge a lot more. And you know what? I'm going to be in Congress. Or in California where people love cars and appreciate a man who can keep them running. I might open me up a little place north of San Francisco and I'll work in the mornings, and in the afternoons I'll go out fishing for sea bass. Fifty-pounders. Sit out there in the sunny salt air and think about you stuck in a snowbank and waiting for the tow truck from Little Falls. Good luck, losers.*

"It was so good last year," said Mr. Bruner. "Everybody said so. It's just so meaningful, I think."

"I didn't read the Declaration last year," said Mr. Detmer. "Had a bad cold last year."

"Is that right? I could've sworn it was last year—"

"Nope. Had a cold. I guess that's what gave them the idea they could do without it. They asked me to shorten it. I said, no."

"Good for you."

"I mean, it is what it is. The Declaration of Independence. It's the birth certificate of our nation. They said it's too long for kids to listen to. I don't think so. I was brought up to sit and listen, but kids nowadays have the attention span of a katydid. Everybody wants things shorter now."

Mr. Detmer stood up. "Gotta run. The missus wants to get a seat early so we can shake hands with the governor."

And then he looked out the window. "Lord have mercy. What have we here?"

Clint looked back over his shoulder. It was Angelica, crossing the street. She was carrying her torch, wearing her seven-pointed crown. Kevin was with her now. His T-shirt said BLOOM.

"Looks like Clint's girlfriend traded him in for a newer model," said Mr. Diener. The grumblers all chuckled. They were staring at Clint's back, expecting him to react, turn red, weep for jealousy, something, but he sat and drank his coffee and took another forkful of eggs.

I am a peaceful man, but tonight I will do my work
And slip into your house and cut your throat, you jerk.
You will hear my footsteps and think it's a joke
And then the razor makes a clean stroke
And you will find yourself in a land of smoke and ruin
And Satan smiling at you—"Hey, good to see you.
   How you doin?"

And then a hand landed on his shoulder and he looked up to see a piggish man in a blue suit and tie. "Hi, we talked on the phone. I'm Todd from the governor's office," he said. He had a broad snout and dim little eyes and big pink jowls with some bristles on them. He was all ready to go to market. Thump him and hang him by a hook, skin him, drop his guts in a pail, you would have you some darn good breakfast sausage.

20. MR. DIENER'S INVESTIGATION

Miss Liberty had been part of the Fourth since 1913, usually played by a stern, top-heavy matron who marched down the street, torch in hand, as if she were on her way to burn down the homes of unbelievers. Miss Fleisher was Miss Liberty for decades until her knees gave out, a veteran schoolteacher who knew how to instill fear using only her steel blue eyes. It was Clint's idea to cast a succession of Lake Wobegon beauties in the role, starting with his daughter Kira, who walked with a joyful élan, grinned, waved, alongside a float of paper daisies on which rode an old man (representing Life) and a boy (The Pursuit of Happiness) who one year was susceptible to motion sickness and couldn't finish the parade. Angelica was the latest Miss Liberty. When she subbed for a friend last year several women onlookers reported to Clint that she clearly was not wearing a brassiere. And Mrs. Diener said that, in observing Angelica lift her robes to step down from the float, it was clear that Miss Liberty was not wearing undergarments.

"I had sat down to the curb to tie my shoe and she hoisted

up her robe to step down and I looked up and there was no London, no France. And for your information, she waxes. Very weird."

This was seconded by Mr. Berge, who was reasonably sober at the time.

"You could see her coosie," he said.

"Her what?"

"You know what I'm talking about."

"What did you say?"

"You heard me."

"Where in the world does that come from? 'Coosie'?"

"All girls have one, that's all I know."

Clint suggested that many young women wear flesh-colored underpants and in any case he was not going to call up a fine young woman and ask her a personal question like that.

Mrs. Diener was not satisfied. "Suit yourself," she said. She gave her husband an earful and he looked up Miss Pflame on the Internet and found out that she lived above the Condor Club on Geranium Street in a rough section of St. Cloud and his brother-in-law Virgil, who knew people who knew other people, made inquiries and found out that Miss Pflame had frequented a clothing-optional dude ranch in Wyoming and had written about it! Bragged about it. On the Internet. Naked people on horseback. Think about it.

"A nudist?" said Mr. Diener. "In our parade? As the Statue of Liberty?"

"Plenty of perfectly decent people are nudists," said Clint.

"Would you? Would your daughters?" Mr. Diener's watery

green eyes looked almost snakelike, a tiny forked tongue flickered from those pursed lips. "We've put too much into this to take the risk of some public scandal blowing up in our faces ruining everything."

"A public scandal?"

"Virgil found out that Miss Pflame had participated in demonstrations in St. Cloud. One was to protest the arrest of a man who distributed free condoms at a condominium complex and another was to protest the expulsion of a high school homecoming queen who turned out to be a boy named Taylor. "Miss Pflame has a one-track mind," said Diener. "You want Miss Liberty marching in the parade and waving a sign in favor of Premarital Sex?"

"It isn't premarital sex if you don't plan to get married," said Clint.

"Not a joking matter, Clint. This town has some standards and we're not going to sit by and let it go the way of everything else nowadays. You don't see our young people lounging in the streets smoking marijuana and our young women having sex and then going off and getting abortions. Do you? No, you don't."

And then Mr. Diener bore in on him. "And you don't see married men running around with young women and dumping their wives like they were used cars, do you? No."

The old rattler had him in a corner there. Clint wanted to push back but he wilted, he turned away—"I'll talk to her about it, I'm sure everything will be fine," he said, waving his hand weakly.

So Mr. Diener knew about him and Angelica. And if he knew, then everybody in town knew. Everybody. So why not go to California? Angelica was going with Kevin but Kevin wasn't written in stone and if she knew Clint was nearby and available, she would drop Kevin like a bad dream—why not go? He was disgraced already. Irene was steamed. Bunsen Motors was sliding toward bankruptcy. What did he have left to lose?

Oh do not leave without me, woman whom I adore
Though I know about rejection, having been left many
  times before,
But I am your best lover, as you have said before.
Oh take me tonight, my darling—away to the western shore.

A heroic venture, to leave his entire adult life behind all at once, but what about Irene? His lover of last night. His valiant wife tending her tomatoes, weeding, watering, smoking away the aphids, pinching off the runners, so as to put something rare and exquisite before him—a fresh, homegrown tomato, sliced, lightly salted or drizzled with oil. A man doesn't just up and walk away from a garden in July. A garden he's been cultivating for thirty-two years. So there's a drought. Water as you can and wait it out. It rains here. This isn't a desert.

21. PASTOR INGQVIST STEPS IN

A high of 78 was forecast, then revised to 84, which raised the spectre of heat prostration, so Billy P. went off to round up firemen to organize two more first-aid stations and the Catholic Knights of the Golden Nimbus went off to collect ice. "All you can get," said Clint. "If necessary, buy it."

The lawns and gardens of Lake Wobegon were lush from a long drenching rain on the 2nd and the morning of the 3rd, and the geraniums glittered fiercely in their pots and the flower beds shone with fresh enthusiasm. The town park alongside the lake was freshly mowed from the swimming beach to the narrow sward behind Ralph's Pretty Good Grocery and the Mercantile and the dirt alley behind them. A little boy sat in the shade of Ralph's awning and unwrapped a Butterfinger bar with great delicacy. Wally's pontoon boat, *Agnes D.*, was tied to the town dock, its deck and canopy freshly washed, little flags fluttering at the stern. Hjalmar and Virginia had rented it for the day. Their daughter Corinne was coming all the way from upstate New York with her boyfriend, Leeds Cutter, whom nobody had laid eyes on but who was said to be handsome and able to jump up on a table from a standing start, just crouch and spring and there he was. Other pontoons were at the ready and runabouts and a 40-foot scow was pulled up on shore and three men in orange jumpsuits labeled AERIAL DISPLAY INC. were wheeling cartons aboard it with red labels: EXPLOSIVES—EXTREMELY DANGEROUS. KEEP AWAY FROM OPEN FLAME, EXTREME HEAT, OR STRONG VIBRATIONS.

The Lake Wobegon patrol car ("Protect and Secure") was parked out front of Lake Wobegon Lutheran Church, and Judy Ingqvist, glancing out the parsonage window next door, thought maybe her husband the pastor had had a heart attack, but no, the constables had only come to tell him about a bilko artist named Schwab who had worked some Lutheran churches in western Minnesota, pretending to have a conversion experience and hugging people and taking their wallets.

He was thought to be the same thief known as the False Usher, who ran off with collection plates.

"Collection plates are slim pickings compared to people's wallets," said Pastor Ingqvist. He read the flyer the constables had printed up.

> Today our town welcomes 1000's of visitors for our Internationally Acclaimed Fourth of July. Truly it is a "red-letter day" for Lake Wobegon. As we show our warm hospitality, let us also be vigilant. Watch for strangers who appear to be nervous or agitated and glancing around. Do not hesitate to ask persons unknown to you where they hail from.
>
> If officials determine that danger exists and an alert is needed, a public announcement will be made, as follows:

"Will the winners of the rhubarb pie contest kindly report to the judges' table?" This will notify you that an alert has been declared. If so, you should gather your family together immediately and congregate with PERSONS KNOWN TO YOU. Let your local law-enforcement officers handle any situation that may arise. They are trained and prepared. Thank you for your cooperation.

Lake Wobegon Dept. of Public Safety

"Looks like you've thought of everything," said Pastor Ingqvist. He wore a seersucker jacket and white shirt and jeans and a straw boater. He was on his way to the football field to visit the horses.

Clint was back at the football field, leaning against the canteen stand, sipping coffee, watching the teamsters brushing the Percherons and putting the gilded bridles on. CNN had called. A producer named Ricky. Very excited. They were in the truck on Interstate 94 nearing St. Joseph. "Why isn't Lake Wobegon on our map?" he said. "Long story," said Clint. He gave them directions, offered to meet them in one of the mapped towns. "On our way!" said Ricky. "Beautiful horses," Clint said to one man who was brushing a horse's fetlock and he grunted and didn't even look up. And then Mr. Griswold came bustling up, carrying a shopping bag, in white slacks and a golf shirt and a Cheap Sport Coat of Many Colors.

He grabbed Clint's arm in a tight grip and said, "That crazy woman Georgia Brickhouse is on her way. You know that?"

Clint shook his head.

"Who invited her? She's coming with some Christian honor guard, from Liberty Baptist High School in Paynesville—ever hear of it? Boot camp for troubled fundamentalist teens. An old turkey farm and they turned the sheds into barracks. Out in a big field behind barbed wire. Yeh yeh yeh. You never heard of it? They advertise on the Internet—if your kids don't seem interested in the opposite sex and you think they might be homos, you can send them to Liberty to be deprogrammed. That's what Georgia used to do, deprogram potential lesbian teenagers. And now she's running for Congress. Can you believe it? Yeh yeh yeh."

"I'm thinking I'm not going to run."

"No no no, Don't go negative on me. Lot of excitement out there. Talked to the cheerleaders and they're on board. How about your brother introduces you? When do you want to announce? How about right after the Living Flag? We'll get the press together and you stand up and make your announcement and everybody's waving their flags—here," and he handed Clint a card. "Take a few questions, and we're off and running."

The card read: "As an American veteran, a businessman, a father, and a proud Midwesterner, I have watched with dismay as our leaders in Washington have gotten entangled in a bitter partisan deadlock that makes it impossible to do the people's business. There is a need for new blood with an independent vision and a willingness to work together for a stronger America. And that is why I have decided to announce . . ."

Clint shook his head.

"Change it any way you like," said Griswold. "This Brickhouse woman and this weird cult she's part of—we've got to step in and take her on. Can't let her hog the spotlight, not even for a minute. Take my word for it. You gotta go straight at her before she convinces people she's halfway normal."

The man had a habit of looking off your shoulder as he talked to you, first one shoulder and then the other, as if scouting the area for intruders.

"I'm talking to the cheese producers, gonna get them on board. They've got a committee, Americans for Food Action. You don't have anything against federal subsidies, do you?"

Clint guessed he didn't.

"I got the gun guys pretty much rounded up. You're a hunter, right?" Clint nodded. "Yeh yeh yeh. Great. You're all set on gay marriage, right? Right to life? Right?"

"I don't know."

"Yeh yeh yeh. Nobody knows. But we gotta calm those people down. You know. Brickhouse has got 'em jumping out of their underwear."

Clint wanted to tell the man that he wasn't so sure about running for Congress. Appreciate your enthusiasm but it's a big step to take, and my wife is opposed. And my business is on the rocks. And I am having an affair with a 28-year-old yoga instructor. Or was, until recently.

And just then Pastor Ingqvist slipped up behind him and put a hand on his back. Clint jumped. Pastor slipped his arm around him. "Just wanted to tell you what a great job you do, Clint," he said. He looked at the old coot in the bad sport coat. "David Ingqvist, I'm Clint's pastor." The man blinked. "I know," he said. "I've been checking up on Clint. I know all about him. He's going to announce for Congress today."

"Actually, I'm not—" Clint said.

"That's great." Pastor Ingqvist slapped him on the shoulder. "You got my vote. When's the big rally?"

"Today," said Mr. Sport Coat.

"Not going to happen," said Clint. "Irene doesn't want me to."

Griswold clapped him on the shoulder. "Grab the bull by the tail. Strike while the iron is hot. No time like the present. Electing you would be like selling air to a drowning man. People are waiting for somebody like you."

He stepped away, headed uptown.

Clint felt the light spray of the horseman's hose and stepped back. "What's going on with you?" said Pastor Ingqvist. Griswold stopped twenty feet away as if he had one more thing to say and then walked on. "Not all that much," said Clint. The horsemen were sweating, stripped to the waist. They wore bandannas around their heads.

"I'm listening."

Clint looked around and leaned closer. "I've committed homicide," he said. "I choked a man with my own bare hands. Choked him and then I threw his body in a ditch and I pissed on it."

"You didn't either."

"Did. This morning. I killed Berge. Had all of him I could take and then he gets right up in my face and gives me more and I just reached over and strangled the son of a bitch."

"This isn't funny—"

"According to Scripture, if you contemplate murder in your heart, it's the same as if you actually do it. So why didn't I do it?

That's what I'm asking myself. No jury in this county would have—" But Pastor Ingqvist was having none of it. "If you want to talk, I'm here to listen," he said. "I'm not here to judge you. And it isn't about Berge, it's about a woman. According to what I hear."

"David—"

"You don't have to explain anything to me. I'm not your judge. There isn't anything you've done that I haven't contemplated a hundred times. We're all in the same boat. But what are you hoping to get from this?"

There was silence all around them, everything seemed to have gone dead.

"Put the Seventh Commandment aside for a moment. What's your reasoning here? How is this supposed to make anybody happier?"

"But she does. She makes me happy. That's the point."

"So can Irene. Give her a chance. Don't throw away forty years."

"Thirty-two years."

Ingqvist didn't smile. "Sin is confusion and it causes terrible pain. You're too old to go through all that."

And then who should appear but the murder victim himself, looming up like death on toast with a peace offering, a bottle of Powers whiskey.

"How about some flavoring for that coffee?" he said.

"No thanks. I'm busy, Berge. Beat it."

"Helps keep the flies off you."

"It's not even noon."

"So?" Berge put the bottle to his lips and took a long draw, swallowed, and smacked his lips. "Good Irish whiskey. You know, it was Saint Patrick who drove the Norwegians out of Ireland. He did the snakes and then the Norwegians. He poisoned their fish with lye, but the Norwegians they just called it lutefisk and thought it was wonderful. So he pissed on their potatoes but they just made lefse from it and thought that was quite a treat. So Saint Patrick said, 'This isn't worth my time; they can go to hell.' And that's how the Norwegians got to Minnesota."

He told this to Clint, his red pocky face six inches away breathing whiskey and coffee on him, and Clint turned away.

"I went to school with you. You got no right to look down on me." Berge backed off, in search of shade, muttering to himself. He was used to being ignored.

"Let's talk about this tomorrow," said Ingqvist.

"If I'm here tomorrow."

He was sitting next to Irene in church one Sunday weeks before and Ingqvist was droning from the pulpit about how God meets our every need—a sermon called "God, I'm Starved"—and then something snapped at him, and it was Irene. He'd fallen asleep and started snoring and she poked him in the ribs. Rather hard, he thought. You could wake a man up without leaving a bruise, couldn't you? He sat up straight and in that moment he realized that his funeral would likely take place in this very room and his body would lie in a casket at the head of the aisle, maybe a flag on it, honoring the old Navy vet, and he remembered San Diego drenched in sunlight and the *tacquería* at the beach and the month of training at the Presidio in San Francisco. He'd gone into the Navy a virgin and finally, at age twenty-two, in a bordello on Lincoln Boulevard, that lovely Chinese woman showed him the basics. Cheyenne. So sweet. Genuinely kind. His earliest instruction in sexual matters came from a book, *Marital Hygiene*, that his brother handed to him when he was fifteen and said, "Mother wants you to read this," and turned away, beet red. The book had a few illustrations of male and female anatomy, and its thrust was clear: If you have sex without God's blessing, you will catch an unspeakable disease that eats your brain and you wind up an idiot in a bathrobe with pee running down your leg, so you wait until you meet the Right One and have a sacramental marriage and everything is fine.

Meanwhile, he wanted to get laid as soon as possible. This was terrifying. Mom gave him special elastic underwear with a note: "This will help you subdue any carnal impulses, my darling. I am praying for you." So he wore it and it had the opposite effect. He fantasized about girls' bosoms and the mysterious intersection of their legs, which *Marital Hygiene* represented as a cavern leading to an underground chamber where babies hatched.

But what he had imagined to be a harrowing descent into the bat cave of self-destruction turned out to be an elegant little dance no more mysterious than a two-step, with various interesting twists and decorations, and what worked well, Cheyenne showed him, was kindness and delicacy in bed. Take it easy. Don't grab. Let the drama build. And it will. And now, sitting in church, thinking about her slight body, her elegant little breasts, her black bush, he began to rise in his pants, just as it was time to go forward for Communion. He sat with his legs crossed and motioned for Irene to go ahead. "What's wrong?" she whispered. He shook his head. Nothing. Just the old business about the flesh. I'll get over it when I'm dead.

22. COULD'VE

Q: So where had he gone wrong?

A: When he came back to Minnesota and, in a weak moment, sacrificed his interests for (what he thought were) the interests of others. The undoing of his liberty. And that was the making of a libertarian: a wrong turn toward inside-out sacrificialism that twists your life like a pretzel.

He could've moved to California when he was 23. He was already in California, in the Navy, all he had to do was stay. He planned to go to art school on the G.I. Bill and he went home to Lake Wobegon to tell them his plans and say good-bye and his old girlfriend Irene Rasmussen sent word via girlfriends that she never wanted to lay eyes on him again because he had broken her heart. So he drove out to see her. They sat under the cottonwoods and she said, "Why didn't you write to me more? I wrote to you. Long letters. You sent me postcards." He told her he had been busy having a great time in California and there was too much to write about, he didn't know where to begin. She said, "Well maybe I wish I had been having a great time too instead of sitting here and waiting for you." He said he was sorry. She said, "You aren't, not really. You are completely self-ish. I don't know what I ever saw in you. California changed you completely. I hardly recognize the Clint Bunsen I went to school with. You got all stuck on yourself. It's tragic!" And she wept. And so he put an arm around her. Then both arms.

Irene had a lot of class, she was no dummy. She preferred classical music to country-western and she read Jane Austen in-stead of romances and she didn't overeat the way other girls did. She intended to stay lean. She could shoot baskets. She beat him once playing Horse. She could play a couple pieces at the piano: one was by Chopin and the other by somebody else. She had a lot going for her. But he didn't love her. He realized that now, looking back. He'd been too busy all these years to think about his feelings and now maybe it was too late. Because back then, when she accused him of selfishness, to show he was not, he said, "What do you want me to do?"

"Show me you care."

"I do care."

"Prove it."

"How?"

"I want you to make love to me," she said.

Well, what could he say? *"No, thank you very much, I'd like to but I promised my mother I'd be home early"*? He was sorry she felt neglected; he thought she was dating Joe. "Not really," she said. "We went to movies and he wanted to go further but I told him I was waiting for you."

No girl had ever offered herself to him; he didn't know what to say. "Are you sure?" he said.

"Of course," she said. So he took her up to his uncles' hunting shack near Cloquet and there under the glassy gaze of a deer and a cougar they made love very sweetly and in the midst of her passion, she cried out, "You've done this before, haven't you! I can tell! I knew it! I was waiting for you and you were out there fooling around!" He lied and told her she was the first he ever loved. He was naked, lying atop her, easing himself into her. Over and over he whispered that he loved her. They lay in each other's arms afterward and fell asleep and the next day her father had a talk with Daddy and Daddy spoke to Clinton. "You can't take liberties with a young lady, Clinton, unless your intentions are honorable. I trust that your intentions were honorable."

Daddy stood at the porch screen, looking out at the green grass, his back to his son.

"I was planning to go back to California, Dad. I didn't mean for it to happen. Honest. It was her idea." He was teary-eyed at the thought of not going to art school and taking a course in sculpture, which he was good at.

"If you go and leave Irene here, you can't come back, Clinton, it's as simple as that. I've told you plenty of times: You have to take responsibility for the outcome of your actions, whether you intended them or not." So they eloped to Wisconsin. A judge in Hudson married them, his secretary as witness, and Clint wrote "Just Married" in the rear window of his car because he thought somebody ought to and she made him wipe it off. On the way to the hotel, she asked if he believed in God. "I think so," he said. She said she didn't. She used to but not anymore. He was shocked. He had heard of atheists and now he had married one. And then it turned out she didn't want to go to California and have a great time, she wanted to stay here with her family who drove her crazy. And then his dad died and Clarence needed him at the garage and there was no chance to go back to California. And so he never got back to California. *The saddest words of pen or tongue: I meant to go when I was young.*

A wrong turn. He almost didn't take it. His last day in California he went to Santa Barbara, applied to art school, and met Ronnie for lunch. A big orange sun and low clouds in the mountains, a freighter lying at anchor far out on the Pacific, and under the palm trees the Café Judah in a low stucco building that opened its arms to you and offered exuberant salads with fresh tomato and sweet onions and crisp leaves, not limp and defeated like the Midwestern salad. He sat at a table on the patio and watched a tall woman with great long legs walk by, sunglasses, full of energy and mystery. Ronnie was his classmate who drove out in his old Plymouth along with Larry the Leaner, nicknamed for his habit: He never stood if he could lean. Both of them thick as bricks. Got warehouse jobs and stole junk food from the supermarket so they could afford to buy beer. But Ronnie had warned him. "You go home, pal, and you won't make it back here. Irene'll get her claws in you and that's all she wrote." Larry agreed with him. "Tell 'em you're too busy to go visit. You go home, you're sunk." Prophetic words from fools. And a few years later Ronnie and Larry got better jobs and fell into the arms of smart women who rescued them from idiocy and now they were Californians and Larry was doing quite well in mobile phones and when he came home to visit, he dropped in to see Clint and said, straight out, "What happened to you? How did you get defeated like this? Who beat you up?"

But his daughter Kira went. Attended Concordia for three years and then landed a job managing a café in Monterey. Saw the ad online, called the owner, he hired her. Irene told her she couldn't go until she cleaned her room, and Clint told her to walk away from it and hit the road. "If you postpone going until you get everything cleaned up, you'll never go," he said. He walked her to the car he had bought for her and shoveled her bags in the backseat and kissed her good-bye.

She said, "Why are you so eager to get rid of me?"

"I don't want you to miss out on your life, kid."

His heart was breaking. Little Kira his volleyball star, the Can-Do kid, the good student, the good daughter who didn't run around and always called if she was going to be out past 11 p.m. and who enjoyed her parents' company and who (though she didn't know it) was the glue that held her parents together. And now she was going to the West Coast, work in a café, meet some guy, maybe the dishwasher, maybe the owner's idiot son, and that guy wouldn't be good enough for her and he'd leave her bruised and desolate and she'd walk weeping in the rains of Monterey, but he smiled and gave her a long, tight hug, and she got in the car and drove away, her little white hand waving out the window, and he went in the house with tears in his eyes and stood at the kitchen sink and ran cold water from the tap and scooped it up to his face.

"What's the matter? I thought you wanted her to go," Irene said.

He wept because without Kira there was no good reason to have a home any longer. Not that he could think of.

He wanted her to go and get all the richness of life—passion, grandeur, bravery, adventure—everything he had tried to protect her from—he didn't want her to make his mistake, come trotting back home to board her father's sinking ship, sit in an office at Bunsen & Daughter Motors, marry some available boy with mechanical aptitude, never experience true independence, get old in her childhood home. Shades of the Colleys! Mrs. Helen Colley sent her daughter Mary off to Stanford and six years later when the grandpa succumbed to an infected hemorrhoid and the family fortune turned out to be a catacomb of debt, young Mary returned and got old fast living in a welter of family stuff, rooms jammed with mystery boxes and busted furniture piled on piles of old newspapers and catalogues, two old ladies, mother and daughter, living as sisters in the narrow labryinths between mountains of junk, the stench of cat urine and the flicker of an upstairs florescent light, the voice of Caruso, the whirlpool of dementia pulling them down together, a promising young woman sacrificing her life to her mother—you only had to remember that sad old rotting hulk of a house with vines growing out of the roof and you were glad to see your daughter decamp for California. Go and godspeed. Have a big romance and then another and another, go off in sunshine or darkness and know that we are not watching and noting your expensive new jeans and interesting hairstyle, your loud laughter, your vivaciousness among strangers (compared to your dutiful daughterliness at home)—go have a life, darling, come back when you feel the urge.

The night before she left, he and she walked by the lake eating ice cream cones from Skoglund's and he gave her a little speech. "Boys want to get in your pants. That's their main idea. So be sure you choose a good one, one who won't see yours as the first in a long series of pants. But a funny one. So that after he gets in your pants, you can have some fun talking to him. You don't want to lie there with your pants off and listen to him talk about real estate." "Oh Daddy," she said, embarrassed. That was a good sign, he thought.

23. IRENE

She had showered and dressed and watched Clint and Clarence head uptown together and thought maybe she'd like to run away from home today. She hated the Fourth and also she had an inkling that Clint was bewitched by the Pflame woman because he had left the house that morning without noticing the platter of deviled eggs she had made, nor the potato salad. She made it all for him, just the way he liked it. It wasn't for the Fourth of July—there was a truckload of potato salad downtown, gallons of glop, the ratio of mayo to mustard 4 to 1, instead of 2 to 1, and hers had chopped scallions and paprika. Not that anyone cared. Evelyn Peterson used to care about potato salad but she was dead. And evidently Clint didn't care anymore because he was over the moon about Miss Pflame, the Internet goddess.

He was so gone with that woman he had no idea how much his own wife knew, that was how far gone he was.

She'd asked him last night, "Tell me if this is sweet enough," and gave him a little slab of rhubarb pie she'd made, and he ate a bite and then went out on the porch to check his phone messages. He was all caught up with that woman.

Irene had made six strawberry-rhubarb pies the day before, for the winners of the three-legged race, the arm-wrestling, the egg toss, the chicken race, the shoe-lacing contest, the Tug-of-War (Men Under 40 versus Men Over), and the fat men's race, six or seven fattycakes lumbering red-faced a hundred yards, their breasts bouncing and sweat pouring off them—Clint had tried to cancel it on safety grounds, but Viola said, No way, it was a high point of the Fourth for her. And a prize pie for the pie-eating contest. As if an idiot who had stuffed the most pie down his gullet would care about winning a pie. But Arlene was in charge of prizes and it was a tradition.

Last year, the pie winner was Duke Carlson, who downed eighteen slabs of blueberry pie, kept them down for the required thirty seconds, and then disappeared into the toilet for a few minutes and came back grinning and accepted his prize, a pie. Ridiculous. Why couldn't we go back to doing the saltine contest: You eat a dozen, and the first one to whistle is the winner.

The three-legged-race winners last year were Dale and David Walters and Jim and Johnny Jirasek, a tie. The Jiraseks and the Walterses had been battling for supremacy in the three-legged event for the past five years. They trained for it. They could run three-legged as fast as just about anybody could run two-legged.

And another pie went to the winner of the arm-wrestling held under the last big elm in the park, which took an hour, large men grunting, big fists locked, and after endless rounds the championship came down to Earl Larson and a big galoot from Millet.

They glared at each other and put their elbows on the table and locked hands and Mr. Berge slapped the table and the men strained, their huge shoulders swelled up, their backs bent, their faces turned red, sweat popped from their foreheads, the crowd got rowdy, minute after minute passed, people jumping up and down, screaming, the two combatants forehead to forehead, two men who'd done heavy labor all their lives and milked cows and hoisted lumber and hauled rocks, fighting now for supremacy, sweating, grunting, and then a child laughed out loud and that's when Earl let a fart. It sounded like a gun went off and lifted him out of his chair and it took the starch out of him and the Man from Millet pinned his arm and threw his head back and laughed. The smell in the air was like buzzards had died from eating rotten eggs. The winner collected his pie and walked away, the loser walked away, everyone walked away, and nothing more was said about it, but half an hour later, people walking under that tree looked at each other and said, "The sewer's backing up."

The egg toss was a crowd favorite, married couples tossing a fresh egg back and forth, taking a step back for each successful catch, lobbing the egg back and forth, higher, higher, step back, back, back, a long toss lands in the lady's bosom ker-splat, a man misjudges and the egg hits him in the shnozzola ker-splort, and finally it's down to the last three couples, tossing the egg ninety and a hundred feet, and one splatters, and now there are two, and now we start to see that this is how marriage works, actually—the hurling of fragile living matter back and forth, the art of the catch. And then a man backs up for a basket catch and misjudges and the explosion of the egg, and we have a winner, which as in actual marriage is measured by survival.

Irene took the deviled eggs and potato salad over to the motel to put on the buffet in the so-called Hospitality Suite for the big shots who probably weren't even coming, according to Cindy Hedlund who was there already, whomping up the cocktail sauce for the shrimp platter. The big cabin—Cabin No. 1— smelled of Lysol and pine soap. Viola had been up since 5 a.m. hauling refuse out to the barn where Art kept refuse in a bare room, no stacks of magazines in the corners. The governor was famous for his sense of caution. After Congressman Olson had gotten nabbed in a public toilet, the governor had reduced his intake of liquids. His advance man had called Viola and told her that a private toilet was important. Also signage. There should be three or four large billboards welcoming the governor and his name should be spelled out in letters at least four feet high. Unfortunately the town had no such billboards. Clint told her to forget it—by the time the governor discovered that he wasn't welcomed in four-foot letters, he'd already be here and unlikely to cancel on a technicality. Viola wasn't sure. Dorothy had brought in two long cafeteria tables and set up a Hot Pot for the sausage and put out several boxes of Ritz crackers and some cheese. As much cheese as a governor would want, probably.

Viola sat capsized on an old couch which she had covered with a pink sheet. Cabin No. 1 would have to be the entire Hospitality Area, she said. Cabin No. 2 was beyond cleaning—it needed demolition. She was worn out. "This whole shebang ought to be bulldozed," she said. "That's going to be my project this year."

"I know where we could find matches," said Irene.

"Don't tempt me."

Cindy was putting too much ketchup in the shrimp sauce, not enough horseradish, and chattering about her daughters and their various triumphs in Minneapolis. Cindy had a low hairline and you wondered if maybe she shouldn't have it waxed a little. She had taken up wearing big earrings and maroon fingernail polish since she started selling real estate. She was visualizing success, she said, and could feel that it was visualizing her.

And then Viola said, "I probably shouldn't say anything about this but I wondered if you'd heard these rumors about Clint."

Irene smiled pleasantly. "What rumors?"

"You know. Just rumors. Someone said you and Clint were going to separate. I personally hope it's not true. I'm glad he's resigning as Chairman. He's been working too hard, if you ask me."

"We're going to be just fine," Irene said. And then she laughed. "But if we weren't, I'd still say we were." She looked at Viola. "You know how it is."

"I asked my sister-in-law to bring potato salad for the picnic today and she shows up with two big tubs of mush she bought at a gas station on the way up," said Cindy. "Can you believe that? It's like I asked her to bring meatloaf and she brought dog-food. What's the big mystery about making potato salad? You don't know how to boil potatoes? Or a few eggs? You can't chop celery? I don't get it. I told her, 'Laurie, you forgot how to make potato salad?' She said, 'What's wrong with this?' So I told her, 'If you care about people, you ought to serve them decent food, not something made in a factory three months ago and loaded with preservatives,' and she got all sniffy. She said, 'Well, if you don't want us to come, just say so.' I want her to come, but don't bring garbage, okay?"

Irene said that that was the way it was these days. Young women were proud of not knowing how to cook. A sign of liberation or something.

She and Clint had eloped, a big drama back in 1976. Their families, the Rasmussens and the Bunsens, had loathed each other for years since a Rasmussen tried to kill a Bunsen with a shovel in an argument over cattle getting into a cornfield, and her parents had forbade her to see him under any circumstances but she loved him because he was kind, he was no dope, he had interesting things going on upstairs, and he was mature and seemed unlikely to wind up on a barstool or running away with Jewel the cocktail waitress, so she went and shacked up with him and returned the next day and her mother wept and her father thundered—and two weeks later the young people found a justice of the peace in Hudson, Wisconsin, and tied the knot.

"Some people simply should not marry," her mother had told her. "On account of bad blood." Now Irene was starting to see the wisdom of it. He had resented her affections all these years and finally he was about to lash out. History repeats itself. We want to believe in a New Day and a New Deal but if the water is bad, you're going to keep getting sick from it.

Cindy Hedlund gave her a book, *Making Your Marriage Work for You*, that described three types of marriages: the conflict-avoidance marriage, and the validating marriage, and the volatile marriage. Hers had started out conflict-avoidance and turned volatile somehow without her knowing it. A man's emotional crises are subterranean. You go along with your life and one day the foundation collapses. He was a good man and then the Internet came in and he started living a fantasy life. It was all beyond her, how a little screen could come to take the place of real life. What was the appeal? And then Clarence decided it was time for him to retire and Clint to buy out his share of Bunsen Motors, which was fine except that poor Clarence was never cut out for business and sat in his office and read novels while Clint broke his back repairing cars, meanwhile the used-car business dwindled for lack of a crackerjack salesman. You needed a hustler to move those cars and Clarence was a dreamer. Used cars are where you develop new customers and build loyalty. Well, it hadn't been built. And now Clarence and Arlene wanted to pull up the tent stakes and move to Florida for crying out loud. And Clint was supposed to pay for it. And right about then was when Clint took up with Miss Pflame. What a gruesome moment that was, discovering the letter from her about what a wonderful lover he was. An e-mail he printed on creamy paper like he meant to frame it or something. Jeez. You're almost 60 years old and you've finally gotten the last of the kids launched and on their way and you think, Good, now I can resume my life, and whammo, your partner is out dancing in bed with some tootsie he met online. It bruised Irene's good nature and rubbed it raw. A treacherous passage. She woke up every morning feeling that she was walking a minefield, and a coffee spill could trigger the explosion, a misplaced newspaper, clumps of mud on the kitchen floor. He had recently suggested she see a doctor about depression and she told him he should see one about irrationality and that was where they were, fussing at each other, ever on the verge of decamping and flying solo for awhile. But last night was very nice. Last night was what she wished the next ten years would be like.

Her younger sister Jeanine was married to Harry for twelve years, a depressive man who refused to seek help, and she divorced him (whereupon Harry got much better) and married Louis who made her very happy until he went down from a heart attack, on a fishing trip in Florida, just keeled over dead and fell overboard. Sank like a stone. They never recovered the body. Three months later Jeanine fell in love with a fisherman named Angelo whom she met on a bus to Duluth. He was missing the little finger on his left hand, torn off by a rope. He had been to China twice, had captained a submarine chaser in the North Atlantic, now he was captain of a luxury steamboat on the Mississippi. His crazy uncle in Duluth had died and left him a warehouse full of stuff people had stored and then forgotten about, and he expected to walk away with a couple million dollars. The Caribbean beckoned to him. He'd buy a 40-foot yacht and learn scuba diving and wend his way from Hispaniola to Antigua and Barbados. On the bus it seemed he suggested that she could come along. He said, "We could live on the boat and just go where we wanted to go. Free as the wind." He had beautiful hands. He braided a little bracelet out of leather for her and he put it on her wrist.

She was corresponding with him regularly. "There are men out there," Jeanine said. "Don't ever forget that. There is no reason any woman should be alone."

Viola wanted to go home and take a long, hot bath. She was worried about Art who had called her this morning and seemed agitated about who might be using the Hospitality Suite—"No damn politicians and no media," he said over and over. "He ought to move to Montana where he can shoot guns and not upset people," she said. She looked around at the Hospitality Suite and laughed. "This was my idea," she said, "and Clint said it was foolish and he was right. Nobody's going to come up here. What was I thinking? It's all for nothing."

"You and I can come up here and have a good stiff drink," said Irene. Cindy said to count her in too. "Hospitality begins at home," said Viola. "Why do we put out the red carpet for people we don't know and will never see again? We ought to treat each other better." A profound thought that hung in the air for a moment and then evaporated. "Bye," she said. "See you at the Flag."

Cindy was arranging cans of soda pop in stainless steel trays and dumping bags of ice cubes around them. Irene spread patriotic paper tablecloths on the long table and taped them down tight and arranged folding chairs into little conversational circles. Cindy, for some reason, considered her a confidante and this morning she was anxious to unburden herself about a man she'd met online in a chatroom called Married But Looking. "I just do it for fun," she said.

"Oh my God," said Irene. "I don't want to know." But Cindy plowed on. "I could have died. He was a Lutheran pastor. He went to Concordia the same time I did. I think I danced with him once, back when they didn't allow dancing. It was a party in an

English teacher's house. His name is Arnie and now he's in Nebraska and he just told me how his life had gone bad—wrong job, wrong wife, wrong place—and he is just yearning for something else. You could hear it in his voice. Yearning. You know what I mean?"

"Of course. It's as common as the sore throat. Tell him to go find a good romance novel. That's what they're for."

But Cindy and the poor dope in Nebraska were kindred spirits and they had talked and talked for hours and she'd said things she had never told anybody before. "You're the only one in this whole town I can trust," she said.

"Go no further. I am not to be trusted," said Irene. "My husband is involved with a young woman who is actually in town today—think of it—she has come here—and I am in a mood to shoot somebody, so don't tell me about you and your problems. I have plenty of my own. Sorry to be unkind, but there it is."

"Oh my gosh," said Cindy. "You are so brave." And she burst into tears. "What women go through. I can't talk to Roger. He is in another world."

"This is the only world we have," said Irene.

It was two o'clock, time to go see about the Living Flag. She felt obligated. She wished the Fourth was all over. She hated the whole thing. Always had. It wasn't about patriotism at all, just a bunch of men making noise, blowing off rockets. A day for the George Bushes of the world to wave the flag and parade around and pretend to be big shots. And the stupid Living Flag. Putting on the red, white, and blue caps and standing in formation to make the stripes and the blue field of stars. Did Clint realize how much people hated doing that? People all jammed in tight on a hot day and sweating like pigs and the caps smelling of mildew. Who was this for? *How did this serve the cause of human intelligence?*

And then there were the hormones in the air. The young women of Lake Wobegon, darling girls who once knelt around the campfire singing "Kumbaya" and "Dona Nobis Pacem" as sparks flew upward, and now they were practicing to be street-walkers and the Fourth of July was their Coming Out Party—she had had this fight with Kira. It wasn't Clint's problem, he was oblivious. It was she who had to confront the child standing bra-less in a little tanktop and shorts—*I have nothing against showing off a nice pair of legs. A little décolletage? Fine. But look at yourself in the mirror. You are showing your belly button and so much below your belly button, you could sell advertising.* She'd fought with both her girls about this—less with Tiffany, who was chunkier and self-conscious—but Kira had a beautiful body and a big ex-hibitionist streak and the skirmishing was intense one summer—*Are you wearing a bra? You are? Let me see. Where did you get that, out of a porn shop? Did some boy give you that? And your under-pants—doesn't that feel weird to go around with a string up your butt?* Clint saw nothing, heard nothing. Daddy's girl could do no wrong. So Irene had to fight all the battles. *No, you will not be getting a tattoo on your lower back. Not while you live in this house. I don't care if it is small. No no no. No to a lip ring too. No to dyeing your hair, it's perfectly nice just the way it is.* She tried to keep her girls decent through their tender years until they smartened up. Nothing wrong with Bermuda shorts, girls, and a nice T-shirt with a brassiere under it. Be clean and pleasant and comfortable with yourself. Read good books, study, travel, be of service. And be yourself, not a character in a movie. But when the Fourth of July rolled around, out came the loose tank tops and teeny tiny shorts—a carnival of flesh. *Yowsa yowsa yowsa. Take a look! Teen flesh! And butt cracks!!! We got em! Hey hey hey. Check it out! Hurry hurry hurry. GIRLS GIRLS GIRLS.* The town was flooded with young men, dudes in muscle shirts and flocks of geeks, clouds of testosterone in the air, and the maidens went crazy from the smell of it. They emerged in twos and threes and headed downtown for the festivities, and people turned in amazement— *Emily! Our valedictorian! What is she doing in that little red bra and low-rider jeans? Did she forget to put on a shirt? Oh my goodness. Where is her mother?*

What was it about the Fourth of July? Some windborne chemical urging mammals to couple up and breed. And alcohol, of course. Flying the flag of Our Nation excused all sorts of abuses. If you wore a flag pin in your lapel, you were free to be as disgusting as you liked. Raw youths from Millet came cruising the town on the Glorious Fourth and the girls of Lake Wobegon went out in tank tops and low-rider jeans and drove their mothers wild—to see their girls out with bare midriffs down to their you-know-what—*Why? Because boys like it?? Boys'd like it if you stripped naked and jumped up and down but why do it? We want you to go to college and have a career, not earn your living dancing on a bar and men stuffing ten-dollar bills in your crack. Oh darling.*

What was it about the male species that their brains slipped down into their pants? And yet—and yet. Last night had been lovely. He loved her. Deep in his heart he did, though Miss Pflame had turned his head and planted seeds of confusion—he did love his wife. He was not beyond hope. And she should fight for him just as she had fought for her daughters. You can't stand by and say, "Oh well. What will be will be." Sometimes you have to grab the ones you love and shake them—*brbrbrbrbrbrbrbrbrbrb*—and tell them to shape up or else.

But what is the "or else"? Give him an ultimatum and send him packing, the big cheater? A single lady of 60 whose résumé basically is "Raised three kids in Lake Wobegon, MN—ever hear of it?" does not command respect in the great world these days so her options would be limited. She could stay here in her beat-up house and be the Divorced Lady, volunteer for Grace at the library, whoop it up with the girls at Moonlite Bay on Friday nights, or she could sell the house ("Family Dreamhome: 3 BR stucco house w/ porch on handsome half-acre lot in peaceful small town in mid-America. Owner is brokenhearted and must move soon. Best offer.") and maybe get enough to rent a condo in Tampa and wait for Social Security to kick in. There wouldn't be a bucket of money coming from Bunsen Motors, that was clear. She'd worked hard all her life and divorce would put her in a hard place. That was the simple fact of the matter. Boo-hoo. Poor me. She ought to shake up the philanderer and wake him from his dream, and for that, she thought, she really ought to get a gun.

Irene had never held a gun in her hand except at a carnival booth, shooting water into a plastic clown's mouth to make the little horse run in the derby and win a plush bear, but it couldn't be so hard. Idiots shot other idiots all the time. A gun would be good. Talk only goes so far. When Johnny was doing Frankie wrong, she didn't ask him to go into counseling, she went to the pawnshop and got a big .44 and marched down to the hotel where he was shacked up with Nelly Bly. She shot through the hardwood door, rooty-toot-toot. Unfortunately she put Johnny in the graveyard. Irene didn't intend to kill Clint, just bring him to his senses. It was time he learned: You can't have everything. Take your choice. Make a life with me or get a bellyful of hot lead.

Art had guns at the motel. She just needed to bust into his cabin and find one and load it. Or not load it. She could decide that later.

24. THE FOUNDERS ASSEMBLE

Under a big maple in the park, next to the drinking fountain, the historical figures were waiting patiently, Lincoln and George and Martha and Uncle Sam and the *American Gothic* couple. It wasn't easy to find people to fill the roles—not many Wobegonians had theatrical aspirations—and the ones Clint persuaded to do it were grumpy right before a parade, especially George Washington, whose wife Martha was actually his sister-in-law—his own wife refused to do it—and his pants were too tight, about to split in two. Martha rolled her eyes—her sister had offered twice to let the pants out in the inseam, but no, he wouldn't have it.

"She must've washed 'em in hot water."

She reached for his fly. "Just open up the snap."

"Don't stick your hand in my pants. People are looking."

"I'm Martha, your wife, remember? I can grab your pants if I want to." She got his waistband and tugged him toward her. "You're the father of your country—I want to see what you've got down there."

He pulled away. "There are children around here—"

When he wasn't George Washington he was running the grain elevator, but he'd been Washington for eight years now, substituting for Earl who had to have hip-replacement surgery, and he'd read books about Washington and thank God he came along when he did, otherwise we'd still be hooked up to the English, a class-addled race addicted to warm beer and cricket, a game in which the pitcher throws the ball in the dirt and a guy swings a shovel at it and the games last six hours and everybody wears white and nobody knows what's happening.

And he bumped into Abraham Lincoln, standing alone, in his black frock coat, white shirt, string tie, and stovepipe hat. His fake beard, which was coming unglued on one side. "Watch where you're stepping," he said.

"Sorry. Got a wardrobe problem. How you doing?"

"You see a toilet around here?"

"They got Port-A-Potties in the park," said George Washington.

"You'd think they could provide something here—" He looked around. "I gotta go so bad I can taste it."

"I can see that. Your eyes look yellow."

"Very funny."

"Go pee in the alley."

"Oh sure. Right."

"Go ahead. I'll watch your back."

Lincoln was looking at a mangy mutt across the street. The dog had bitten him a year ago and was looking at him hard as if trying to put a name to the face. He had been laying for Lincoln a long time.

"Oh shit," said Lincoln. A troop of twelve Camp Fire Girls was advancing toward him smiling, with their group leader, a large woman with a grin you could cut down trees with. The girls wanted their picture taken with the Great Emancipator if he didn't mind.

"I need to go see a man about a dog," he said. "You want a picture, you better hurry." He was starting to shift from foot to foot. "Smile. Look happy," said the Leader.

Nearby, Paul Revere sat uneasily on a horse, two lanterns in one hand, reins in the other, and his mount dancing in a circle, tossing its head, though John Adams was holding the bridle. If horses can smell fear, then there was plenty to smell. Paul's face was flushed, his heart was pounding under his ruffles. "Maybe I'll climb off and see if he settles down," said Paul. "Sit tight," said Adams. "You climbing off is going to get him all riled up."

"Why can't I just walk like everybody else?" said Paul.

"People expect you to be on a horse. Stick with the plan," said Adams.

25. THE LIVING FLAG

The Living Flag was forming on the football field just as—wonder of wonders—the CNN crew arrived in town. Word spread fast. *They're back.* And crowds flowed toward the field. The Percherons stood tethered under the canvas tarps on the running track and the crowd filed into the bleachers, big families strung together, kids like ducklings tucked in close to their mothers, the dads pushing grandmas in wheelchairs—*Oh my gosh*, thought Clint. *Handicapped facilities.* He sent Carl to open up the high school. They could ship the cripples up there to take a leak, if necessary. On Main Street, the black CNN van with a satellite dish and a long steel arm, folded, on the roof, cruised past the Chatterbox driven by a grim-faced man with a shaved head and mirror shades. He pulled up in front of the Sidetrack Tap—Dorothy was watching from the window of the café—*Wrong, wrong, wrong! Wrong parking spot! We don't want Mr. Berge on national TV. Somebody's got to get them to move that van.* She called Clint.

By the time the four CNN men had put their boots on the ground, Clint and Viola Tors were heading to the scene. The shavehead had the cargo door open and was about to extract a box—"No, no, no," said Clint. "Back here. By the reviewing stand. It's all blocked off."

"And there's a Hospitality Suite," said Viola, "with fresh shrimp. Better elevation. And it's shadier."

"This the parade route?"

A smiley man touched Clint on the shoulder. "I'm Ricky," he said. "I'm the producer."

Ricky wore black jeans and a black T-shirt that said NEWS across the chest. His smile included all of his front teeth, top and bottom, and a good deal of pink gum as well. His hair was trimmed to a soft grayish buzz and he had a silver ring in his left ear. Clint thought, *Fine. This isn't the first man you've ever seen with an earring. No big deal. Don't focus on it.* But Ricky was a piece of work. He grabbed Clint's forearm and said, "I think we're going to do something utterly marvelous today." He took a deep breath and said, "I love this town. I've been here ten minutes and already I feel love. I always wanted to live in a town like this. Friendly people. I'm from Philadelphia and I love Philly but when it comes to good people you just can't beat the small town. And that's what we're going to do today. The news is full of violence and rage and sex scandals and today America is going to get a look at its true self, its goodness. We are going to do goodness today!"—he addressed the last part to his crew who stood waiting for instructions, a short squat man with a coil of power cord around his neck and a skinny kid supremely bored with an iPod plugged into his ears.

"Goodness. The human heart. A sense of community. The

American family. That's what we're going to show today," said Ricky.

"We scheduled the parade for four o'clock," said Clint. "But we're flexible."

"Perfecto!" said Ricky, grinning. "Couldn't be better. We're doing a live remote. Live. Not taped."

Live. You mean—live? "Live as you and me," said Ricky. "It'll be beautiful. But we don't know when they'll switch to us, so we need to stay in position. High alert." He motioned to his crew, and the shavehead and the skinny kid started hauling blue road cases out of the van and the squat man opened a switchbox on the side of the van and the satellite dish rose into the air at the end of the steel arm.

Clint could feel the day coming together at last. His swan song as Chairman, on national television, live. *Somebody find Berge and lock him up,* he thought. You don't want 57 million people to see some whiskey-laden bum walking sideways toward the camera and telling the president to go stick it up his ass. *Stay calm,* Clint told himself. *Take charge.* He told Viola to tell Miss Falconer to get the choir ready. He told Carl to find Lyle and tell him the parade might have to loop around a few times.

"Loop around?"

Yes. Exactly. A loop. Just in case CNN's coverage was late. Clint wanted the parade to get on TV, especially the Percherons and the big circus wagons.

Mr. Sport Coat was observing from behind Clint's shoulder. "I'll have a T-shirt made. 'Bunsen for Congress.' Take me two minutes. Have ten T-shirts. You and nine of your closest friends.

Slip into the parade and march past the camera. If they're live, there's nothing they can do about it. Nothing."

Clint shook his head. Not a good idea.

The Living Flag organizers walked through town and hollered to people in their backyards, "CNN is here. Let's make the Living Flag look good on TV. We need people! Can't do it without you! Come on down!"

They moved along, coaxing and urging, moving the sheep toward the football field. Clint was on the horn, ordering ice from Little Falls. An old lady had fainted by the lake. CNN was busy. The squat man was assembling a control console beside the truck and the skinny kid had hung an awning over it and Ricky was sitting looking at the CNN broadcast feed on a screen and talking over headphones to somebody named Sam.

At Leonards Field, the red caps and white hats were distributed, broad-brim straw hats, and then the blue hats, and everyone wanted blue because they were the last to line up, and then the stripes started assembling, three abreast, and then the blue rectangle.

Father Wilmer poked his head into the Sidetrack and announced that the Flag was forming, and Wally said, "Yeah, I'll be down if I can. I don't know. It all depends."

"We need everybody," said Father Wilmer. "CNN is on the scene and we don't want it to be puny."

"Okay, but I've got a business to run, Father."

Father looked around the dim barroom, newly mopped and disinfected, the lights bubbling on the jukebox. "Close it up. It's a holiday," he said.

"No holidays in the bar business. Just the occasional lull."

"Somebody said they saw Art walking around downtown," said Father.

"Art is in Montana," said Wally. "I know that for a fact."

"You sure?"

"Sure, I'm sure."

Todd the governor's man took Clint aside. "I'd rather you didn't make a change in plans without consulting me," he said. "The governor is committed to being here. He's on his way. He's expecting to be in the parade. You can't invite the governor of Minnesota to come all this way up here and then shove him off in a corner."

Clint took a deep breath and counted to ten, but ten wasn't enough, so he counted to twenty, meanwhile he looked the man straight in the eyes, which were pink and piggish. And his breath smelled of cigarettes.

"You're a guest in this town, mister. Don't forget it."

Todd put his face closer to Clint's. "Not talking about me. Talking about the governor of Minnesota." And he poked Clint in the chest.

"You poke me once more and I'm going to see to it that the police find pictures of naked Boy Scouts in the glove compartment of your car. And if you went up for fifteen years, mister, it wouldn't bother me one bit."

That knocked Todd back on his heels. He tried to grin as if it were a terrific little joke between the two of them but the grin didn't come out right.

"You think we don't have that kind of stuff around here, guess again. So don't push me, asshole."

"All I was saying—" said Todd, but Clint cut him off. "You want trouble, mister, we've got more than you can handle. So don't press your luck." And he turned away. A big washtub of icy water sat in the shade and he fished out a bottle of Dr Pepper and opened it with his army knife and took a swig.

He was proud of himself. Some very nice lines, like something Gene Hackman might've said, or Edward G. Robinson. He crossed the street with a slight swagger, thinking of John Wayne, thinking of how Todd had come here expecting to run into Extremely Nice Lutherans who would kiss his fingers because he worked for the G-O-V-E-R-N-O-R—and instead of buttkissing, the man got a good slap in the chops, which he'd had coming to him for a long time now.

He got to the other side and in the window of the Mercantile he could see Todd standing stunned across the street. He hadn't moved an inch. Clint turned on his heel and headed west toward the park and the stage wagon and the parade elements gathering there.

LeRoy drove up and down the streets in the patrol car, appealing for Flag participants. "Everyone who can, report to Leonards Field," he said in an authoritative voice over the car's loudspeaker. "The Living Flag is being assembled now. I repeat: All residents—this is an official notice—you are asked to report to Leonards Field."

Irene had left Cindy Hedlund at Art's Night O' Rest to wait for CNN. She stopped by home to change into her nice white linen pants and white blouse. She headed downtown where a couple hundred folks were milling around and trying hard not to stare at the CNN truck and Ricky sitting at the control board.

He was smoking a cigarette and gesturing as he talked into his headset. From the gestures, you gathered that the person at the other end was not so bright.

Arlene said, "I hope Clint is going to take a few days off. He looks peaked to me."

"He's always looked peaked." Irene was looking up the street at a woman standing in the shadows under the awning of Skoglund's Five & Dime. She knew right away who it was. She had known for a long time. She thought of walking over to the woman and telling her, "I know who you are and I think you ought to look me in the eye. Know that what you do has consequences for other people. And you are not anonymous. On the Internet maybe but not here."

Oh, but why? If he really thought that some chicky looking for a father figure could make him happy, fine. Go and God bless you. But he wasn't going to be taking much money with him. The Ford garage was worth peanuts and she doubted they could get much for their house. For Sale signs tended to stay up until the paint peeled. Hjalmar and Virginia put their house up for sale and while they waited for a buyer, they dwindled and got frail and were carted off to the Good Shepherd Home, and when Hjalmar's mind went, Virginia cut the price almost in half, and two years later, it was bought for half of that by a hermit who ripped up Hjalmar's beautiful lawn and planted peonies and ginkgo trees. Sic transit Hjalmar. So if Clint walked out on her, he might have to hitch a ride. He and his chicky might have to live in her car for awhile and apply for food stamps. Nothing like poverty to dampen a hot romance.

At the football field, Irene was given a white hat and wound up in a middle stripe between Cliff with his birdcage hairdo sprayed with lacquer and teased into a white globe around his pink scalp and Mr. Diener who she had never cared for but there he was and what could she do—you couldn't have everybody angling for a better position or the Flag would never get made— so she sucked it up and planted her feet next to his blue sneakers and looked straight ahead.

"I've been hearing a lot of talk about your husband," he said. "I don't like to pass on gossip but I figure you ought to know what's going around."

"I pay no attention to gossip," she said through clenched teeth.

"I don't either necessarily but I think that if Clint is running around with a young woman from St. Cloud, he deserves a good talking-to and it seems to me you're the one who ought to do it."

"The woman is standing over there if you want to go talk to her," said Irene.

Mr. Diener turned and looked.

"You can't change people," she said. "Past a certain age, a man is going to do pretty much what he chooses. Why waste your breath?"

"Sometimes a man loses his mind and he has to be brought back to reality."

"It's going to take more than a lecture from me, believe me."

And there she had to stand, while the Flag was built stripe by stripe, by Gary who stood in for Father Wilmer who was feeling light-headed. Gary was bouncing around 15 feet in the air in a cherry-picker on a truck from Mist County Power & Light and talking over a bullhorn: "Stripe Number 4, straighten your lines! You reds, you're not there—you're up here! We got too many white people, we need more red ones! All you tall white people, I want you to be red so the red stripes stand out more— all you short reds change places with the tall whites—let's do this without talking, people! People, listen to me. We have a national TV network here—you remember what a success it was last year—so let's get this thing going. This might be seen around the world—around the world—think of it—and we don't want the world to think we are unable to form a straight line even after we've been asked to eleven times—it's very discouraging, people." The Flag fell silent. "I don't have to be here, people," cried Gary. "And CNN doesn't either. Lots of other towns have Fourth of July celebrations too. We're not the only fish in the pond. Where's the community spirit? Where's the love of country?"

"Aw, quit your bellyaching," muttered Mr. Diener. He was peering at the woman in the shadows. She seemed to be on a cell phone.

Irene watched her. She looked very cool and collected. She was talking loudly. Irene picked up the words "Leaving tonight" and "I don't know" and "It's up to him."

Irene got back to Art's Baits & Night O' Rest and not a soul was around, though the shrimp was on ice in Cabin No. 2 and beer filled the cooler and a bottle of rosé wine. Viola had left the keys sitting on the TV set. Simple as that. There was the key to Art's cabin. She walked onto his porch and opened the door with the BEFORE YOU KNOCK ON THIS DOOR TO ASK A QUESTION, KINDLY CHECK THE LIST OF RULES POSTED IN YOUR CABIN sign and went in. The place stank of cigarette smoke and dirty laundry. Boxes stacked everywhere, on the sofa, on the floor, and narrow passages through the boxes to the bathroom, which was unspeakable. The place reeked of loneliness. This is what happens to people who live alone. They den up and growl at intruders. There are no guests, only intruders. She had always disdained Art and now she had sympathy for him, the old devil. He didn't clean or bathe, having nobody to clean or bathe for, and he was simply waiting to die. He cared nothing about material things, it was all junk to him, and here it was—dressers full of battered spoons and bundles of soiled ties, dried-up shoes, arrowheads, nylons (Nylons? Nylons), Necco Wafers, fistfuls of buttons, fishing lures, stale candy, sparklers, used postcards, razor blades rusting in their packages, a great deal of coinage, chunks of chalk, a box of tassels, lots of driftwood—he didn't care about any of it, was simply filling space to give his life some shape—and in one box marked DO NOT TOUCH she found a revolver in a plastic bag with a box of shells. Smith & Wesson. It felt good in her right hand, also in her left. A nice wood grip. You could point this at a man and he'd know you meant business. You weren't just nagging at him now. Nothing says "STOP" like a pistol. A universal language.

It was so easy to load. A little plate with an indent for the thumb: You pushed it forward and the cylinder flopped out to the left and you stuck the brass cartridges in and slapped it shut.

She held it out in front of her and aimed it at the carton of tassels and shot *BOOM* and bits of cloth blew up in the air just like a man's flesh would if you shot him. It'd tear him up pretty bad. Not that she would ever do that to Clint. But he'd know what a gun can do, having been in the Navy. If she pointed this gun at him, suddenly the fantasy would be over and everything would become very real.

26. SHOWTIME

lint located the choir on the beach near the changing shed. They stood in three straight lines, heads down, and Miss Falconer was standing silent, looking them over, as he approached. He was about to say hi when she slapped her fist into her hand and said, "I am ashamed of you. Each and every one of you. I ask you to stand in formation and I go away for two minutes and I come back and you are throwing sand at each other. You people. It's almost more than I can bear. You have this opportunity to sing on national television for millions and millions of people and to represent our community and you cannot be trusted to be alone and unsupervised for two minutes!!! Where is the maturity? You seniors think you're big stuff, and you can't even keep order. And you know something—some of you years from now will look back on this year as the best year of your life. That's the truth. For a lot of you, it's all downhill from here. So enjoy it while you can. And if I ever catch you throwing sand again, you're going to be leaving this school a lot sooner than you think." She stopped when she saw Clint.

"We're ready for you," he said. "Let's see if we can't squeeze you in on the parade route."

At the football field, bullhorn in hand, Gary was in full cry. Irene had escaped along with a few others and he was trying to hold the Flag together. "If any of you think you can do better, come on up. Be my guest. It isn't as easy as you may think, trying to get people to stand still in formation. You whites—Stripe Number 1—you right here—you're starting to fall out. Did I say to fall out? No, I did not." He thanked people for their patience even as he was exhausting it and told the blues to squeeze in as tight as possible around the folks with the star hats. "C'mon, take a deep breath and move in tight, people. This doesn't have to take all day. Let's do it. C'mon, lady—move in close there. He won't bite you." And small-town people, who never crowded onto a bus, who hate crowds, who would naturally stand about 37 inches from somebody they're talking to, squeezed in a little tighter, and Mr. Diener squeezed next to Gloria Dietzmann whose hair smelled of sauerkraut and who was complaining about her legs. Her sister Marie used to yodel "There's A Star-Spangled Banner Flying Somewhere" and it was always a big hit, modulating higher and higher and then a big double-time finish, and she imagined she had a big future as an entertainer and moved to California, but yodeling, unfortunately, is only good for short bursts—a whole evening of it is too much—and it took her ten years to figure that out and now she's playing in a bar in Lincoln, Nebraska, and looks about 75 though she's only 61.

Gary was ratcheting on and on—"Let's squeeze in tight, people—let's connect the dots—I know it's a hot day but let's just exhale and squeeze in tight—let's make this the best Living Flag that we ever made." And then they had it. And then Berge cried out, "Three cheers for the red, white, and blue!" So they cheered, "Hip hip *hurray!* Hip hip *hurray!* Hip hip *HURRAY!!*" And then Mr. Detmer called for the Pledge of Allegiance and they did that. Someone yelled out, "How about 'The Star-Spangled Banner'?" so of course they had to sing that. Some soprano started it too high and the old ladies were screeching like they needed oiling. There was an epic poem by Mr. Stenerud, poet laureate of the Knutes, "Tip Your Hat to the Flag," including the lines "when time just seems to drag" and "though other nations brag" and "let not your footsteps lag" and "this is no jest or gag" and "though protesters rail and rag" and finally

So let us e'er be vigilant,
Let not our efforts fag,
So that our kids and grandkids
Will tip their hats to the flag.

And then there was the sound of heavy wheezing on the public address system and an old whiskey voice said, "Breathes there a man with soul so dead, who never to himself hath said, this is my own, my native land." And it was Art. He wore camouflage pants and an Army jacket with several gold medals and campaign ribbons and a pair of reflective sunglasses. He had gotten off bus and made his way back home like an old abandoned dog and stepped into the Sidetrack Tap and found it empty. No Wally. And then he remembered how years ago he was thrown out of the Sidetrack for cursing at Democrats and when he got back in, for revenge, he wired a battery to the drain of the urinal and then sat at the bar waiting for Wally to take a piss. Wally had a steel bladder but eventually he went to the pisser and Art flipped the switch and waited for the scream and then he was going to yell, "Sic semper tyrannis" and run like hell. He waited a couple minutes and Wally came back. "Took you awhile," said Art. "Yeah, I got to reading a book someone left in there," said Wally. So Art waited and waited and had a few beers and then he had to go pee. He was pretty sure he had turned off the switch but he thought, "Oh, what the heck, I'll use the stall," but someone was in the stall, and suddenly he had to empty his bladder urgently. He went to piss in the sink and then heard footsteps and switched to the urinal and made contact and felt a hot burning sensation in his groin and let out a yell. The memory was vivid still. He looked at the beautiful display of liquors in the glass cabinet, Kahlúa and Drambuie and sloe gin, green and red and amber, stuff he'd never thought to drink before—he was strictly Jim Beam and beer for a chaser and peppermint brandy if he had a cold but here was a pantheon of liquors untasted and what better time than now? He poured himself a splash of Finnish vodka, just to rinse his mouth, and then he had a little swig from each one—a licorice drink and a sweet whiskey liqueur and some strawberry concoction—and then he started pouring liquor on the floor and throwing bottles against the glass cabinets—"That's what I think of you!" he yelled. "Look out! I know who you are and I will not be stopped!" And that put him in a mood to go out and witness to his townsmen.

"Most of you folks consider yourselves patriots," he said to the Living Flag and a few hundred onlookers, "but how can you say you love your country if you don't follow the Constitu-tion?" He had found the bullhorn lying on the steps—Gary had gone off to take a leak—and now Art had something to say.

The Living Flag was starting to erode around the edges. "And how can you celebrate freedom when a man's own motel is taken over without his permission and his own possessions are re-moved from the premises?" cried Art, wild hair and all, eyes raging, an arm up in the air, and what appeared to be a pistol in his pants pocket. "There are individuals in our midst who don't belong here and it's time to root them out!" he said as Gary removed the bullhorn from his hand. Art careened a few steps and stopped—"I am not leaving!" he yelled. And then he was gone.

27. IN THE GARAGE

Clint was herding the choir toward Main Street when his cell phone rang. An urgent report from Billy P. on the hill: The cannons could not fire on account of cars parked in the line of fire—someone had removed the yellow No Parking tape and the cannoneers were upset and about to pack up their gunpowder and go home—

Cars to the right of them, cars to the left of them,
Someone had blundered—
"Who is in charge of the parking?" he wondered.
"Tow the cars! That's an order!" he thundered.

And the phone rang again. It was Angelica asking if he could find her a place to change into her Miss Liberty outfit and ten minutes later he met her in the alley behind Bunsen Motors and led her in through the shop to Clarence's office. She carried the robe, the crown, and tablet in a shopping bag. She had brought an iron too.

"Where's Kevin?" he said. She said Kevin was having a fit.

He didn't like crowds and he didn't want her to march in the parade. He wanted to get a move on. They were supposedly driving to South Dakota tonight. "I hope he likes to make love with you," he said.

"Let's not talk about it. How's the car business?" she said.

"Terrible. Never worse."

"Maybe you ought to get out of it."

"The thought has occurred to me."

A red Taurus sat in the showroom with red, white, and blue bunting hung over it, and a sign: FORD—FOLLOW THE DREAM.

"Not the car I was dreaming of," she said, "but maybe I could drive it and find my dream." She took his arm. "What's your dream, darling?"

His dream had been this tall woman with reddish hair and a silver pendant around her neck. "Is Kevin in his camper?" he said. He had already checked with LeRoy who located the camper in the yard at Art's Baits, parked next to the Hospitality Suite.

"Yes. Sulking. Which he's good at, poor baby."

She looked down at Clarence's old gray metal desk, the green lounge chair, and the framed pictures of his children, the plastic Model T, the souvenir coconut from Hawaii, the little bronze trophy for service to the community, the jar full of coins, the desk calendar from Lindberg Funeral Home, and said, "I would guess that he doesn't do much work at this desk." Clint nodded. He opened the big bottom drawer and lifted out a stack of paper. Crossword puzzles, clipped from the newspaper and pasted to white paper, all of them finished, in ballpoint pen. "My brother likes to save all the crossword puzzles he's done. There are more in a box in the closet."

She laid out the great green robe on the desk and ironed it and unplugged the iron and kicked off her sandals and started unbuttoning her blouse. "I should let you be," said Clint.

"Oh? Why?" she said. "I've missed you."

"What about Kevin?"

"I don't even know if he and I are still together."

"You don't know?"

"I'm not feeling clairvoyant today. It's that time of month."

She took the blouse off and folded it and then slipped her jeans down over her womanly hips and folded them and then reached back and unfastened her bra.

"It's going to be hot under that robe," she said. She put the bra on the stack of clothes and slipped out of her pink panties and stood for his inspection, hands on her hips. It was her all right: her lovely suggestions of breasts, so subtle and delicate, and the dark conical nipples, her flat abdomen with the deep navel, the wild bush below.

"Are you marching naked today?" His voice was a little high.

"I'm wearing a robe."

"But underneath?"

"What you see is what you get."

"Do you think that's a good idea?" Dumb question. Dumb fatherly question. What an idiot he was. The woman was offering her nakedness to him. He lusted after her nakedness and she was giving him this as a pure gift, and it would be their secret under the hot gaze of the town. He and she would know and nobody else. An invisible bond between them. *Naked Woman Marches in Fourth of July Parade.*

She sat down on Clarence's desk. Her naked hinder plopped down where so many purchase agreements had been signed, so many hearty handshakes, and she smiled a wan smile and said, "I want to run away with you."

"Now?"

"Independence Day. What better time?"

She was serious, apparently. She gazed into his eyes as if she were his high school counselor advising him to go to college and she told him that he was unhappy with his life in Lake Wobegon. The marriage was dead. His children were grown and out of his life. The business was failing. He no longer considered himself a Lutheran in his heart. He had no true friends here, only old acquaintances, nobody he could unburden himself to. He wanted a change in his life. She was the agent of change. She was moving to San Francisco in a month, to waitress at her cousin Sydney's restaurant, the Fillmore Grill, and eventually to go back to school. She wanted to get an MFA in creative writing. Sydney had found her a studio apartment on Irving Street, very nice, right on the streetcar line. She'd move in on Labor Day. San Francisco was a golden place. Salt air and sunshine, never too hot, never too cold, a city of perpetual spring, new beginnings. People sitting outdoors in February, drinking coffee at coffee shops. Her neighborhood, the Inner Sunset, had little bookstores and cafés, Thai and Japanese, Italian, Lebanese, a world of delicacies awaited. They'd live in her studio apartment and he could take his time figuring out what he wanted to do. First, learn to hang out. Sit. Watch the world go by. Be secure in your own being. Accept the meaningfulness of your own existence, apart from your function in the economy and your reputation in the community. Accept being you.

"That's the name of the neighborhood? 'The Inner Sunset'?"

"There's the Inner and the Outer Sunset. The Outer is west, right on the ocean. The Inner is east of Highway 1."

"I was there when I was in the Navy. We had training in deck guns there."

He could see the slight figure of the Chinese woman in the bluish light as she bent over him and asked if it was all right. *Oh yes, it was. Very much so.*

"I don't mean to tell you what to do, but I think it's time you think about what you want instead of what everybody else wants. Why deny yourself? If you don't take it now, when will you?"

He didn't have an answer for that. He was drifting, falling through space. Infidelity is a bad habit: Once you start, where do you stop? Look at David Diener, divorced twice and en route to the third. Married young, a shy, bookish young man who was overwhelmed when young Marcia showed interest in him and they were married seven years, and one day he was out fishing on the lake and a woman swam up with a bad leg cramp. He helped her into the boat and massaged the cramp and went through the misery of divorce and married the swimmer, Melody. And about seven years later he was fishing again and he and his buddies went to the Moonlite Bay supper club for deep-fried walleye and he laid eyes on a waitress, Marva, who wore red pants, was tall and beautiful and funny and young and when she bent over to set down his hamburger and fries and he looked down her shirt, his brain turned to jelly. He cajoled her into having a drink with him after work and afterward they sat in his car and kissed and he fell in love with her. He sent her a poetry telegram. A messenger came to her door, dressed as a Greek god with golden hair, in a loose-fitting tunic, and he opened a box and released five hundred golden butterflies and recited "Come live with me and be my love and we will all the pleasures prove" and it was Craig, an old high school classmate of hers, and she started dating him and broke David Diener's heart and he went into therapy and the therapist, Molly, was warm and funny and two years later they were married. The man is on a roll, but who would want all those complications, the weepy scenes, the packing, the lawyers.

"I am seeing you sitting in a coffee shop in San Francisco," she said. "It's a warm day in February and you're reading the newspaper. You're wearing a beret and drinking espresso. There's a yellow notepad on the table and you've written on it with a fountain pen. I think it's a poem but I can't be sure. You've lived in the city for three years and you can't imagine living anywhere else."

They heard the click of the front door and Clint jumped. Angelica got into the robe and put the crown on and Clint eased out the door into the showroom. His brother stood looking out the big plate glass window at the street. Parade-goers were streaming by.

"You disappeared," he said.

"I was just on my way back."

"Is there something I ought to know?" said Clarence. In his older brother voice. Low and commanding.

"About what?"

His brother turned and faced him. "What's going on with you?"

"I am living my life. Trying to."

"What's the problem then?"

And then Miss Liberty emerged and stood beside him in her great green robe, her seven-pointed crown, her golden torch, her tablet with JULY IV, MDCCLXXVI written on it. "Ready for my close-up," she said cheerily. "You must be Clarence. I'm Angelica." She put the torch under her arm and shook his hand. "I'm a friend of your brother's."

"I wish somebody would clue me in," said Clarence.

"I hear you like crossword puzzles," she said. "Well, this is sort of a puzzle but without the clues, so nobody really knows if he gets the right answer or not."

"Let's go do a parade!" said Clint. He offered Miss Liberty his arm and out the door they went. Clarence watched them go. His brother clearly was in trouble and he was supposed to rescue him as we are trained in Boy Scouts to do—Never Turn Away From Someone In Trouble—that was baked into them by Einar their old Scoutmaster—but how do you rescue someone from himself? Clint had been out of control with this Fourth of July business for several years now. The lavish spending on circus wagons and cannons and horses—good gosh, Clarence had covered for him, made excuses to people—"He just wants what's best for Lake Wobegon. Wants the world to know about us"—but the bottom line was: Clint was a loose cannon and needed to be reined in.

And then Clarence looked in his office. A shopping bag on his desk. A woman's clothes in there. The young lady with Clint. Her clothes, her underwear, for crying out loud. And then it dawned on him. *Miss Liberty was buck naked.* She was walking around in a green robe and nothing on underneath, just her and her sandals.

She had to be stopped before she did something foolish and brought the whole Fourth of July crashing down around her head.

28. THE BIG PARADE

The parade was assembling and Clint walked along the line, checking the units off one by one. The first big bandwagon was in place, a real Gargantua, forty feet long, fifteen high, big as a semitrailer but with brilliant red and green curlicues and furbelows on the sides, a sixteen-horse hitch, two hairy-legged teamsters in the wagon box, and a six-piece band on top, warming up. "You look fabulous!" he shouted up at them. The musicians looked a little dazed in the sunlight, like nocturnal cave dwellers in captivity.

Behind the bandwagon stood the VFW honor guard and two schoolchildren bearing a long silk banner (STAND BY YOUR COLORS—BE TRUE TO YOUR OWN) and the white Chevy Impala convertible with a banner on the side, OUR GRAND MARSHAL, FATHER WILMER—Viola had tried to get TV weatherman Danny Tripp for grand marshal by way of Danny's hair stylist, but Danny had just signed a six-figure contract to do weather in Salt Lake City so he had no interest in public-service stuff—he was out of here! So the Committee voted in Father Wilmer, over his protests. "I am only a village priest, I'm no big shot," he said. And there he was, standing by the Impala, still reluctant. "I honestly would rather not," he murmured, brushing the long wisps of hair across his bald spot, fidgeting like a schoolboy.

"We voted to honor you and we are going to do it whether you want to or not," said Clint. "Don't take it personally. We're honoring the parish. Sit up there and smile and wave. It's only a parade. Do your part."

Father Wilmer whimpered something about really, really not wanting to and Clint grabbed him by the back of his jacket and shoved him into the car. "Sometimes we have to do things we don't want to do and this is one of those times, Father." The priest tripped on the door frame and Clint had to grab the seat of his pants and boost him up toward the ledge on the backseat.. "Please let me sit down on the seat. Not up there," Father pleaded. "You are going to sit up there and damn well look like you're having a good time. Damn it. No more out of you or I'm going to slap you one. I mean it."

Behind the Impala, impatient, ready to go, stood twenty young women of the Tammy Jo Dance Studio Happiness Troupe, shuffling quietly on their taps. "Let's see smiles! Everybody wants to see smiles!" cried Tammy Jo. "Nobody wants to see frowns." And then another Impala with Senator K. Thorvaldson, the oldest man in town, 96 according to himself, but some people thought that carbon dating might show him to be ten years older than that.

Then the 4-H float (LIBERTY, AMERICA'S GLORY. GUARD IT WELL. SO MAY IT EVER BE.) with kids in tricornered hats holding muskets made of broomsticks. And then the second bandwagon, and the third.

The fourth brought up the rear, another forty-footer, with a twelve-piece band who would play "Just A Closer Walk With Thee." The bracing smell of horse perspiration and fresh manure, the big horses standing in place, heads up, nostrils flared. Thrilling. It was hands-down his favorite part of the parade—also the most expensive—and he looked at the crowd of placid onlookers and saw here and there the grinning faces of others moved by the sight of powerful horses hauling gaudy wagons with hot bands atop them.

Behind the big wagon was a Model T with a bright pink banner on the side, BONNIE SCHELLENBACH, MISS PORK, and a pretty young woman in a white organdy gown, with a sash (MISS PORK) across her bosom. She was a cousin of the Magendanzes. She looked pretty miserable.

Uncle Sam paced back and forth in his special shoes with two-foot stilts attached. "Sure could use a beer," he said. Last year he'd been stuck behind a bagpiper playing "Amazing Grace" who kept such a slow pace that Uncle Sam lost his balance and toppled over in midstride which of course elicited a big cheer from the crowd.

He reminded Clint that it doesn't work to walk slow on stilts. "You have to keep some forward momentum with stilts, otherwise you're sunk."

The *American Gothic* man stood, pitchfork in hand, in the bright sun, blinking, his bald head already burned a faint red, and Mrs. Gothic stood glaring at him. "I told you to put a hat on," she said.

"You ever look at the painting? There's no hat on him in the painting."

Miss Liberty approached them. "Am I supposed to be with you?" she said. Mr. Gothic shook his head. "You're way up there with the governor," he said. "You're not with us, I know that."

Mrs. Gothic watched Miss Liberty hike toward the head of the parade, around the gold-booted red-jacketed Will Jones Drum & Bugle boys stepping out to "Yankee Doodle," and she turned to Mr. Gothic and said, "That woman does not wear anything under that robe. She didn't last year either. I can tell by the way the robe sneaks into her crack when she walks. And you can see her nipples. She is naked."

"You don't think she's going to streak the parade, do you?"

"You're hoping she does. I know that. Statue of Liberty running naked through the streets—right up your alley."

Susan B. Anthony was standing nearby and she agreed about Miss Liberty being up to no good. "Quite a comment on our society, if you ask me," she said. "Nice weather brings out the worst in people, somehow. It's been shown time and again."

"I don't see why people get so upset about nipples," said Mr. Gothic.

"Any more remarks from you and I'll put that pitchfork where the moon don't shine," said his wife. He felt a little *plip plip* on his head as if a bird might have dropped something. "Do I have something on my head?" he asked. "Hair," she said.

Miss Liberty arrived at the head of the parade, which was on McKinley Street beside Krebsbach Chevrolet, and there, behind the twenty-man color guard, their big flags fluttering in the light breeze, was Uncle Sam, leaning against a lamppost, eating a hotdog.

"Isn't that hard, walking on little stilts?"

"Not so bad, once you get the knack of it. It's the standing around and waiting that kills me."

Lyle sat in his golf cart behind the color guard. He had gone home this morning and left the stage wagon to others and they had done a fine job without him and so he was miffed about that. He wore a blue beanie with a little American flag atop it and two bigger flags mounted on the front bumper of the cart and strings of little paper flags all around the canopy. He was trying to get his walkie-talkie to work and it kept squawking at him. "I told you. I'm here, dammit!" he yelled into it. It squawked again. "What?" he said.

"I think they want you to move to the rear," said Uncle Sam. "The governor's late. Clint wants to get the show on the road. Let him bring up the rear." He looked at Miss Liberty. "Who needs the governor when they have us?" he said. He wiped the mustard from his upper lip and stepped toward her, his arm bent, extended, and she took his hand. They stepped into position and as they did, he could feel, his hand in hers, brushing against her, that the woman was not wearing a brassiere. Mercy. Young women! There were no rules anymore. Oh well. And now he could feel excitement in his red-and-white-striped pants. There definitely was interest down there. He was going to have to get his mind on other things.

Lyle drove his golf cart around the corner and down the line of the parade, past the first circus wagon to where Clint stood in the middle of the street, a man in a dark suit next to him. "He's three minutes away," said the man. Clint ignored him. "Go back to the mayor's car," he told Lyle. "Tell them the governor's going to ride with her."

"I was told he would have his own car," said the man in the suit.

"It's the white Chevy convertible," Clint told Lyle.

"So what else do I do?" Lyle said. Clint told him to see to the rear of the parade, keep it tight, don't let those people lag behind. And make sure the big wagon with the hot band and the elephant hanging on brings up the rear. The elephant would hold a flag in its tail, saying THE END. Cute.

Thomas Jefferson and Benjamin Franklin came hustling up, Franklin straightening his wig. "We're late, we couldn't find a parking space," said Jefferson.

"There was a parking space reserved for you. Right over there. Behind the church."

"I forgot my parking pass."

"What do you need a pass for? The space was marked 'Jefferson.' That's you. Right?"

"Maybe the governor's driver is looking for a place to park," said Todd.

"It's almost five o'clock and I'm starting the parade," said Clint.

"Give us five more minutes." Todd put his hand on Clint's shoulder. Clint took the hand off his shoulder. "We have a pie-eating contest later. Maybe he could participate in that. There's also a three-legged race."

Todd got a solemn look on his face. "We're talking about the governor of the State of Minnesota."

"I could get a manure spreader. How about we have him ride in that?"

Todd leaned in close and said, "You're the one looking for an endorsement, buddy, not me. I'd watch my step if I were you."

Clint walked over to the big wagon and called up to the teamsters—"You all set?" They gave him a thumbs-up, and he looked up and down the line. Everybody seemed to be in place except for the two Founding Fathers who were heading for the History unit. Amazing. Eight bands at parade rest, and four big teams of wagon horses standing in place and tossing their big heads, switching their stumpy tails, and a clown rocking back and forth on his unicycle, and around the corner on Main Street, the hushed hum and murmur of the crowd sweetly waiting for something to happen—Gary and LeRoy estimated thirty-two thousand people on hand, a new record for attendance—yellow schoolbuses stretched from the Sons of Knute Lodge all the way to the creamery—acres of cars by the grain elevator and the so-called industrial park—gangs of college kids rambled around—fifty seniors from the Good Shepherd Home sat under a canvas pavilion by the bandstand.

"We forgot! Hold on!"—it was Viola, out of breath, holding up her hand, pointing to her wristwatch.

"Delivery Day! We were supposed to have four minutes of silence at 4:36! It's past five o'clock."

"What do you want me to do?" he said.

"I don't know."

"Do you want me to hold up the parade?"

"No," she said.

"Then I won't," he said.

"Add 'em up and move 'em out!" he hollered into his walkie-talkie. Nothing happened. It was the old After You Alphonse syndrome—people couldn't start marching without looking around and making sure others would march with them—"Are you ready?" "Yes, let's see if they're ready. Okay, they're ready. Is he ready? He's ready. Okay, is she ready? She's ready. I guess we're ready. Do you think we're ready?"—Clint pressed Talk. "Add 'em up and move 'em out! That's an order. Go!" And he could feel in the soles of his feet the great parade gather itself up and take a deep breath and then the roll and rattle of drums from the Will Jones Drum & Bugle Corps and the basso grunt of the drum major and his *Heeee-ya—HUHHH* and the cadence of marching feet.

Uncle Sam stepped out, grinning, tossing handfuls of silver stars in the air, hand in hand with Miss Liberty, behind the eight-man color guard as it swung around the corner—not a geezer in the bunch, all eight in fighting form—and a great cheer went up from the crowd packed onto the sidewalk for four blocks to the bleachers. Flags flew over the heads of the crowd, a boulevard of flags, and small children hoisted onto their parents' shoulders waved tiny flags—a solid wall of humanity with little faces poking out between the legs—Miss Liberty grinned to see it. She let go of Uncle Sam's hand which was pressed against her right boob exploring it and she raised up her torch high and swung it in time to the rattle of the drums behind her. It was maybe her last parade. Farewell, Minnesota! It was like a dream, all that energy and passion flowing her way, and her naked under the robe and ready to receive it. It'd do these Lutherans good to look at a naked woman even if they don't know she is. The crowd was waving to her and she waved her tablet at them. "Hurray for freedom!" she hollered. She chanted, "Life! Liberty! Happiness!" The color guard was poking along and she swung out in front of them. "Hey!" yelled Uncle Sam but she was in full stride, weaving from one side of the street to the other, her torch keeping time. The people were all transfixed by her and the day, everyone beaming and grinning, and she thought, "What if I dropped my robe?" They were so excited: Why not give them something to remember for the rest of their lives? The body is God's handiwork and he'd given her a good one. Why be ashamed? The tap dancers came along, twenty heads bobbing, dancing to "Tea For Two" or was it "Stars and Stripes Forever"? And then the Soybean Queen and then the Whistling Mothers, twenty-two ladies in gray skirts and capes, marching along and whistling "Colonel Bogey March" and doing a bang-up job of it. The crowd had never heard female precision whistling before. They listened, awestruck, as the Mothers went through their maneuvers, wheeling and fanning into a revolving circle and then into concentric rectangles and when they started whistling in four-part harmony, it knocked the socks off people, they whooped and yelled, and then the Mothers were gone and up came Mr. Topps the Human Gyro, an old man in red tights who balanced on one finger on a chrome gazing globe. Likewise phenomenal. And the Car Club and a pink Oldsmobile with a mouthful of chrome and a sweet Mustang and a '57 Chevy with the great fins, followed by a sad-faced clown with a big red beezer and a monkey on his shoulder. And the Future Farmers chorus in blue jackets, singing:

We raise the crops that make your kids grow tall.
Plant in the spring and harvest in the fall.

Work late at night and rise at early morn.
We plant the corn, we plant the corn.

Clint watched them go by and all the miseries of the past weeks fell away and he felt glee. Utter glee. Roll on, America! He'd done his best and it was passing before his eyes, all the color and grandeur like a tapestry he'd painted. And him in his tight white pants with gold buttons and rose-embroidered shirt and LIBERTY button fit in perfectly. He had been a Spectator all his life and now he was in the Parade. That was it! Don't let life pass you by. Get your boat in the river. Roll with it. Let it roll. He hadn't seen a Norwegian bachelor farmer all day but if they wanted to drive a load of pigshit down Main Street, fine.

"How's it going?" Irene yelled in his ear and he jumped.

"What you doing here? You hate parades!"

"Came looking for you," she said. And she took his left arm in hers and crowded up next to him. She had a canvas bag around her shoulder and he could feel a piece of hardware in it, a garden trowel or pruning shears. "I gotta keep an eye on you," she said. "Defend you against your girlfriend." And then Wally the Human Pinwheel went cartwheeling by and eight Percherons and a circus wagon painted with bronze faces in feather headdresses and a band atop it playing the "Minnesota Rouser" and he stepped into the street to check on the units behind and when he came back to the curb, Irene had melted into the crowd.

29. THE GOV ARRIVES

The ocarina band from Our Lady of Perpetual Responsibility was supposed to follow the first big bandwagon and then Clint said no. They had rehearsed a very nice arrangement of "Dona Nobis Pacem" in case he changed his mind but he had not. "The band on the wagon is going to be blasting away on 'Muskrat Ramble' and your 'Dona Nobis Pacem' is going to be lost," he explained to Sister Arvonne, but he underestimated her. She did not intend for all of that rehearsal to go for naught. She mustered her twenty ocarinists in the church along with the twenty girls of her Joyful Noise choir and she hustled them by a back route to the tail end of the parade, behind Mayor Eloise Krebsbach's white convertible. She knew Eloise very well. Eloise was her prize pupil. Eloise was not going to let an old Lutheran like Clint Bunsen stifle a Catholic children's ocarina band and choir. No, ma'am.

The crowd of forty children in their pressed white shirts and blue capes, shoes shined and hair combed, arrived at the white convertible sitting by the entrance to the Wally (Old Hard Hands) Bunsen Memorial Ballpark and there was Eloise in a pretty red frock and a garland of daisies on her short black hair. Sister Arvonne had donned the old black habit, the wimple, the whole kit and kaboodle, for the occasion—people like to see a nun in a nun outfit, not in jeans and a sweatshirt which she wore most of the time. "We're going to be back here where we're more appreciated," she announced. She made the volunteer firemen back up the truck to make room for the children, and she got them shoehorned into position just as Lyle wheeled up in a golf cart and told her she was in the wrong place. "The governor's back here," he said. "You're up behind the bandwagon."

She could hear the drum-and-bugle corps stepping off and the crowd cheering in the distance. "Plans change," she said. And then she heard the rustling of costumes and turned and here came fifteen Sons of Knute in their Viking regalia, the Sergeants at Arms carrying spears and shields, the Knights Exemplar in their horned helmets with plumes and their swords and blue silk sashes, and the Grand Oya in his sash covered with badges, the fringed silk ceremonial apron, the ceremonial mace, and his horned helmet fringed with fur. The Sergeants carried between them a Norwegian flag large enough to conceal a Sherman tank.

"We thought we'd be happier back here," the Oya explained to Sister Arvonne. "We didn't feel wanted up front. The parade's all about TV now." She nodded. "Pardon my French but we're just a bunch of old Norwegian assholes and they're looking for youth and beauty."

She beamed up at him. "But when was it ever different?" He

nodded back. "You put your finger on it, Sister. Story of the human race. When you're over the hill, you're over the hill." His big nose had red veins streaking down it and a cluster of them in the big bulb at the end. A mole was tucked to the side like a black fungus.

She had never spoken to a Grand Oya before. The Knutes were known to hold anti-Papist views and they smelled of fried herring, but on this sunny day they were quite jovial and grinned at the Catholic children and let them inspect their swords and shields. "I guess this is the rejection section," she said.

The Oya was a nice man with firm ideas about obsolescence. "When you're old, after your kids are grown up, Mother Nature has no more use for you," he said. "Get out of the way and mind your own business. That's my principle. Fishing and drinking beer, that's my idea of the good life." He was starting to explain to her the Codex Angularis which Saint Knute, the Viking Christian explorer, had found in a Gnostic temple in Egypt in 1024 and brought back to Vinland and translated from Aramaic, an account by a lesser apostle of Jesus known as Saint Sandy who maintained that Jesus was first and foremost a fisherman and had no truck with hard work—"Jesus said, 'Blessed are they who fish for they shall have more time'— left out of the Sermon on the Mount unfortunately"—and was just getting warmed up when Irene Bunsen walked up. She and Sister Arvonne were pals from way back. "I wish I'd thought of this before," she said. "I should've dressed up as a nun. Why not?" And then a black Lincoln SUV pulled up ahead of them and a highway patrolman rolled down the window.

"Got the governor here," he said. Lyle pointed to the white convertible. "Get him in there," he said. "The parade just started."

The governor emerged from the back door, a well-practiced smile on his face, eyes alight. "Great to see you again," he said to Irene who had never seen him before. He pressed Sister Arvonne's hand. "God bless you," he said. "Hey! Great to be here!" he said to the children who didn't know who he was. "You all as excited as I am? Looks like you are!" He had the old charmola working, all right. His grin came right up to the gums. Clearly he was someone of distinction. His blue suit was perfectly pressed, not a wrinkle on him, not even on his pants—Did he take them off on long car trips, Irene wondered. Perhaps so. He waved to a knot of people standing in the shadow of the ballpark. They didn't wave back. The outfield was studded with black pipes standing upright, black wiring everywhere. Three men in orange jumpsuits were on the grandstand roof, setting up what appeared to be a giant American flag made of colored sparklers. The governor gave them a big double thumbs-up. One of them yelled, "What?" He cupped his hands. "You're doing a heckuva job!" he hollered, winking at the Knutes. "Same to you!" the man yelled back.

The governor climbed into the backseat of the white convertible and perched himself on the back shelf alongside Mayor Krebsbach, just as Todd came running up, out of breath. "I tried to hold your place for you," he said, "but they decided it had to go. Anyway, everybody is excited you're here. People've been talking about it all day." He looked around. "Would you mind if the governor and I have a moment alone?" he said to the lady in the red dress. The governor leaned over and Todd stood on tiptoes and whispered in his ear. "The guy running the parade is an auto mechanic with a hair up his butt about running for Congress and he might ambush you about that. Let me handle him. Plus which, Georgia showed up five minutes ago. Stay loose."

"Georgia's here? Why didn't you tell me?"

"She surprised us. She was supposed to be in Waseca. She flew up on her broom."

"I don't care for surprises. I've told you that."

"Don't worry. I'm on the case. She won't lay a hand on you. We've got tranquilizer darts if necessary." Todd smiled at the mayor. "Good to see you," he said. "Have fun, you two."

He nodded to the driver, a skinny man in reflector shades, hair greased and combed back. "Move 'em out," he said. "Who're you?" said the driver. "Can't move 'em out until the people ahead of us move."

And then the 4-H float in front of them lurched forward with fourteen Busy Beavers holding up their giant flag quilt, and the governor grinned heartily and waved his gentle beneficent wave to the knots of people, families, gangs of teenagers, along the curb as the car swung around the corner past the back door of some sort of lodge hall where, he noticed, an old man was blowing the contents of his left nostril onto the sidewalk. A little tot slept in a stroller and his mother chomped on a giant bratwurst. A man in a denim jacket stood against the building, drunk. Six people stood in line at a portable toilet from which came the sound of male urination. People with glazed eyes peered at the governor as if at a strange creature in a zoo and he looked down and realized Todd had forgotten to hang a banner on the side of the car. What an idiot. The guy was a moron. End of the road for Todd. Today his ass would get fired, the little turd. A woman held up a sign, "Georgia for America," and looked beyond the governor, a big grin on her face. From behind him came the quavery hum of the ocarina band like a cloud of horseflies on his tail—"Beautiful day," he said to the mayor, "great crowd—great what you people have accomplished here"—and then he heard a woman caterwauling to his rear. He did not need to turn around to see who it was.

Irene held her position in front of the ballpark as Georgia swept by, standing tall on the American Legion float (IN HONOR OF THOSE WHO MADE THE ULTIMATE SACRIFICE), six corpses at her feet, their bodies twisted, bright red blood spattered generously on them, and it looked for all the world as if she had bludgeoned them herself and was ready to take on newcomers. She wore a white ruffled blouse and knee-high red plastic boots and bright blue tights on her corn-fed thighs and across the two artillery shells of her bosom was written CONGRESS. Her mane of wiry blond hair was pulled back in a knot and her broad warrior face looked eager for engagement with America's enemies. She wore a tiny microphone on a headset and her voice boomed out: "I am ready! Bring it on! I will be in place, ready to fight for you, on Day One! Day One!" A brigade of Georgia supporters thronged alongside, handing out literature to bystanders, as the candidate shouted her message over and over and gave a crisp hand-to-the-forehead salute to each flag she spotted along the route, even the small ones. There were a great many flags and she tried to keep up with them, saluting, saluting, her back nice and stiff, feet firmly planted, announcing her readiness to serve, as two big loudspeakers behind her blared out a choir singing "In the beauty of the lilies Christ was born across the sea"—she was bigger than life, and also heavier, and when the float turned the corner and hit a bump she lurched to her left and planted one red boot on the groin of a corpse who let out a strangled cry and half sat up and clutched himself in agony—though fallen, he was still a man and had feelings in the matter—Georgia stood straddling him, saluting flags left and right, preparing for her close-up on CNN.

Alongside her float, the Human Pinwheel came slowly cartwheeling by, hoping to get on TV and advertise himself—he needed the work. Georgia glanced his way and pointed at him and jerked her thumb like an umpire, OUT—and three of her guys moved up and collared the bum and hustled him away.

"Go out there and unplug her!" Mr. Griswold grabbed hold of Clint's shoulder. "Yank her switch! Tell her the rules say no amplified sound."

"Too late," said Clint.

"You gotta challenge her. Can't let her rant and rave like that. She's about to get on national TV."

"I'm going to take the high road. You challenge her."

Mr. Griswold adjusted his cuffs as the Ultimate Sacrifice float approached and he stepped into the street.

"Ready and able," the big woman cried. "Ready to fight for you!" The corpse was sitting up and she stepped over him and stepped down on the pavement. "Hey, big mouth!" yelled Mr. Griswold. "Turn off the loudspeaker! We're tired of you and your noise!" He jumped up onto the float and grabbed the microphone. "She's a fake!" he yelled. "Georgia Brickhouse is—"

She was on him like a buzzard on roadkill. She yanked the microphone away and grabbed his arm and twisted it. "Beat it, pip-squeak. This is America and I'll make as much noise as I want so just shut your own mouth," she yelled and turned around and raised her right fist and her supporters chanted, "Brickhouse! Brickhouse!"

She gave Mr. Griswold the straight-arm and shoved him aside, heading toward the TV camera and satellite uplink dish she spotted up the street.

Miss Falconer was heading for the cameras too. The spot Clint assigned to the choir was a block and a half away from CNN— too far—way up near the Sons of Knute Temple. "Seize the day," she decided, and so she was leading forty choristers in blue-and-gold satin robes on an invasion of the sidewalk opposite the CNN truck—"Choir coming through!" she cried, perfectly coiffed, prim, her bejeweled glasses on a chain around her neck, tapping people on the shoulders with her baton—"Make way for the choir! Coming through! Thank you! Thank you!"— her choir perspiring in their robes, squeezing into the cracks in the crowd—"Go somewhere else!" a man yelled. "No room! No room!" But she elbowed by and he was engulfed by blue and gold and the choir, intact, but in some disarray, stood opposite CNN, Miss Falconer with pitchpipe in hand—"Our first number will be 'O Flag Of Freedom, Grandeur Bright,' " she cried. "Diction, people! Diction!"

The CNN crew was still waiting for the word from master control in New York—Ricky chain-smoking, murmuring on a cell phone, glued to a headset, watching a monitor—shavehead manning a shoulder camera in the cherry-picker, the squat man with a hand-held in the street, the sullen teenager, head wrapped in big headphones, at the audio control—all of them psyched-up, ready, coiled, waiting, waiting, as the parade passed them by—a drum-and-bugle corps playing a raggy version of "Yankee Doodle" with backbeat flourishes, the queen of the soybean growers smiling and waving stalks of produce, the governor turning full-face to the camera and grinning heartily, eyes twinkling, transcendent, redeemed, freshly waxed, as if he had never ridden in a parade before—he basked in the brightness of all those eyes turned toward him, he could hear the word "governor" repeated hundreds of times, simultaneously, like purring. And next to him, eclipsed by his glow, the mayor of Lake Wobegon looking small and ordinary, like a personal assistant, a coat holder. Or his wife. He turned up the wattage of his personality as he came closer to the camera. He raised his chin and looked awestruck as if he were approaching the holy city of Jerusalem. Radiant beams shone from his face, his jowls disappeared, he threw back his shoulders and exuded joyful love of his fellow man and all of God's green creation, as the ocarina band shuffled behind, and then someone yanked on his sleeve. It was an old coot with little flags sticking out of his cap. "Hey guv'nor," he growled.

"Get out of here, Art. You're drunk," said the mayor. Art ignored her. "Hoping you can come up and see my motel," he said. "They tried to take it away from me but I got it back. Got a bottle of whiskey to wet your whistle. I know how to treat people right." He walked alongside the car. "You talk to the president, right? That's what I hear." The man's breath was enough to strip wallpaper. "I got an idea I want you to pass on. Instead of bombing Iraq, Air Force ought to drop manure on them. Take those big tanker planes and fill 'em up in Iowa and cover the country with shit." The old guy walked alongside the car, hanging on to the governor's sleeve. Where was Todd? Where was the security? Those guys clung to you like lint all day and when you needed them they'd gone off for lunch. The governor looked beyond the old drunk and tried to wave to the crowd but the old guy had a death grip on his arm. "You know about Muslims. They consider pork unclean, so they'd right away imagine it was pig shit, otherwise why would we drop it? Right? And so they'd all be ranting and raving and praying to Allah but meanwhile you'd be fertilizing the country so in a few years it'd become the breadbasket of the Mideast. You win the war without killing anybody and you do some good for the long run. What about that?"

And then the old guy cried, "Hey! Why do you wear your watch on your right arm? That makes no sense at all." He started to peel the watch off. Great God in heaven. He was the governor of Minnesota and he had to fight a drunk for his watch!! He looked back—no Todd, no highway patrolman—and he told the drunk, "Get the hell away from me." The drunk held on tighter—"What'd you say?" The drunk turned and yelled to the crowd—"I'm trying to tell my guv'nor sumthin and he tells me to get the hell away!"—he stuck his face up close to the governor's—"Who pays your salary, chickenshit? Tell me that. Who paid for that watch? Me. The taxpayer."

"Hey, Governor!" It was Georgia Brickhouse, dismounted

from the dead man whose left testicle she had stepped on, striding up the CNN side of the street, red boots, blue tights, white blouse of Congress, her adherents chanting her name. She yelled, "Governor! It's me! Georgia!" And the high school choir, thinking the TV cameras were on, raised their fists and chanted—

WOBEGON
We said it once, we'll say it again
WOBEGON
Wobegon, Wobegon, that's our team,
You are the curds and we are the cream.
So pick up your trash and step to the side
Lake Wobegon will not be denied
Go, Leonards!

30. THE COLLISION

ut master control was not ready for Lake Wobegon yet. Ricky said, "Sorry, folks! We've got to do it all over!" and raised his index finger and waved it clockwise. Three feet away, Clint got on the horn—"Bring 'em around again," he told Carl who was stationed at the parade's end at the park. "Ours not to reason why. Recycle the parade. Send them back around." He meant for the parade to circle back by way of Elm Street and sent LeRoy dashing up there to clear traffic but Carl in his excitement waved the first units to make a sharp U-turn and head back along Main Street where they met the rest of the parade approaching who had to sidestep to the left, bands and wagons and horses and all, and soon there was a two-way parade—"I love it!" cried Ricky—the mighty sixteen-Percheron hitch towing the wagon with the band playing "Tiger Rag" passing the haywagon with the Lake Wobegon Whippets aboard, twelve ballplayers in uniform, bats on their shoulders, looking glum, followed by the "Yankee Doodle" fifes and drums, the Pork Queen waving to the Queen of Soybeans, and Miss Liberty gallivanting along behind Uncle Sam lumping along on his stilts,

and Abe and George marching arm in arm, Martha having retired due to painful bunions, and the Gothic Woman and Man
With Pitchfork marching in tandem, followed by the old Chevys
and Pontiacs of the Car Club, and the Ladies Sextette on a fork-
lift, lip-synching "To Know Him Is To Love Him"—a fine mess
of images on CNN's monitor—"Beautiful!" Ricky cried. "Keep
going! It's perfect." Flags swirled as honor guards swerved to
avoid each other and the eight-horse hitch pulling the Arabian
Nights wagon passed the Future Farmers chorus and Miss Liberty's robes swirled around her, the seven-pointed crown slightly
askew, she waved her torch as she passed Clint and blew him a
big kiss and then there was the governor of Minnesota approaching in his convertible, a small grim woman by his side and a
giant red-blue-white Congress person striding along, trying to
catch up with him, pushing small Catholic children out of her
way, shoving a nun—the governor glanced over his shoulder
like a hunted animal—the huntress was shrieking, "Governor!
Governor!"—she wanted a photo, her and the gov, holding
hands aloft—a team—working together to protect our country
from terrorists—and the psychic Miss Liberty felt the dark aura
of his dismay. His face was a cry for help—and now Miss Falconer sensed her moment and the choir in blue and gold sang,
with ferocious diction, *O flag of freedom, grandeur bright, shine
O flag of yore with radiant beams of glory's light from freedom's rocky shore*—to Miss Liberty the governor's energy field
said: Trapped. Between his robotic radiant face and the harpy on
his tail and the TV camera beaming the show to the far corners
of the world and his dream of becoming vice president of the
United States, he was wedged tight and hard in a small space that

did not permit him to run free—her heart went flying out to him—he and she had been lovers in a previous life, she sensed—perhaps in a Conestoga wagon on the Oregon Trail, they had seen each other through the flames of a cooking fire and taken a walk at night through shoulder-high grass and lay down in it and joined in passionate congress—she wanted to offer him comfort now and inspiration. She held her torch high and called to him, "Courage, my darling!"—just then Ricky shouted, "WE'RE ON!"—actually screamed—he'd been waiting four hours for this moment and air pressure had built up inside him—and the governor's car slowed so as not to run over the squat man with the handheld—and Angelica struck a pose for the governor who was clambering out of his car, trying to escape the clutches of Georgia Brickhouse. *O flag of light we bless thy name and to thy Maker pray, protect us from the tyrant's shame on Independence Day.* He opened the door and stepped out onto the pavement, the car moving at 2 m.p.h. and he lost his balance and caromed off the front fender and Miss Liberty reached out to him and he took her hands, a radiant look of expectation on his face and stepped on her gown which fell to the pavement and she stood naked except for her red sandals, her torch held high. *O flag of love within thy folds lies freedom's mighty rod that raised up high in truth embolds a song of praise to God.* Clint saw this out of the corner of his eye, her bare back and legs, and beyond the governor Georgia standing frozen—a nudity alarm had gone off in her head—but the governor was still smiling his radiant parade smile at the naked woman with the torch and he bent down to retrieve her robe just as she bent down too and their heads bonked hard and he got the worst of it—he straightened up, bug-eyed, poleaxed,

and then dropped to his knees, his face, which now looked some-
what wolfish, was just even with her abdomen and he grimaced
and fell forward, his forehead against her navel and her hands
on his head, and a dozen people with zoom lenses on their digital
cameras captured it, what appeared to be (which it was not) a
sexual act in a public place, a public man addressing a woman's
privates. *O flag of knowledge let us tell the world of freedom sweet,*
O blow the horn and ring the bell, its joyful song repeat. Lights
flashed on many cell phones. And that was the picture that everyone saw over and over everywhere in the Western world for the
next few days—a dazed man in a dark blue suit and red tie kneel-
ing before a young naked woman, her long back and her womanly hips and firm buttocks, engaged in some sort of activity in
her groin area which she, holding a torch high in the air, seemed
to enjoy, and an angry Amazon behind him, horror writ large
on her face and CONGRESS across her chest—it went straight to
the Internet and people who'd never been to Minnesota e-mailed
it to their friends and they sent it to their friends and without it
ever being noted in the *Times* or the *Post* or the *CBS Evening*
News it entered the Great Swamp of National Consciousness and
the governor's name became one that you associated with S-E-X
and bigwigs in Washington crossed the governor's name off
their lists instantly and his career skidded off the road and into
the sea and though he himself would go on walking around and
serving on boards and panels and consulting on things, he was a
dead man from that moment. He had been crushed by Liberty's
thighs.

A yellow-and-black butterfly had landed on Ricky's control
board and distracted him—he picked it up gingerly by one wing

and it fluttered away—and then New York was yelling, "What's going on out there?" and then he cut away to the cherry-picker and a high shot of the Will Jones Drum & Bugle Corps and "I'm a Yankee Doodle Dandy" but in the delay an image was burned on the national retina that joined Marilyn Monroe in gold lamé singing "Happy Birthday" to John F. Kennedy and Monica Lewinsky radiant in the crowd welcoming Bill Clinton. Within minutes, twenty-two seconds of video was up on YouTube and a frontal view on various subterranean websites which spread like mushrooms and what was so riveting was not the woman's buttocks, handsome though they were, but the man's expression of wonderment as if he had been closeted in a monastery for years and now he knelt in adoration of the female form, and pressed his face against her, at least until the Amazon (his wife? his mother?) hauled him off her and read him the riot act.

31. IRENE ARMED AND DANGEROUS

I
t was a wonderful parade, according to everybody who hadn't seen the Statue of Liberty naked—she was naked only for a few seconds before Clint Bunsen rushed to her side and re-draped her and led her away—they loved the circus wagons, the mighty steeds, the blaze of pageantry, the bands. Irene did not see it. She had walked south along Main Street and smelled pig manure, rich and sour, and there, parked on the street, a plastic tarp over the box, were three old bachelor farmers in a pickup truck, passing a bottle of whiskey around. They looked at her as if they'd never seen her before.

She walked up to the window. "Where you going with that?" she said in a friendly tone of voice.

Mr. Boe was at the wheel. Rheumy-eyed, grizzled, snaggle-toothed Mr. Boe. "Going to join the parade," he said.

"No, you're not. You're going to turn around and drive out of town and take that wherever you got it," she said. They laughed. Apparently they'd never been ordered around by a woman. So she pulled the pistol out of the bag and pointed it at Mr. Boe and cocked the hammer. He rolled up the window. She

243

tapped on the glass with the pistol barrel. He started the engine. She tapped hard. He rolled the window down a little. "This shoots through glass, I believe," she said. "And if you don't do what I say, I'll blow your brains out." She had never said those words before. A first for her.

Mr. Boe turned to consult with his friends and Irene reached in and turned off the ignition and pulled out the keys. "You see what happens when you don't listen?" She walked away. The lake was two blocks to the east. She'd walk down to the shore and throw the keys in and then go looking for the Statue of Liberty. The woman was not going to waltz out of town scot-free. No, ma'am.

Susan B. Anthony was resting in the shade of the Statue of the Unknown Norwegian, sitting on the grass, her shoes off, and saw Miss Liberty being towed away by Clint Bunsen and had no idea what had happened, and neither did most other people, even those who'd gotten a glimpse of pink naked flesh—it was all over so quickly. The governor fled, his face twitching, and galloped up the street in search of the black Lincoln. Todd ran along beside him and the governor yelled, "You're history, shithead." The governor ran up the alley behind Ralph's Pretty Good Grocery and the highway patrolman had brought the car around to the front. "What'd I do?" cried Todd. The governor poked him in the sternum. "J'ever think to put a goddamn sign on the side of my goddamn car, you jerk?" Todd gulped. And then someone laughed nearby and the governor turned and saw through a window in the back of the Mercantile people watching TV and the woman with the seven-pointed crown and the torch—the robe tumbling to the ground and her bare back and proud young buttocks and the camera zooming in on the governor as he held her by the hands and the goofy grin on his face as if he had never seen a naked woman before—the people in the store whooped and laughed.

Clint had seen the whole thing, standing behind Ricky. He saw Angelica on a collision course with the governor and his big foot on her gown which fell with a whoosh and she was naked in the mob, and then the slapstick head butt, and the governor on his knees, and her gorgeous rump so firm and proud and the delicate cleavage below it, an immaculate and inspiring sight, and then he was at her side, picking up the robe and parking it on her shoulders and saying, "Come, my darling" and helping her away through the stunned seniors in rows of folding chairs and around the corner of the Chatterbox, Dorothy in the doorway snapping pictures of the passing parade, and past the fire department garage where the volunteers stood around the truck drinking beer and watching CNN. One of them saw Angelica and whooped and whistled and she took Clint's elbow and they walked in stately fashion to the Lutheran church and in the back door. "I'll go get your clothes from the garage. You okay?"

"Yes, of course."

"Good."

"I'm sorry," she said. "The dang robe was too long, I've been hoisting it up all day. My arm got tired."

"It's okay," he said. "It's not as if people had never seen a beautiful woman before."

He left her in the annex and trotted down the alley to Bunsen Motors, his walkie-talkie squawking in his back pocket: "Clint, come in. Come in," said Carl. "Art's on the warpath. He thinks you took over his motel and you told the governor to stiff him. He's pretty mad."

32. PREPARING FOR FLIGHT

He let himself in the back door and got Angelica's bag out of Clarence's office. His cell phone was ringing. He looked at the ID screen. The Associated Press in Minneapolis. Damn. The Honor America show was getting started in the park. He could hear the choir singing on the public address system—

Shining Mother, we salute you,
Perfect grace of golden years.
Loving Mother, see your children
Bid farewell with shining tears.
Through life's dangerous lonely voyages,
'Long the coasts of grief and fear,
In our hearts we e'er remember
How you taught and loved us here.

His phone rang. It was Griswold. "You disappointed me, Buddy. Today was the day—"

"You're breaking up, sorry, bad connection." He hung up.

And then his phone rang again. Irene. "Where are you?" she

said. He told her he was heading home in a few minutes. "That's not my question. Where are you now?"

"What does it matter?"

"I'm only going to say this once," she said. "You go away with that girl and you're never coming back. Just so you understand. No freebies. So make your choice. I'm just telling you. You want to run away, go, and have a good time, but when you go, you're gone. Where are you?"

"I don't know what I'm going to do but whatever it is, I'm coming back."

"No, you aren't. You're running away. Tell the truth."

"I don't know what I'm going to do."

"You're running away with a 28-year-old yoga instructor is what you're doing. And if you do you're not coming back. Where are you?"

He said nothing. He looked around. One last look at the old shop, his workbench, his tools laid out in rows, the service manuals. Odd to think that he had spent his youth and middle age here, raising cars on the lift, lowering them. He walked into the showroom. There was Daddy's high desk with invoices sticking out of the pigeonholes and there was Daddy in his big white hat and golden smile, waiting for the sun to shine. The boy tiptoed to his side and touched his arm and said, "Happy Fourth of July, Daddy." And Daddy said, "Happy Fourth of July to you, Clinton." And he took his boy's hand and he said, "Did you enjoy it?" The boy nodded. "That's good." Daddy looked away, sad and forlorn, he missed Bonita his contortionist pal. He said, "What do you want to be when you grow up, Clinton?" and he said, "A fireman" though he didn't. Daddy said, "Firemen are happy people because they help others." And then he pulled a flask of whiskey out and took a slug of it. "Life is hard, Clinton. You have to get happiness where you can find it."

Bang! And now he was 60 and being careful on the stairs and not eating big dinners anymore and asking people to repeat what they just said and looking at the page with blurry eyes. And where was the happiness? Daddy died at 60, eaten up suddenly by colon cancer. In May he was his old bouncing self and in June he sickened from colon blockage which he thought was constipation. He couldn't poop. He took mineral oil and got bloated and gassy and on the Fourth he sat on the porch and wept. The parade was routed up Taft Street for his benefit and he sat in his rocker and feebly waved a hanky at the majorettes who curtsied to him and the brass band who played "Tiger Rag," his favorite, and a sad-faced bozo trotted over and squirted him with a trick flower, and Hjalmar Ingqvist of the State Bank marched up with a photographer and gave Daddy a bronze plaque which Daddy took out to the garage that evening and bashed with a ballpeen hammer and flattened the lettering—*To Clement Bunsen in recognition of a lifetime of meritorious service*—Daddy didn't want an award: He didn't want to die, which was what the award was for. It was a death prize. He wanted more life and to see Bonita again and intertwine with her as Frank Sinatra sang. One more time! Just one more! Please.

And now here was his boy trying to figure out his problems, trying to be good and be happy, and a cold wind had blown in and a still, small voice that said: *Let me give you the big picture, fella, you are over the hill, and we've got no further use for you, so get out of the way. You're dead wood.*

But no, it was Irene's voice asking him where he was.

He said, "I'll be home soon." She hung up. When he got back to the Lutheran church, Angelica was nowhere to be seen. He poked his head in the Fellowship Room and looked down the hall of the Christian Education Wing and then heard the floor creak up above. She was in the Sanctuary, looking up at the Lord Jesus Christ in stained glass, holding a lamb. She had dropped her robe again. She stood naked at the Communion rail.

"You'd better put these on," he said, holding up the bag.

"Want to come to California?" She said that Kevin had taken off. He told her he was leaving if she didn't come immediately and she told him she had to march in the parade. He said that if the parade was more important to her than he was, then okay, he was out of here. And he was.

She turned to face him. "I worry about you, darling. You are so, like really depressed, and you have to bounce back somehow. Maybe it's diet. I feel like I ought to be taking care of you. If you accept depression as a way of life, you die. Why do you work so hard to get what you don't even want?" she said. "You're the Man and you aren't having any fun. Really. Have you ever done yoga? Seriously."

And then he heard a distant whistle blow. And the urge came over him. The urge to be fluid, get a move on, leave your regret and failure behind, something good may lie ahead. Drive west. Get to the Black Hills. Wyoming next. The snow-capped Grand

Tetons up ahead. The railyards there along the river, under the cottonwoods. A campfire. Other gypsies gathered in the flickering light, their RVs pulled up in a circle. People roasting chicken and peppers on sticks, lolling about with cartons of red wine, talking about Mexico. Maybe some cagey old Bedouin will plop down and read your tea leaves and tell you where to go to find the gravy train. Jesus never commanded anybody to work hard day after day. Jesus said, Don't worry about what you shall eat or what you shall wear. Don't worry about money. Jesus did some teaching and preaching and healing and hiking, and he was a great fisherman, but he didn't have a day job at the vineyard.

"Are you having any fun?" she said.

He told her that he was brought up to look like he wasn't having fun—it was considered undignified, also bad luck—but that inside he was, really, no kidding, having a good time, but could she please get dressed now?

"Kiss me," she said. So he did.

"Did you ever enjoy living here?" she said. She held her arms out. "What was the most enjoyable part you can remember?"

Well, he enjoyed the Fourth, though not as much as when he was 10 years old. And that's who he was doing it for, 10-year-old boys, not for his own pleasure. You were supposed to do this, weren't you? Make sacrifices? Give to kids what your forebears had given to you. So he'd thought about running for Congress but the Brickhouse woman had a ferocity he didn't have. A woman on the make, a shakedown artist, and fascinating to him and seeing her today took the fight right out of him. He was a lightweight and glad to be one. Running for Congress

seemed as foreign to him as playing the sitar. But O God Angelica had her arms around him and his face lay against the side
of her neck and her long hair. He kissed her again and again, on
her throat and her collarbone and up behind her ears. "I wish I
could take you with me," she said. "I want to rescue you from
yourself."

"I want to go, but I want to go the right way."

"I think it was meant to be," she said.

"I don't know," he said.

I always wanted to see the white castles of Spain someday
But the plane that flies to Spain has flown away
So I may never see Seville, Barcelona, or Madrid
I could have once but I never did.

33. IRENE CATCHES UP

He stood there nuzzling her like an old horse, wanting to start his life over again with her and be 23, just out of the Navy, heading for art school. He could see it now, sort of—the drive west, a tourist motel somewhere in South Dakota, the kind where you park your car at the front door of the cabin, then up at dawn and the land rising to the high plateau of Wyoming and maybe a stop at Yellowstone to see Old Faithful. He would suffer terrible remorse but she would see him through it and meanwhile California lay ahead, shining, the pastel towers, the orchards, the powerful breakers of the rolling sea, and they'd find a little seaside town and he'd find a garage. A good mechanic will always find work. Folks in the bullshit professions have to struggle—write up their bullshit résumés, make friends with bigger bullshitters, learn what kind of shit is valued and how to produce it, maybe buy a bull—but a mechanic can walk into a shop and establish his bona fides in ten minutes and once they know you can do the work, nothing else matters. He could earn a nice living in Parnassus and maybe he and Angelica would stay together and maybe not. Not up to him. But he would be free.

He'd walk into a café and sit down and the waitress wouldn't come over and say, "I like those shoes better than the ones you were wearing last week. You got those from a rummage sale, right? I knew it. They were my uncle Ralph's. Blue boat shoes. SueAnn had a hard time throwing those away because they were the shoes Ralph died in. He was on his way to go fishing and he got as far as the dock and he felt bad and he sat down with the bait bucket in his lap and he died. Bang. Just like that." Maybe he'd go to church and maybe not, but it wouldn't be anybody's business, just his. Maybe he'd be a Republican and maybe he'd quit thinking about that stuff and get a bike and become a bicyclist. And five years from now people in Lake Wobegon would say, "You wouldn't believe who Lillian ran into in California. Clint Bunsen! Yes! He looked good, she said. Very tan and trim and he bikes cross-country. Dips his rear wheel in the Pacific and bikes east all the way to the Atlantic. Came through Minnesota and for some reason didn't stop and say hi. He's got a nice little cottage, she said. Spanish style. Terrace, a little garden. He said to say hi, she said."

"I'll go get us a getaway car," he said. "I'll meet you at the garage in fifteen minutes."

"You sure you want to go?"

"Come meet me at the garage. I'll get us a nice car." And now he was back in Durango at the gas station and Mom was on the phone and now he was going to tell her the truth, that he did not want to go home. He felt heat back behind his eyeballs. He was about to weep.

He dashed back to the garage. He grabbed the keys to a used

Mustang on the lot and he dashed off a note to Clarence—"I'll call you tomorrow and explain everything"—and he found an old brown duffel bag and he started throwing tools in it and got it half filled up and was looking for another bag when the back door opened and Irene strolled in. She locked the door behind her and she walked through the shop and into the showroom.

"Turn out the light," she said from the next room. "Art is on the warpath and he's looking for you, darling. He found the Hospitality Suite and he is incensed, he called up and said he knew it was your doing—"

"Where is he?" Clint stood in the doorway.

"On his way here, I suppose."

It was twilight outside. In the park a tenor was torturing "Bridge Over Troubled Water," making it twist in pain. On the street people streamed away from the park, blankets in hand, to find a good spot to watch the fireworks. Three young women loitered across the street who apparently hadn't attached themselves to young men, or had come detached, and they were elaborately cool, as if pantomiming themselves having a wild good time, but he could tell they had their eyes out for opportunity. *O love, O love, where have you gone?*

"Don't lie to me," she said. "Tell me the truth. You're going away with her."

"The truth is what I'm trying to find out."

"You're going," she said. "That's the truth. But the fact is that you have to get past me first. I'm your wife. I'm not somebody you can just toss aside like an old brown banana." And she reached into her shoulder bag and pulled out a pistol.

He hadn't noticed the shoulder bag. And he hadn't noticed her blouse. It was white, silky, and it was cut low. Daringly low. Unusual for Irene to go out dressed like that.

"Oh darling, I can't let you do it. If I were angry at you, I could, but I'm not, so I won't. I'm not angry, I'm tired. You're wearing me out. You and I went through so much together, don't make us go through even more. Please."

He needed to sit down. Right away. He walked to the Taurus on the showroom floor and sat down on the front fender. She didn't look like she'd shoot holes in him but how could you tell? She looked very calm. She stood by Daddy's old desk, the pistol in her right hand, her back to the front door, and beyond her, crowds moving in search of excitement, the beautiful uncomprehending people ignoring the Big Story.

"I never had my chance to be foolish, Irene. I want to go back and do it."

"Fine. Let's do it together. I'll be just as foolish as you. Maybe more."

He thought: *Maybe I should jump up and walk straight toward her, just walk over and take the gun away. She's not going to shoot me. Walk over, take the gun away, and say good-bye.*

She said, "Listen to me. We raised our kids here. This is our life here. Don't be in such a hurry to throw it away. And don't say it was nothing. It was something. You came home after work and three little kids could hardly wait until they saw you come down the walk. You dressed up as the Big Bunny. Remember? We had our Christmases here. All those birthdays. What was that about? You and I fought here. You yelled at me once to Just

Grow Up—remember that? People heard you a block away. You watched football on TV back when you used to watch football. We got sick here, we had sick kids. I nagged you to quit smoking. I had that awful bout of depression where I curled up in bed for a week after I taught Vacation Bible School. You cried in that house. Twice. In thirty-two years. I was there, I remember it. Once on Christmas Eve the year your mother died and the other was when Kira left. We had fights here. Those grim fights over money. The time you told me you never wanted to see my father again. The time you stayed out all night and told me you were at a friend's and I found the motel receipt in your pants. Honey, we went through it all here. We weathered the storm, babes. We made it. So why start all over with somebody else? Darling, you'll have to go through everything with her that you went through with me, but darling, when you finally get settled—like we are now—you'll be eighty-five and gone to rack and ruin and here you are with me, you're sixty, we could have twenty-five great years. Why not?"

He shook his head. "I'm all done," he said. "I've got nothing left. The tank is empty." He was waiting for her to suggest counseling. "I was in California, darling. And I came home to say good-bye. My mother asked me to come home and give her a hug and I did and now look at me. I am sixty years old and I have lived over three decades of a mistake and, Irene, that is longer than a mistake should go on."

He didn't think she'd shoot him. On the other hand—oh my God—maybe she was thinking of shooting herself. And the thought of it—her raising the barrel to her temple in one swift

move and pulling the trigger and spattering herself on the wall—
that would be the end of him. He'd never survive it. He'd live
the rest of his life as a pale weeping shadow.

Ten feet away, the people streamed by, and they couldn't see
the two figures there in the dimness, but if her gun went off, the
mob would gather and break in and find one of them dead—and
now Angelica was approaching the door.

He was about to point this out to Irene when there came a
banging in back, someone shaking the locked door. And then a
big *whump* of boot against wood, and the door cracked open.

"BUNSEN!"

The voice of Art, exploding in the shop. "BUNSEN!" A few
footsteps on the gritty concrete floor. "I know you're in here,
you bastard." A few more footsteps. "Go ahead and run but I'll
find you—"

He walked to the door and stuck his head in. He saw the dark
form of Art standing by the workbench with a rifle in his hand.

"Hey. John Wayne. Welcome to the movies."

"Came to tell you to get your crap out of my cabins, Bunsen.
All that shrimp and fish for you and your liberal pals. I'm onto
you. That fridge you brought in. Where'd that come from? Electric company, that's where. Get it out. Now."

"Go talk to Viola, cowboy."

"Talking to you, Bunsen. Think you can walk into a man's
house and take it over, think again! And one more thing—give
me back the gun you stole." He banged the rifle butt on the
workbench and made the hardware jump. "This is America, in
case you didn't notice! Not the Soviet Union. Not yet."

Irene was standing beside him. He saw the reflection of the gun in her hand. She stepped in front of him.

"I've got your gun right here, you old booger, and I'll give it back when I'm done with it. So just turn around and go out the way you came or else I'm going to put a hole through you."

Art said nothing for a moment. "Oh yeah?"

"Yeah."

"Like to see you try it, lady." But he didn't sound like he meant it. He'd never been married so he didn't know how to fight with a woman. He had no useful experience. "Who are you? Is that Irene?" he cried. He stepped forward to get a better look and she pulled the trigger.

The sound seemed to lift Bunsen Motors a foot off the ground. Clint's head shrank to the size of a pea, then gradually got back to normal. The old man stood frozen, the rifle clattered to the floor.

There was a hum in the room, the hoist was rising. Evidently the bullet had hit some control mechanism—the hoist rose, two solid steel tracks in the air—no. Clint had hit the switch on the wall with his left hand.

Clattering in front—somebody banging on the showroom door. Clint turned—it was Angelica, face pressed to the glass, hand shielding her eyes, peering in. Irene strode to the door, gun in hand, and opened it. "Come in," she said. "I'm the wife."

34. FINALE

Art had never been shot at before and the shock of it capsized him completely. He sat down on the floor semicomatose and Clint lifted the rifle off the floor. "May I offer you a cup of coffee?" The old man said he thought that would be nice. Ordinarily he didn't drink coffee this late, but he could use some now.

Clint filled the coffeemaker and listened to the voices in front, Irene trying to explain to Angelica what had happened and who the old man was and why she fired the warning shot into the ceiling, which Clint thought was a good story, he just wished he weren't in it.

"I'm sorry if you thought he was going to waltz out of here and into your arms," Irene told her, "but that's not how it works. If you want him, you can take him, but I'm going to have to shoot him first. You don't get to take him whole and fresh. I'm going to shoot him in the foot, or maybe in the butt. He can't walk out of here without a mark on him. You just tell me where to shoot him. If I blow part of his hinder off, they can fix him up with silicone but he'll lose some muscle so he's probably going to be a leaner. Hard to get that balance right. In the foot—that's going to be painful—lot of delicate little bones—and he's going to be gimpy, no way around it. Or I could blow his ear off. That sounds bad but it might actually be more merciful."

He winced—she wasn't kidding. (Was she kidding?) No, she wasn't.

The back door was fifty feet away but he didn't feel like running. And do what? Call the cops? Hop a freight? Wait around in the woods for things to blow over?

"Is this a joke? That is so sick. How can you even think about doing that?"

Click-click. Irene locked the front door. "It's an eye for an eye and a tooth for a tooth. Primitive justice. Very simple. You don't get away for free. There's an exit price. I know men. They have powerful imaginations. He could get in a car with you and two hours later he imagines he never was married, he has no children, no obligations—men are hitchhikers. Well, this one is going to walk out of here with a reminder. I'm going to put a mark on him."

"You're serious," said Angelica.

"You're a bright woman."

"I don't want any part of this," said Angelica. "I am not into violence in any way, shape, or form. If this is a joke, it's a bad joke. I'm out of here." But she didn't move. He stood, smelling the coffee as it dripped into the carafe, wishing she would think of something.

"I love your husband. I don't need to own him, I believe that everything we do for love enlarges us and makes us free. Your husband is a hero to me. He has suffered this town and yet his eagerness for life is undiminished. He has not given up hope. He is eager—"

"Butt, foot, or ear?"

He thought he'd choose a shot in the butt if it were up to him, which evidently it wasn't. The ear? No, she wasn't a good shot— she could easily take out some of the frontal lobe and leave him a vegetable, dim-witted but filled with anxiety. The foot— painful. Probably for years to come. He'd spend his life sitting and lying and he'd turn into a blimp. A butt shot—of course so much depended on the angle. A straight shot was likely to hit the pelvic bone and maybe richochet into the gonads and you'd be a nutless guy who walks funny.

Of course it would sting and there'd be possible infection, maybe one of those virulent new staphylococci that snaps you in two like a matchstick, and of course there'd be the public humiliation—"His wife got tired of his philandering and cut him a new asshole. Clint. That's why he ushers at church. Can't sit down. Can't drive, can't go out for dinner. Has to wear a bag, she scared the piss right out of him"—but chances were good he'd heal up and be able to re- sume normal activity, whatever that might be.

He helped Art up from the floor and got him parked in a chair and poured him a cup of coffee but the old man's hands shook so bad, he couldn't hold a cup, so Clint lifted the cup to Art's lips, sort of like Communion. "This is coffee, made for you, Art," he whispered.

" 'Preciate it, Clint."

A whiff of Angelica's perfume swept through the room and she touched his shoulder. A thrilling touch. "Good-bye, dar- ling," she said. "I'll always care about you." He gave her the keys to the Mustang. "It's the red one, alongside the building. A gift. I just put in a new transmission. It'll get you there."

"Thank you."

"Would you mind giving Art a ride home?" he said. "He's at the motel. There's a sign. It's just north on Main Street, a little beyond the swimming beach. On the right."

"You want me to give him a ride?" she said, as if he'd asked her to hold a squid in her arms.

"It'd be a big help. He's seventy-eight. He's sort of shaky since Irene took a shot at him."

"I don't understand you people," she said, but she took Art by the arm and steered him out front—"Goodbye, Angelica," said Clint. "Drive carefully. Oh, I forgot—it's a stick shift. Is that okay? Standard transmission?" "Oh God," she said, and the door clicked shut.

Ah, mi amor, I will think of this sweet love of ours
Every night I look up at the stars.
I wish you as many happy days as there are leaves on my oak tree
And that on some of them you will remember me.

It was almost dark and the park was full of people, like cicadas chittering, and cars parked along the county road to the north, cars up on the hill, people waiting for the rockets to go off.

"Let's go home," she said, and she handed him the gun. "You take it. My hand is tired of holding it."

"You weren't really going to shoot me, were you?"

~~R~~EAD MORE OF THE CLEVERLY HILARIOUS
~~GARRI~~SON KEILLOR IN VIKING AND PENGUIN BOOKS

~~Pontoon~~

~~The f~~irst new novel of Lake Wobegon in over seven years, *Pontoon* is nothing less
~~than a~~ spectacular return to form—replete with a bowling ball-urn, a hot-air balloon,
~~a flying~~ Elvis, and, most important, Wally's pontoon boat. As the wedding of the
~~decade~~ approaches the good-loving people of Lake Wobegon do what they do best:
~~drive~~ each other slightly crazy.   *ISBN 978-0-14-311410-9*

~~La~~ke Wobegon Summer, 1956

~~La~~ke Wobegon Summer, 1956 depicts the most harrowing time of life in Lake Wobe-
~~g~~on—adolescence. With his trademark gift for treading "a line delicate as a cobweb
~~b~~etween satire and sentiment" (*The Cleveland Plain Dealer*), Garrison Keillor cap-
~~t~~ures postwar America and delivers an unforgettable comedy about a writer coming
of age in the rural Midwest.   *ISBN 978-0-14-200093-9*

Wobegon Boy

John Tollefson leaves Lake Wobegon to manage a public radio station at a college for
academically challenged children of financially gifted parents in upstate New York.
Though he makes a pleasant bachelor life for himself in New York, he feels rootless,
restless, with nothing at stake. Can a romance with a historian named Alida Freeman
give his life the nobility and grace it lacks?   *ISBN 978-0-14-027478-3*

Leaving Home

In this collection of Lake Wobegon monologues, Keillor tells readers more about
some of the people from *Lake Wobegon Days* and introduces some new faces.
                                                     ISBN 978-0-14-013160-4

AND DON'T MISS OTHER GREAT WORKS BY GARRISON KEILLOR:

Homegrown Democrat
A Few Plain Thoughts from
the Heart of America
ISBN 978-0-14-303768-2

Good Poems
ISBN 978-0-14-200344-2

Good Poems for Hard Times
ISBN 978-0-14-303767-5

A Prairie Home Companion
The Screenplay
Foreword by Robert Altman
ISBN 978-0-14-303823-8

Love Me
A Novel
ISBN 978-0-14-200499-9

The Book of Guys
Stories
ISBN 978-0-14-023372-8

WLT
A Radio Romance
ISBN 978-0-14-010380-9

We Are Still Married
Stories and Letters
ISBN 978-0-14-013156-7

PENGUIN BOOKS

"I hadn't made up my mind and luckily for you I didn't
have to."

He thought he could smell rain but it was only the lake. And
now a burst of flame from the hill, the cannons firing. The crowd
raised a mighty cheer. He imagined a big storm coming up and
bowling balls dropping from the sky and one ball smashing his
head in two, cracking the skull neatly in half, one eyeball per
sphere and the two spheres lying in the dirt looking at each
other. He quickened his steps toward the safety of home.

They walked home in the summer night as the first rockets went
up. Fireflies flickered in the tall grass. Their neighbors stood on
their front lawns to watch the spectacle and somebody yelled,
"You're missing the fireworks!" and they waved and walked on.
They got home and Arlene and Clarence came over and then
Lyle and Carl and his wife and Billy P. Clarence said, "I heard
somebody streaked the governor. A lady." He hadn't seen it
himself but Arlene saw it on TV. So Clint told him the whole
story. His lover Angelica had come to town with her new lover
Kevin who had a fit and took off and meanwhile, marching in the
parade as the Statue of Liberty, she had approached the governor
who, for reasons unknown, had walked up the front of her robe
and torn it from her body, leaving her buck naked on Main Street
smack-dab in front of the Mercantile and the high school choir,
but he, Clint, had snatched her from public view and hid her in
the Lutheran church and intended to run away with her to California when Irene surprised him packing up tools in the garage
and leveled a gun at him. When poor old Art came in, rifle in

hand, she shot a hole in the ceiling and scared the piss out of him. And when Angelica came to pick up Clint, Irene offered him to her on condition that she (Irene) could shoot him first, either in the foot, the butt, or the ear. Angelica turned down the deal.

"I can repair the roof tomorrow," Clint said.

"So you're sticking around?"

"Looks that way."

"Quite a story," said Billy P. "Glad you're okay," said Carl's wife. The others just nodded and smiled and watched the fireworks.

He considered whether to tell Clarence that they were Hispanic no longer, but no—Clarence hadn't believed it anyway, and if he did, well, the illusion might loosen him up a little and germinate some life under that Norwegian icecap.

Clint got out a case of beer and a bottle of white wine and Irene popped popcorn and put chips in a big wooden bowl and they sat around on the porch back in the old life of howareyou-notsobadcantcomplain and everythingisaboutthesamehowsyour-self. A pretty good summer. The parade now, that was hilarious. That governor—his name escapes me—got his undies in a twist, that's for sure. Naked? So what? I looked at her, didn't bat an eye. What's the big deal? Why get all worked up over it. There's enough of that as it is. People getting on each other's nerves and that's why God invented fishing. To get you away from the telephone so you won't worry, which you do anyway. How can you not? The corn needs more sun and Wally's Evelyn has lymphoma, the poor man is in agony as he pulls the tap at the Sidetrack and makes small talk with the clientele, he is looking into the abyss, but what can you do, not much to be done, what will

be will be, and aren't watermelons chea[ ] too. Boil 'em up with sugar, mash them i[ ] and screw on the lid, you got jam. Nothi[ ] Anyhoo. July. The old lady wants to go see C[ ] price of gas now. Ya can't go motoring in the [ ] used to. I told her, "Why spend money to go [ ] Canada when we can be perfectly unhappy he[ ] Gimme a cold beer and a brat with mustard and I'm [ ] to eat four at one sitting and now I'm a one-brat [ ] beers, one brat. With age comes wisdom. Sit outside, [ ] the crickets, look at the stars, who needs more? Kids d[ ] with their radios on, neighbors sit out back talking. I w[ ] until 2 a.m. the other night. Never used to stay up so late [ ] you need less sleep as you get old, don't you know. So much [ ] do, so little time. I heard that somewhere. Speaking of which, [ ] believe it's time we should be heading home. Good night. See [ ] you tomorrow, Lord willing.